Raging Spirits

***

Angel Smits

ImaJinn Books

Raging Spirits
Published by ImaJinn Books

ISBN: 1-933417-04-8

10 9 8 7 6 5 4 3 2 1

PUBLISHER'S NOTE:
This book is a work of fiction. Names, characters, places and incidents are products of the author's imagination or are used fictitiously. Any resemblance to actual events or locales or persons, living or dead, is entirely coincidental.

Books are available at quantity discounts when used to promote products or services. For information please write to: Marketing Division, ImaJinn Books, P.O. Box 545, Canon City, CO 81212, or call toll free 1-877-625-3592.

Cover design by Patricia Lazarus

ImaJinn Books
P.O. Box 545, Canon City, CO 81212
Toll Free: 1-877-625-3592
http://www.imajinnbooks.com

He really couldn't be a shapeshifter, could he?

A breeze whipped up with the coming storm, and the scents of the forest danced around them. That and the warm scent of him. She breathed in, taking him inside, settling him in the empty place in her soul.

"Do you ever make wishes?" she asked.

"Don't be silly." He pulled away and resumed walking.

"I do," she called after him.

He stopped and turned back, as if curiosity was too much for him. "And what do you wish for?"

She hesitated only an instant before moving toward him. When nothing more than a breath's distance separated them, she reached up and placed a finger against his jaw.

"For this." She stood on tiptoe and pressed her lips to his, pleading silently for him to feel—to *let* himself feel—something besides anger.

A growl escaped from his throat as his arms enveloped her and pulled her tightly to him. The hard, hot length of his body pressed against hers took her breath away.

This was madness. She willingly reached out to him, and he responded with a heady sensuality that turned her knees to water and jumbled her remaining sanity. He was too dangerous. She couldn't trust him.

Then why did she ache so? Why did it feel safe and right when his arms held her? Drained and slightly out of touch with reality, she let him kiss her, let him touch her, let her body melt into his. She slid her arms up over the muscles of his chest and held on tight.

"What are you doing to me?" he whispered, lifting his head only a fraction of an inch.

"Nothing," she said, parroting his earlier words and pulled his lips back to her.

He returned to devour her with his kiss, engulf her with his arms. She let herself experience him, giving back with as much passion as he did. Suddenly, the feel of his hair between her fingers changed. It was courser, stiffer. Different.

She pulled back, looking into his shadowed face. "What's happening?"

"Between us or to me?" The thick gravel of his voice surprised her. "Don't ask questions you can't handle the answers to."

This one's for you Ron. Remember—I will haunt you. Thank you for all the support, patience and love you've given me since I started this quest. I love you.

Acknowledgments

This book would have never come to be without all the help from a very special group of people. Thanks for making Thursday nights magic everyone. You are the best.

Other Books by Angel Smits

Memory Whispers

Prologue

Old, gnarled tree roots broke through the cement, making the walk up to the old house in the dark treacherous. She glanced at her watch. Two minutes before midnight. She reached the front porch just as a gust of wind showed up. The old, broken porch swing creaked and a pile of dried autumn leaves jumped into the air and swirled around her. She grimaced as a spasm of pain took her by surprise. Her fingers curled around the porch rail until they appeared white in the moonlight.

Then as quickly as it had begun, the wind stilled and everything in the night around her fell silent. Everything. Not even a cricket or stray cat tried to break it.

She took a deep breath as the pain subsided as well. Gripping her bag tighter, she stepped up onto the porch. Finally, a sound as the wood groaned beneath her feet.

She'd just lifted her hand to knock when the door abruptly opened. Dim light fell at her feet in a small puddle of gold.

"Did you bring it?" the old woman standing in the doorway whispered.

She nodded. "It's right here."

"Come in then." The old woman grabbed her arm and pulled her inside. The door slammed with a loud thud, and she hadn't even seen the woman move.

The old woman was tiny, which surprised her. She didn't know why, but it wasn't what she'd expected. The woman's white hair and her skin's pallor were the only light in her dark attire and the dimness of the house.

She looked around as the woman hurried about, leading her down numerous halls and through doors.

Finally, they entered a round, windowless room. The old woman closed the door. She threw three bolts into place, each making a loud thwack as they hit home. Then she spun around, her talon-like fingers extended. "Give it to me. Hurry child."

She struggled with the cumbersome purse, but finally she pulled out the small wooden box. The polished surface gleamed in the dim light, and for the first time she noticed all the candles set about the room. She frowned. Had they been there when she'd come in? She didn't know and that frightened her.

Before she could stop her, the woman grasped the box, hurried across the room and set it in the center of a tall marble table. On each end of the table an ebony pillar candle glowed, its flame dipping with the breeze caused by the woman's movements.

"Now." The old woman spun back around to face her. "Do you have the other things?"

"Yes." She dug in the purse again and pulled out a small paper bag. "Everything's there."

"Excellent."

Despite the closed up room and the numerous candle flames, the room grew cold as she handed the bag over. She shivered as the cold seeped clear to her bones.

Everything happened so quickly. She blinked and the woman handed her the box again. Glancing at her watch, she realized that nearly an hour had passed. How had that happened? Time seemed to have vanished. She slipped the box back into her bag and tried to recall what the woman had done. All she remembered was candle flames and the table.

The woman escorted her back to the front door with slow shuffled steps. For the first time, she realized the woman hunched over as she walked, and was that a cane? Where had that come from?

At the front door, she breathed a sigh of relief, ready to escape the house. She'd accomplished her mission. Stepping out into the night, she didn't even look back when the door slammed shut behind her.

The wind sang around her and bent the oaks nearly to the ground. But she didn't feel it. She felt nothing except a solid coldness settle deep in her chest.

One

The gale force wind whistled through the eaves and rattled the glass in the window. Clarissa Elgin slept fitfully, a part of her awake, watching the storm with growing trepidation. Suddenly, a gust blasted against her bedroom window. The glass shattered, and the broken frame slammed against the wall.

The breeze tugged at her, tearing at her hair and nightgown. She grabbed for the sheets, the blankets, the mattress's edge, but to no avail. The wind pulled her from the bed. With ease, it sucked her through the broken window, and she tumbled weightlessly through the dark night sky. A scream froze in her throat.

Fascination mingled with her fear. Beneath her, elms, willows and majestic pines whipped in the same wind that carried her through the heavens. Thick, heavy branches twisted and danced like wild lovers in the night. Rooftops, a vaguely familiar church steeple, and a myriad of glowing streetlights whizzed by, dwarfed by the height at which she flew.

As quickly as it had begun, the wind ceased, and she tumbled toward the earth. The buildings rose to meet her, and she shut her eyes in anticipation of the coming impact.

But none came.

Her descent slowed, and opening her eyes, she found herself inside a tiny, deserted diner. Before she could question why, she drifted slowly down to her feet beside the long counter.

She'd never been here before, and she looked around with relief and interest. Once-shiny chrome covered the walls and a scarred red Formica counter ran the distance of the room. Red vinyl stools sat at equal intervals along one side and matching booths lined the perimeter.

The whole scene could have come straight out of an old movie.

A large plate glass window formed one wall of the diner. Outside, night held the distant city tight in its predawn grip while a single customer sat at the counter. His face was turned away from her, but she found her gaze drawn to the thick, dark mane of brown hair tumbling over his broad, leather-clad shoulders. He turned then, giving her a silhouetted view of his features. He reached for his coffee. As he sipped the steaming brew, Clarissa's gaze roamed over the rugged contours of his handsome face. There was a strength and sadness there that triggered her curiosity.

He didn't look at her. She wasn't even sure he knew she was there. He didn't speak at all. Not to Clarissa or to the waitress who leaned against the counter and studied him appreciatively from beneath lowered lashes. Seemingly unaware of his audience, he continued to stare into his coffee.

Slowly, drawn to him and the aura of sadness around him, Clarissa walked to one of the stools beside him. He turned his head and his gaze raked from her head to her toes and back again. Looking down, she realized she still wore her pale blue nightgown and heat built inside her. A flush warmed her cheeks.

His dark eyes seemed to reach out to her. She crossed her arms over her chest, seeking protection from his predatory gaze and the answering sizzle it created in her blood.

A reluctant smile tugged at his lips, and his right eyebrow arched in question. "Interesting outfit to be running around town in at this time of night."

The deep growl of his voice brought the image of a lion to mind, and Clarissa trembled in the wake of the sound. "I didn't have much time to dress."

She watched as he drank the last of his coffee and signaled for a refill. The waitress topped off his cup, and Clarissa wondered only briefly why she didn't offer her one. The woman shoved a silver basket toward the man, and he tore open two paper packages and dumped the contents into his cup. The incessant clink of his spoon grew louder. Its pace slowed as his eyes grew distant.

A crash shattered the quiet as the door suddenly burst open. A man ran in. Clarissa gasped. He wore a black ski mask, but she saw the wild spark of madness in his undisguised icy-blue eyes. A chill gripped her and she shivered in the thin gown.

The punk pointed a handgun at the waitress. "Gimme what's in the register." When she stood motionless, staring in fear at the hooded face, he screamed, "Now!"

At the sharp command, the waitress pushed the buttons on the cash register. Her fingers trembled, missing the keys, and she had to repeat the procedure several times.

"You." The crook pointed the gun at the man's face. "Empty your pockets."

"I don't have anything valuable." The man stood, seemingly unafraid, as he did as he was asked. A roll of candy mints, a handful of assorted change, a black comb missing two teeth and his driver's license landed on the scarred counter.

"Where's your wallet?"

"I didn't bring it with me. I only came for coffee."

"You're lyin'." The kid walked toward the man, stopping only inches away. The punk slammed his fist into the man's stomach, and he doubled over in pain.

Despite her fear, Clarissa realized the thief couldn't see her. She tried to move, hoping to stop the horror going on around her, but her feet seemed glued to the floor and her limbs were useless.

"This is for bein' stupid." The young man stepped away, raised his gun and his ice-blue eyes sighted down the barrel.

Clarissa watched as he pulled back the trigger. The hammer dropped into place and the bullet emerged.

"No!" she screamed.

The punk laughed. The sound, though muffled by the mask, lost none of its madness. In slow motion, the bullet slid through the air and hit the man's broad chest. Clarissa watched the fabric of his shirt tear, then saw the skin beneath give and blood seep from the wound to soak his shirt. His cry of pain sent terror rocking through her as he tumbled to the worn linoleum floor.

The thief grabbed the money the waitress had removed from the till and ran. The merry jingle of the bell attached to the door reverberated mockingly around them.

"Get a doctor," Clarissa screamed to the waitress who stared at her wounded customer.

"If only..." the man whispered as Clarissa knelt beside him. She tried to stop the bleeding, but the blood came too fast. Her nightgown quickly soaked up the warm, sticky fluid.

"If only I'd stayed home tonight," he rasped. "But she wouldn't let me. Damn you, Rachel," he cursed as more blood pooled on his shirt. "Damn you," he repeated in a whisper, just as his head fell back against the cold floor, his dark brown eyes staring sightlessly at the ceiling.

"No," Clarissa cried, but he couldn't hear her—not anymore. Not...

She sat straight up in bed.

Her entire body felt cold and damp. The blue nightgown

clung to her skin. Looking down, she was relieved to find it wasn't soaked in blood but with her own sweat. The rumpled sheets were wrapped around her legs.

It had been years since she'd had such a strong vision. The last time...No, she refused to face those memories or that pain.

This one had been different, not like any before, she reassured herself. In the past, she'd only been a spectator or the receiver of a message, never a participant. No one had ever seen her before. Why had she been a part of the vision this time? What was the reason? Looking up, she realized the wind was gone and her window was closed, as it should be. Moonlight pooled on the rug. Even the storm had merely been a part of her vision.

She shivered and turned on the light beside the bed. It helped chase the shadows away. Still she spent the rest of the night waiting for them to return.

* * * *

The scents of steamed milk, cocoa, cinnamon, and, of course, coffee filled the air. Normally their familiarity soothed her, but not today. Clarissa bustled back and forth behind the counter of her coffee shop, The Angry Bean, filling orders and avoiding her own thoughts.

By noon, her hair clung to her face in damp blond ringlets, and she'd dropped three of her best mugs. Her nerves were stretched tight.

The crowd had thinned, so she made herself a triple mocha—with extra whipped cream. She hoped the caffeine in the espresso would bolster her lagging energy. She'd yet to take a sip when a voice broke the welcome quiet. "I hope that coffee has more get up and go than you do."

Clarissa looked up and found her friend, Faith Burke, smiling at her from the other side of the counter. She couldn't help smiling back as she automatically grabbed the fixings for Faith's favorite drink.

"Extra whipped cream today." Faith dug in the bottom of her purse for her loose change, like she did every day. Clarissa refused to let her friend pay, and each day Faith dumped change into the staff tip jar as a friendly compromise.

The whir of the steam machine drowned out any conversation, but as soon as it was done, Clarissa waited for

Faith to speak. The silence startled her. She looked up and met Faith's questioning stare. "What?"

"You look awful. What's the matter?"

"I..." What could she say? "I've had a busy morning."

"Yeah, right. Like that's unusual. Take a break with me and tell me what's wrong. Is Lindsey in yet?"

"Not for another half hour." There was no one in line and only a few people sat at scattered tables. The shop was blessedly quiet for the first time all morning. She shrugged. "But I will take the break. Want a cookie?"

Famished and armed with her coffee and chocolate chip delight, Clarissa collapsed in a wooden chair. Unfortunately, she wasn't sure if she'd be able to get back up again. Fatigue engulfed her, and she sipped her drink, praying for a jolt of energy.

Clarissa always believed a good defense was a blinding offense, so she struck out first. "How are those two men of yours?" Distraction was the easiest tool in her arsenal.

Faith smiled, settled onto her chair and snitched a bite of cookie. "Mom and Dad are in town. Dad and Cord are golfing, trying to *bond,* and Mom's spoiling the baby. I'm on my own for a change."

"Working on a new project?"

"Don't try distracting me." Faith playfully shook her finger. "Those dark circles under your eyes are a dead giveaway that something's wrong. What's up?"

"So, when did you become psychic?"

"Funny." Faith knew all about Clarissa's psychic abilities. Clarissa had helped Cord and Faith deal with a rather vicious ghost awhile back, and they'd both nearly died. Clarissa realized how close she'd come to losing her friend. Thankfully, they were not only safe now but happily married.

Still, old fears reared their ugly heads and she drank deeply, swallowing her uncertainty. Should she tell Faith about the vision last night? What would she think? They had been friends a long time, but would she understand?

"Don't try to hide from me." Faith frowned at her.

"I'm not."

"Yes, you are. Come on. Spill it." Faith grabbed the plate and pulled it to her side of the table. "Or the cookie's mine."

Clarissa laughed, knowing full well that had been Faith's intent.

"That's better. So, tell me what's up."

Still hesitant, Clarissa took a few minutes to gather her thoughts. "Okay," she relented as Faith took a big bite. "I was sleeping and had a vision last night. I saw a man get shot." Even to her ears the words sounded distant and unemotional. If only she really felt that way.

This time it was Faith's turn to be quiet, and Clarissa tasted her rising panic, panic that grew in proportion to the shock she saw dawning in Faith's eyes. To distract herself and Faith, she reached out and pulled the plate back.

"Shot? Someone was *shot?* Are you sure?" Faith whispered. "It wasn't a dream?"

"Yeah, I'm sure." Although Faith knew about Clarissa's abilities, she had no way of knowing how impossible it was to confuse a dream with a vision.

"You're positive it was in the future?"

"I think so. In the past all my visions have been precognitive."

"What are you going to do about it?"

"What can I do? Nothing."

"You can't be serious. Clarissa, if someone's going to die, you have to do something to stop it. I know from experience how accurate your visions are, remember?" Her voice rose and Clarissa looked around, hoping the few scattered customers weren't listening to them, especially since many of her regulars were from the police station around the corner. Luckily, no familiar uniforms occupied any of the seats.

How could she explain her fears, her reservations, to Faith? They'd been friends for three years and had never discussed her past. She'd never told anyone of the ridicule and suspicion she'd suffered the last time she'd tried to warn a stranger they were in danger. She shivered at the memories that had driven her to leave Boston and move out west to start a whole new life.

"It's not that simple," she explained.

"What do you mean by that? You have to do something."

"I don't *have* to do anything." Clarissa stood and picked up her empty cup. Anything to take away the edge of fear and pain she knew was coming. "Things don't necessarily change just because you know they are going to happen." She blinked, fighting the hurt that put a lump in her chest.

Faith stared back at her, questions in her eyes. Yet the

way she tilted her head told Clarissa she was trying to understand. "Maybe you had one of those out of body experiences and it...it already happened."

Clarissa had thought about that, too. "Maybe." She knew better, but she humored Faith and sat back down. "I looked through the papers this morning. There weren't any reports of a shooting." All she'd managed to do was stain her fingers with black ink as she read through each of the papers numerous times.

"How do you know it was here in Boulder?"

"I recognized the buildings. I distinctly remember flying over an old church I've seen before." Clarissa dropped the piece of cookie and vaguely heard it thud against the plate. "That's it. The church."

Faith smiled and snitched the last of the treat. "That's what?"

"That's where it is. Near the church. I'm sure I could find the place if I could find that church." The silence grew heavy as Clarissa let the realization and usual fear sink in. "I don't want to get involved in this," she reluctantly admitted.

"I know." Faith swallowed. "But you will. That's the kind of person you are."

"I really hate it when you're right." Clarissa finished gathering their dishes and turned quickly. The heavy, wooden chair fell back onto the floor with a clatter. The few customers seemed barely disturbed by the noise. Relief washed over her. Maybe they hadn't heard any of their conversation.

Faith reached out and touched her arm. "I didn't mean to pressure you. Are you sure you'll be okay?"

"I don't know." That was true enough. Once again, memories threatened to swamp her and send her back into her chair, back into hiding. But the image of the man—his handsome face frozen in newly found death—sent a shiver through her soul.

She slammed the mental doors closed. She would not think about that.

Just then the door of the shop opened and Clarissa smiled in relief. "Time to get back to work." After Faith left, Clarissa purposefully closed her mind to any thoughts of her visions or the man destined to die.

Hours later, she headed for the door, exhausted. Outside the sunset bathed the parking lot in gloom. Her sports car sat in its customary spot, the bright red paint glowing in the late afternoon sun. A cool breeze fingered through her hair and she shivered. It sounded almost as if the breeze whispered her name. Her stomach clenched in anticipation. She spun around to see who was there.

No one.

Still, she felt as if she wasn't alone. She hurried to her car and unlocked it. Slamming the door closed, she smacked the lock down and felt only slightly safer.

Suddenly, a black bird swooped down, brushing its wide wings on the windshield. It settled on the wiper blade and looked through the glass. Amber eyes glared directly at her. She stared in fascination at the softness of its feathers across its spine. Oddly, she wanted to reach out and stroke the sleek, smooth back. Several long minutes passed as the bird perched there, waiting, watching, unperturbed by her presence.

"Caw," it let out a throaty call, and just as quickly, lifted its wings and flew away.

This is ridiculous. She started the car and headed home. Still, the bird intrigued her. She'd never had a pet as a child. Too often animals sensed her psychic abilities and feared her. The zoo animals would pace their cages in agitation if she got too near. Dogs and cats in the neighborhood gladly stayed out of her yard.

A reluctant smiled pulled at her lips as she recalled her grandmother's attempts to compensate. The park near the old woman's house had a carousel. There the animals weren't alive and couldn't fear her. She'd loved to visit the carousel with her grandmother.

The fact that this bird had sat calmly, so near to her, surprised her. Like those old wooden horses, he hadn't seemed to be scared. Shaking her head, she chased away the disturbing thoughts.

She shifted into gear. After several turns down side streets, the city gave way to neighborhoods of tree-lined streets with small older houses. When she passed the Methodist Church, she drove a block and then stopped.

The Methodist Church. The church. She'd "flown" this way last night, she was sure of it. She parked the car in the shade of an elderly spreading elm. For several long minutes she sat in the warmth of the car, her hands trembling against the plastic steering wheel.

Slowly, she opened the car door. Getting out, she moved closer to the tree, closer to the elements of nature, trying to break away from the interference of the cold, modernized world. The heat of the pavement and the steel of the car often interrupted her messages. She'd learned early in life that when the images became too much, a drive in the car would banish them. Though she often thought of the visions as more plague than blessing, today she tentatively sought them out.

She knew she'd come by here, but the images were fading, and it was difficult to remember which direction she'd gone. The cool breeze tugged at her hair and she closed her eyes, seeking any clues the wind might deem to send her. It had been there with her last night.

West. The diner was only a short distance west of here, in a part of town she seldom visited. Gulping back her apprehension, she climbed into her car and turned at the next stoplight.

For several moments, she drove straight west. Then she stopped and turned right once more, then once again as if something drew her down a path. A narrow, broken driveway shot off to the right and she turned into it. There in front of her was the old diner. She swallowed the fear that pushed in on her.

Through the cracks in the old paint, she could see the building had once been white. Looking closer, she saw shades of red, green and blue, and she was almost certain the present color was supposed to be gray. Either that or another coat of badly faded white.

A broken neon sign sat on top of a faded blue awning, its malfunctioning sizzle filling the warm air around her. Dove's Place. It sounded more like a brothel than a diner. Hesitantly, she reached for the car door handle and climbed out.

Would she find him here? If so, what would she do? Before her uncertainty caught up with her, she opened the door and stepped inside.

The odor of something dank and musty filled the little diner. A slow-moving ceiling fan wafted the scent of thick, strong coffee into the mix.

The décor was as authentic as any she'd seen. Aluminum walls, common in the 1950s and every period movie since, reflected her as if through a time warp. The red vinyl stools were just as they had been in her vision. She looked over to the stool where the man had sat last night. He wasn't there. A mixture of disappointment and relief swirled inside her, leaving a knot in her stomach.

Though the stool was empty, she could almost see him there, his strong hands curled around the dingy coffee cup. His shoulders had hunched, as if he were trying to draw within himself, as if wanting to ward off all who approached him. Closing her eyes, she saw the beautiful glimmer of his eyes, and how that glimmer had been abruptly snuffed out.

"What can I get ya?" A rough female voice interrupted Clarissa's thoughts.

"Oh. Uh. Coffee, please." Clarissa looked around for an empty seat and decided to scoot up on the same stool she had occupied last night. As the waitress poured the thick, dark brew into the stained cup, Clarissa grimaced. She didn't want to drink it, but she knew if she wanted answers to her questions, insulting the cook was not a good start. "Uhm, Barbara, is it?" She looked at the small gold badge pinned to the woman's chest. "I'm looking for someone. Do you ever work late at night?"

"Nah, my husband couldn't stand takin' care of the kids that long. No, Madge or Linda works that shift. Why?"

"A...an old friend used to come in here, and I'd like to locate him. Good looking guy, about my age? Dark brown eyes? Long brown hair?"

"Doesn't sound familiar." The waitress wiped the counter with a damp rag, lifting the condiments and cleaning underneath. "If I'm gonna talk to you, I've got to look busy. Ms. Marion isn't exactly an easygoin' woman."

"Ms. Marion?"

"The boss's wife. Ever since he married her a couple years ago, she acts as if she's our lord and master."

"Does she ever work the night shift?"

The waitress laughed. "Nah, that woman don't work—ever—just likes to tell us peons how. Like she ever did an honest day's work in her life."

The conversation lagged while questions bounced around Clarissa's mind. She couldn't ask all the things she wanted. The woman would think she was nuts—and at the moment, Clarissa wasn't so sure she wouldn't be right. She sipped the thick coffee and grimaced, then remembered how the man in the vision had liberally poured sugar into his. It helped a little.

"How late are you open?" she asked.

"Just as the sign says. Twenty-four hours a day. Seven days a week."

"Oh, yes." Clarissa glanced back at the faded sign in the window. It had been there for some time, the letters having dulled in the sun. She noticed several other customers sat scattered about at tables and old-fashioned booths. The jumble of their conversations formed a soft buzz in the warm air.

None of the events matched her vision. She knew he wouldn't be here now. "What time does the next shift come in?"

"Linda's in at three until midnight. Maybe she can help you find your friend." The waitress left the bill next to Clarissa's nearly full cup of coffee.

"I might be back."

"No problem, if you wanna be up that time of night. Not me, I'm up at the crack of dawn. My head's nodding before the late news even begins."

"Well, I'm a night owl. Thank you for the coffee." Clarissa stood and dug around in her purse. "This is my card. Could you have her call me if he comes in?" The woman smiled and slid the card into her uniform pocket. Clarissa wondered if it would vanish in the next wash or if the card would really make it to the next shift. She paid for her coffee, left the full cup on the counter and stepped outside.

The warm fresh afternoon felt good after the stuffy diner. She drank it in, relishing the light mountain air that still amazed her. The heaviness in the diner reminded her too much of Boston and its ancient scents and feel. She shook her head to dispel the thoughts and walked to her car.

The sound of an air pump shattered the peaceful air and startled her. Muffled cuss words followed, and she realized they came from the garage next door. So normal. So ordinary. So, why did the hairs on the back of her neck tingle? She turned, seeking the cause. Nothing looked abnormal.

An old-fashioned general store, with its windows boarded up, stood on one side. Looking down the sidewalk, she saw the remnants of a small town main street. A small town that the city had gobbled up in its growth. Nothing more.

Usually, a place like this, filled with history, gave off vibrations, but this one left her empty, with no impressions at all.

Suppressing a shiver, she hurriedly climbed into her car, anxious to escape this strange place. As she backed out, two men walked behind the car. They passed and when they reached the door of the diner, one of them turned toward her.

Her heart pounded in her chest and sweat drenched her body as her eyes met his.

Frighteningly familiar icy-blue eyes stared back.

The man turned and went inside. Clarissa stared after him. He was the shooter, she was sure of it. But he hadn't done anything yet.

What could she do? She concentrated on the man, committing every detail about him to memory.

Just in case she didn't find his victim in time.

Two

Fear shot out of the sky in the form of lightning. Clarissa expected the sound of thunder on its tail, but its fierce roar still startled her. The mug she held slipped from her fingers and shattered on the tile floor.

Cocoa laced coffee splashed across her toes. She could only stare as the puddle spread around her, the liquid growing, reaching up and poking at the hem of her skirt, fingering the pale fabric like a lover's caress.

She cried out and tried to step away, but the coffee had thickened and held her in place.

"No!" she screamed, the sound of the single word breaking the spell, breaking the darkness. And waking her.

She sat up, hugging the pillow close to her chest, burying her face in its softness. The tears that dampened the case surprised her, but she didn't try to stop them.

The dreams were getting worse and more frequent. She hadn't had any more true visions, but instead, when she slept, the night tormented her, stealing her rest and planting fear in her soul.

She needed to talk to someone, but Faith was away on assignment. There wasn't anyone else she trusted that she could talk to. She couldn't keep on like this, but what could she do? No one else knew about her special sight. No one knew her secrets.

Climbing out of bed, she flipped on the light. The mirror over the dresser reflected her bedraggled image back at her. She stared at the stranger there. How lost and forlorn she looked. "No, damn it." She stamped her foot in frustration. "Whoever you are, get out of my head," she yelled into the night.

Determinedly, she straightened the bedcovers, then struck a match from the tin and lit the lavender candle. Its aroma reached out and caressed her. So easy. So sweet. She breathed in and let it soothe her.

Calmed, she climbed back beneath the covers. Instead of turning off the light, she reached for a book and settled down to read. She needed to refocus her thoughts.

Suddenly, a movement caught her eye. Startled, she looked up and gasped. There in the mirror was the image of a man.

She looked around the room but saw no one. He was the same man as in her first vision. An unfelt wind lifted his hair and fingered through the dark stands. He stared at her with eyes as dark as night and as empty—as if someone had erased his soul.

He tilted his head back and while she didn't hear it, she knew the howl of despair that tore from his throat and shattered the air.

And then she heard a whisper that wasn't a man's voice. A whisper so soft she'd have missed it if there were any other noises in the room. Then the soft, feminine whisper said, "Mine," the sound reaching out and pulling at Clarissa.

She watched in fascinated horror as the man in the mirror threw back his head again. The glass darkened and the image vanished. She shivered and burrowed beneath the thick blankets.

The silence around her told her only one thing.

She was well beyond escape.

* * * *

The line stretched halfway across the bank lobby. As Clarissa waited patiently for her turn at the teller window, she couldn't help wondering if the air conditioner was broken. Even the brass fans hanging from the high marble ceiling did little to help the sweltering heat. Summer should have lost its grip, but it hung on tenaciously, melting the autumn.

Clarissa held the heavy deposit bag in one hand and fanned her heated face with today's paper. After a week, she still hadn't found any reports of any shootings. She was thankful, but she hadn't found the stranger, either.

As a result, her work had fallen behind. She'd neglected things like making bank deposits. That's why the money bag was so heavy this morning. She had to focus seriously on not losing her livelihood. Luckily, despite her lack of attention, business at The Angry Bean had been very good. She smiled in relief as she thought about her shop. Nearly two years in business and she was actually making a living.

"May I help you?" The teller turned her heat-wilted smile to Clarissa as she stepped forward. She pulled the cash from her bag the same instant a door in the back flew open and a young man burst out.

"This is the last straw," he yelled. "I quit." He stalked across the lobby, leaving the big, heavy door behind the counter open wide. Clarissa couldn't resist peeking into the inner sanctum of the bank, an area few customers ever saw. The lush conference room was as opulent as the lobby. Papers and notebooks littered the surface of a long polished table.

She scanned the faces of the people in the meeting as they all stared after him. Only one person moved. A man stood and reached for the scattered papers. Slowly, he put them back in order without speaking a word.

And then he looked up.

The golden-brown eyes staring back at her had haunted her dreams for nights. Her heart twisted and then thudded against her ribs.

"It's him," Clarissa whispered to herself.

The teller glanced back over her shoulder at the open door. "Oh, do you know Mr. Lorde?"

"Mr. Lorde?" Was that his name? Trepidation and excitement welled inside her.

"I'm sure you weren't staring like that at any of the old geezers in that room." The teller chuckled and passed the deposit slip across the counter. "Mr. Lorde puts that look on lots of women's faces."

Automatically, Clarissa grasped the paper and stepped back. She'd found him. He was here, in this lovely bank, safe and sound. Her relief faded as quickly as it had appeared.

Yes, he was safe here. But what about elsewhere? And for how long? Questions tumbled over themselves in her mind.

Why would a man like the one she saw in that room be a regular customer in Dove's Place? The tailored suit he wore was obviously expensive, and he wore it as if born to it. Surely someone that important wouldn't frequent seedy diners. Not that time of night.

Someone stood up from the table and closed the door. Clarissa caught herself as she leaned forward for a better look. The soft snick of the latch seemed all too loud in the quiet foyer.

Now what? She stood in the lobby as other bank patrons walked in and out around her. She vaguely heard their footsteps on the polished tile, faintly heard the gentle hiss of the automatic doors as they opened and closed.

He was in the middle of a meeting. She couldn't just barge in. She hesitated. What would he think or say if she burst in?

She shivered as visions of the past crowded in. She pushed the memories away. This was Boulder, Colorado, not Boston,

Massachusetts. Things were different here. People were different. Faith's words came to mind. Clarissa wasn't the kind of person to leave someone in danger. She pushed her fears away.

"May I help you?" A woman's voice broke into Clarissa's thoughts. She looked up and saw a pretty, neatly dressed woman behind the new accounts desk looking up at her with feigned politeness.

"I...I was wondering if I could see Mr. Lorde. It's very important."

"Oh?" The woman looked doubtful, her eyes scanning Clarissa from head to toe. The frown forming between the woman's neatly plucked brows showed her disapproval. Clarissa resisted the urge to look down. She knew she wasn't dressed like someone doing important bank business, but she hadn't planned on finding him when she'd left home this morning to run a few errands.

"Mr. Lorde doesn't see anyone without an appointment," the woman explained.

"I have to see him." Clarissa walked quickly to the desk. "It's urgent. I can't leave here until I've spoken with him." *Or I lose my nerve.*

Something in her voice must have registered with the woman because she stood, saying, "He should be out of his meeting. I'll see what I can do." She disappeared behind the partition.

Clarissa paced in front of the desk. What if he wouldn't see her? What would she do? Her resolve wavered a moment and she bolstered it with images from her visions and dreams.

It seemed like forever before the woman returned. The smug look on her face sent Clarissa's heart plummeting.

"Mr. Lorde doesn't recall any appointments and is unable to see you today."

"Of course, I don't have an appointment. I just figured out who he is." Clarissa tried to stop the panic rising in her voice and heart.

"Maybe someone else can help you." A trimmed brow shot upward. "He instructed me to give you this. Call Melanie Schaefer at that number. She's his administrative assistant. She might be able to help you."

The woman handed over a business card. White. Utilitarian. Boring. The bold black lettering spelled out David Lorde, the name repeating itself in her mind.

David. It echoed in her thoughts, sounding and feeling right. She felt his warmth as she touched the card he'd held only moments before. Flashes of his image filled her mind. A man with sadness imbedded in his soul. A man with much weight on his shoulders. A man whose very existence could be wiped out if she didn't do something to stop it.

"If you don't mind, I'll wait until Mr. Lorde can squeeze me in today. Tell him it's urgent." Not giving the woman a chance to refuse, Clarissa spun in her heel, grabbed a tattered magazine off the brass-framed table and settled onto the leather couch.

"Well," the woman huffed and disappeared behind the partition again. When she resumed her seat, she merely glanced at Clarissa before returning to the computer terminal.

* * * *

Who is she?

David knew he'd never seen her before, and yet something about her seemed familiar. He studied her through the two-way mirror that looked out on the lobby.

He should have been concentrating on the files for the next meeting, something he'd had little success with today. She moved then, and a stray beam of sunlight from the window illuminated each delicate ringlet of the curls cascading past her waist. He admired their mixed texture of bright gold intertwined with soft white. She absently flipped the mane over her shoulder with a frustrated gesture. Hair like that could wrap around a man, and he almost felt the silky strands binding him to her as their bodies pressed close...

Heat rose in his blood, and he took a step back. Pain stabbed through his joints and he closed his eyes, concentrating to stay in control. No, not now. Not here. Wearily, he rubbed a hand over his face, and he felt the thick stubble on his chin. Damn.

Several deep breaths slowed his heart and the pace of his blood. He focused on remaining calm, forced his mind to control his emotions, to tamp down the longing the woman inspired. He didn't need or want this.

In control once again, he stalked to his desk and jabbed the intercom. "Melanie? That young woman in the lobby, did she give her name?"

"No, sir. She just said she had to see you today. I don't think she's leaving until she does."

David chose to ignore the hint of laughter in Melanie's voice. They'd worked together too long, and he had to admit she was right. The woman was parked on the couch as if she were there for the duration.

His throat went strangely dry as he stood watching her. He reached for the water pitcher on the end of his desk and poured a glass. His hand shook, and the sound of the ice cracking jarred his nerves and made him hastily set the glass back down on the rich wood.

On the other side of the mirror, he watched the sunlight play in the woman's hair and did his best to ignore it. Instead, he focused on the rest of her, trying to find some clue to her identity.

His gaze traveled over every inch of her. The loose green dress wasn't meant to make a fashion statement; it was meant only to be cool. But the low neckline and her bare arms made a definite statement of elegance. Her skin was smooth and golden from the sun, and for some reason, he imagined the scent of vanilla.

Her long, flowing skirt hid most of her legs from view, but the dainty ankles and slim feet encased in the thin-strapped white sandals hinted at trim contoured calves and thighs.

His pulse raced again, and he took another deep breath. He clenched his hands into fists, fighting to remain in control. Suddenly, she turned and David stared into the deepest jade green eyes he'd ever seen.

She knew.

His gut tightened as he read knowledge in her eyes.

She knew he was there.

She could read his soul as if he'd printed it out on paper and handed it to her.

She stood and slowly walked to the mirror without looking away. Delicate, pink-nailed fingers reached into her purse and extracted a small brush. Deliberately, she pulled the brush through her long curls, trapping him in a web of passion as surely as if she'd bound him with twine.

His senses overloaded when she pulled out her lipstick and carefully traced her full, slightly damp lips with a delicate pink shade. The simple action of one lip caressing the other brought perspiration to his brow.

Who was she, and why the hell was she doing this to him?

He growled low in his throat, imagining what she'd do if

he leapt through the mirror and took her. The image formed so strongly in his mind that he had to pull his hands back from the cool surface of the glass.

"Melanie," he roared. The secretary burst through the door, panic written all over her face. "Get her in here. Now." He'd put a stop to this.

He curled his hands into fists and shoved them into his pockets, hiding the cruel evidence that he wasn't totally in control.

* * * *

He was there behind the mirror. She knew he was. His heat pulsed alive and reached out to touch her, at first hesitant, like a newborn wave on the sand. Then, as she ran her lipstick over her lips, his heat grew, reaching out and crashing over her.

Startled, she dropped the tube. It hit the mirror's frame, leaving a pink mark before landing on the tile. Even in the noise of the bank she heard the metal tube as it skittered across the floor.

As she bent to pick it up, a middle-aged woman stepped through a nearby door. "Hello. I'm Melanie Schaefer. Mr. Lorde can see you now."

The woman seemed to sense her nervousness and smiled reassuringly. *She probably thinks I'm intimidated by his status,* Clarissa mused. If only she knew.

As they stopped outside a thick wooden door with "David A. Lorde, Vice President of Accounts" on the brass plate beside it, Clarissa swallowed. Why did she suddenly long to turn and run away?

She knew with sudden certainty that whatever—whoever—was on the other side of that door would knock her world off-kilter. The woman opened the door and ushered her in.

He stood from where he sat behind an imposing wood desk. "Good afternoon, Miss...?"

"Elgin. Clarissa Elgin." She fumbled in her purse until she found a business card and handed it to him.

"Miss Elgin. Please, make yourself comfortable." He took the card and sat down once she did.

She settled back into the soft leather chair and let her relief wash over her. She'd found him in time. Pushing her earlier discomfort aside, she said, "You don't know how relieved I am to find you."

He regarded her with a shuttered stare. "What exactly can I do for you?"

Pausing, she chose her words carefully. She'd never been good at this part. It was a risk, a risk that could backfire on her. It suddenly felt even riskier. "I've come to help you."

"Help me?" He gazed at her in doubt and confusion.

"Yes. I'm not crazy, really." She paused again. "I know this will sound weird, but I have an ability some would call psychic. I've been having visions." She hated the initial explanation. They always looked at her as if she'd lost her mind. Refusing to give in to her own discomfort, she leaned forward. "You were in one of them."

His stare was direct and insolent. "A vision?" He crossed his arms over his chest, purposely putting a barrier between them. "Okay. This could be interesting. What are you up to?"

"I didn't come here to be demeaned, Mr. Lorde. I came here because I have a gift. It's not always a gift I particularly want." Her voice rose as her frustration grew. "But at least I try to use it wisely."

He watched her, a predatory look in his eyes. His long tanned fingers rubbed his chin as he appeared to ponder her words. The soft rasp of his five o'clock shadow beneath his fingers seemed loud in the still air, and Clarissa found her eyes drawn to the movement. What would it feel like to have those fingers touching her? How would his rough chin feel beneath her lips?

Startled at the path of her thoughts, she stood, hoping to relieve some of the intimidation he instilled in her. "As I said, I had a vision and you were in it."

He cocked a knowing eyebrow upward, and Clarissa felt her cheeks warm under the intensity. What was wrong with her?

"When did you have this...vision?

"Just over a week ago."

"Uh-huh." He paused, slowly picked up her business card and perused it again. His gaze flicked back and forth between her and the card. "This isn't the first time a pretty woman has made claims about erotic dreams."

His arrogance made Clarissa cringe. "I hate to disappoint you, but this wasn't a dream." She blew a stray lock of hair out of her face in frustration. "And there was nothing erotic about it." Even as she said it, she decided to ignore the heat in her cheeks. He was a nonbeliever. She'd have to convince him, without giving him any more ideas that this was a come on.

"All right. Let's suppose it was a dream. Why, then, would I see you in that little diner you frequent? On the south side of town? By the old Methodist church. Dove's Place?"

She watched the shock dawn in his eyes. The arrogance slid from his face and was replaced by a cold, dark anger that settled in his eyes and set a pallor beneath his tan. She blinked and the reaction was gone. Instead, he leaned forward and stared coldly at her.

"Look, Miss..." He glanced down at her card and back up again. "Elgin. No one gets into my private life uninvited. I don't know what you're up to, but let me warn you, I'm not someone you want to play with."

She felt the anger in him. Not just at her, but at the world in general. She almost wished for the arrogance, even if it was at her expense. Taking a deep breath, she allowed her mind to fill with the images of the vision, allowed herself once again to feel the horror of it. His anger didn't seem so unbearable compared to his fate.

"I'm not playing games." She leaned close to the desk, catching his gaze with a determined one of her own. "I had a vision about you. It wasn't a dream or a fantasy but a look into the future. I was in the diner with you. So was a waitress. In my vision you were shot. You died in my arms, your blood soaking through my clothes."

She shivered at the all too vivid memory.

She hated using shock, but many times it was the only way to get someone's attention.

A startled look flitted through his eyes before he shoved the mask back in place. "Look, lady. I'm not really up to this right now. I've got better things to do than worry about your dreams."

She paused, hesitant as thoughts jumbled in her mind, appearing from someplace else. "You'll never catch the embezzler."

Now why had she told him that? The words had popped into her mind as clearly as the words he'd just spoken. Earlier, she'd noticed the tension in the staff, but had put it off to the heat. Maybe that wasn't all there was to it. Suddenly she knew what it was. Someone was stealing money from inside the bank.

Suddenly, a cool breeze filtered through the room, and an ice-cold chill reached through the stifling heat and froze the blood in her veins. As she watched David Lorde rise to his feet, she suddenly saw a darkness in him she hadn't seen before. This wasn't the same man who'd died in her arms a few nights ago. This was a man whose life had been hard, a hardness he'd adopted and ingrained within every molecule of his life.

"What do you know about that?" He leaned toward her, his knuckles white on the desk blotter.

"Nothing beyond what I just said." Her fingers trembled, and she clutched the handle of her purse. This whole situation was out of her league. She'd had visions most of her life, but nothing like this.

From out of nowhere, she knew what was going on in his life. Too much knowledge bombarded her mind at once, spinning wildly inside. The embezzlement. The cold hard mask he fought to keep in place. The pain and the anger it could only hide part of the time.

She shivered. Evil, thick and black, brushed its icy wings against her.

"You can tell me what you know now or at the police station." His voice broke into her thoughts. The same growl she'd heard in her dreams echoed around her, and she took several steps backward. The ripples of evil grew in their intensity. She had to get away from this man.

She turned to leave and the room swam before her eyes. She hadn't had visions this strong in years. The last time everything had turned fatal. She couldn't go through that again. She just couldn't.

"Let me go. I don't know anything about this bank. I don't want to know any more about you," she whispered, fear tightening the muscles in her throat. She turned and stumbled toward the door, struggling to catch her breath and get away.

But he wasn't letting her go. Stalking around the desk, he reached out to grab her and halted her flight. Just as his fingers touched her arm, she crumpled. Strong arms slipped around her shoulders and beneath her knees.

She was underwater, trying to surface, struggling to reach the real world. She heard a voice barking out commands. She felt movement and something soft beneath her.

"What did you do? Scare her to death?" A woman's vaguely

familiar voice broke through the thick air.

A deep growl was the only answer she heard before the darkness descended. She heard voices calling to her, but she couldn't answer them, couldn't make her body or her lips respond.

Anger and pain reached out to her, pulling her away. Through the thick fog that engulfed her, she heard different voices. They sounded hollow through the gray swirls. Who were they?

They were arguing. A woman cried and pleaded, a note of pain in her voice. Suddenly, the woman screamed and Clarissa called out to her, "Please, let me help you. Please."

Then the woman's voice grew clear, the fog seemed to thin. "Please. No. David. I...I love you."

The man's voice was clearer now, too. "No, my dear treacherous wife, you don't love me. You just love my money and position and everything it gives you."

"No, David. No." The woman's screams exploded through Clarissa's mind. She heard a gunshot followed by cold, empty silence.

"Now, my sweet, you can't hurt me anymore."

Clarissa stared at a woman's fallen figure. A bright red stain pooled on the front of her creamy, satin jumpsuit. Then, as the image faded away, she heard the faint notes of a music box. Its high-pitched tinny notes faded away, leaving Clarissa cloaked in dark silence.

The blackness should have felt good, but it didn't. It was cold and lonely and she wanted to escape, but it trapped her as if she were buried alive.

Fighting the heaviness in her lungs, she tried to suck in air. Slowly, much too slowly, the darkness lifted and it grew lighter as the moments passed. She pushed herself toward it, longing to see light again.

"I think she's coming to." A woman's voice sounded in Clarissa's ear, and she jerked away from the sound, fearing the return of the angry voices.

"Miss Elgin? Clarissa?" David's voice was a deep rumble, and she turned her head, wanting to hear the familiar sound again. Slowly, she lifted her eyelids and found her sight filled with his alarmingly handsome face.

"What happened?" Was that whispery voice really hers?

"You passed out in my office."

“I’m sorry.” Clarissa tried to sit up, but found her strength gone and her limbs shaky. Though visions often left her depleted, she couldn’t remember the last time she’d been this physically drained.

“Do you want me to call a doctor?” The question came from a middle-aged woman who hovered near David’s shoulder.

“No, I think she’ll be fine. It’s probably the heat. I’m surprised we don’t have more people keeling over in the lobby.” For an instant he turned away from Clarissa and faced the woman. “You can go back to work. Call maintenance and see if they’re making progress on fixing that damned air conditioning. I’ll take care of Miss Elgin.”

“I, uh, must be going.” Clarissa tried again to get up from the couch where David had apparently laid her. Instead of helping her, she found him leaning over her, his warm, strong arms on either side, blocking her escape.

“Oh, no you don’t. I want some answers.”

He was so close she felt the hard edge of his hip pressing against her thigh. The scent of his spicy cologne filled the air around them and drifted into her lungs, taunting her, teasing her with its subtlety.

Reluctantly, she relaxed back against the cushions. Exhaustion tugged at her, and she wanted to sleep, to curl up into a ball and retreat from the world. What little sleep she’d gotten lately had proven painful. That was probably why the simple vision had drained her so completely today.

“I don’t normally have this strong a reaction,” she explained, a weak smile tugging at her lips.

“Reaction to what? Heat? Or being interrogated?”

“Neither. To a vision.”

“Let’s not start that again.” He stood and strode away from her.

She wasn’t fooled. He wasn’t letting her go. He could move with lightning speed. She sat up, taking several long seconds to adjust to the swaying of the room. There was no way she’d get away from him now, and they both knew it.

He paced back and forth in front of her like a caged animal longing to escape but knowing it had no means to leave. Every few steps his hand shot up and slid through his thick hair, leaving narrow tracks that disappeared with the next angry pass of his fingers.

“Look, I can see you don’t believe in my abilities. There’s

really no sense in my staying here. I gave you my card. You know where to find me."

"Wait a minute. You come in here demanding to see me. You know something no one else knows about in my bank. Then you say you know nothing. You expect me to believe that's the end of it?" He reached out and snagged a chair from a nearby table. Turning it backward, he settled into the seat, resting his arms across the back. "Nothing doing."

His dark, angry gaze bored into hers. His wide brown eyes widened even more and his nostrils flared as he breathed in. His shoulders hunched, and with his head lowered, he looked angry enough to charge. She leaned back against the couch, putting distance between them, only slightly reassured that the slim chair back stood as a barrier.

The deep breathing exercises she often used suddenly seemed worthless. Her heart pounded against her ribs, wanting also to be free. Forcing her mind to focus on something besides the anger in his eyes and her own reaction to it, she reluctantly recalled the images she'd just seen. "Are you married?"

Her question came from out of left field and the startled look on his face told her she'd taken him off guard. "Am I what?"

"Married."

Surprise softened his features, and she found herself wanting to erase the anger from his eyes.

"No. My wife died a couple of years ago."

"D...died?" Clarissa looked down at her hands in order to hide the fear gripping her. "How?"

"I don't think that's any of your business." Tension and grief cloaked his voice.

"It's just that...in the vision I heard people arguing."

"Who? What were they arguing about?" His voice was patronizing.

How much did she dare to tell him? Was he...a killer? How fast could she run?

"I asked you a question. Who was arguing?"

She thought for a minute. She didn't know who they were or what they had argued about. The strongest impressions she'd received were about where they had been. She sensed the familiarity they had with their surroundings. Their home. She shivered as the image became clearer in her memory.

"He was angry with her, but I don't know why." She paused,

unsure what his reaction would be to her next words. "He shot her. I heard a music box."

David went ghost-white pale. The eyes that had sparkled with anger filled with the dullness of grief. What nerve had she touched? Guilt?

Jumping to his feet, he flung the chair away. It clattered against the wall. "Get the hell out of here."

The level of his voice hadn't risen, but its tone implied leashed anger. Hatred and pain emanated from him. He turned his back to her, curling his hands into fists, which he shoved into his pockets. "Now! Before I throw you out." His arm extended, one long finger pointing to the exit door.

Clarissa rose to her feet, stumbling slightly. When she reached the door, she couldn't stop herself from looking back at him one more time. He stood there, ramrod straight, every muscle in his body taut and rigid. She couldn't see his face, but she knew his eyes were closed and his jaw clenched painfully tight with a soul-deep pain.

Agony, vicious and cold, ripped through him. She felt it pulsing and alive as it spread around him. She thought she almost saw it, reaching out toward her. Then something icy slid past her, almost a shiver but not quite. She didn't have any idea what it was, and she turned and ran, hoping, praying, to outrun its evil touch.

Three

Flickering white light provided the only illumination in the small security room. The closed-circuit cameras positioned directly behind each teller and at each exit broadcast views of the lobby. David slouched in a chair, his gaze skipping back and forth across the monitors, seeking some sign of anything out of the ordinary. Nothing.

Nothing unusual had happened today—or any day—in weeks. Not unless he counted yesterday's visit from Clarissa Elgin. That had definitely been unusual. But he'd yet to find any connection with her and the bank other than the fact that she was a business customer. How had she found out about the embezzlement...or the murder?

As memories of her warnings seeped into his thoughts, he slammed the door on his emotions, an act he'd perfected over the past three years. He would not think about the past. He'd left that all behind.

He rubbed his eyes, glancing away for an instant. What he wouldn't give for a good night's sleep. Looking up at the monitors again, he watched an elderly woman shuffle through the brass and glass front door.

Everything looked normal, as usual. He yawned, waiting for time to pass. Then the older woman he'd only been half watching bumped into the doorman. Lionel caught her arm and steadied her. Was she all right? She smiled vaguely and continued on her way. He kept an eye on her, making certain she didn't fall.

Light from the chandelier reflected faint blue highlights when she patted her neatly coiffed hair as she passed the large plate glass wall mirror near the door. Slowly, in that shuffling step, she walked to the table where blank forms were kept.

Painstakingly, she removed the white gloves from her hands, revealing curled arthritic fingers. Clasping the chain-mounted pen in an awkward grip, she meticulously wrote on a blank withdrawal slip.

As she wrote, she stopped to fan her face with the gloves she held crumpled in her gnarled fist. Her hand went up to her face, as if testing for a fever. He was just about to alert the staff to the fact that the woman might be unwell when suddenly she looked up.

Her gaze met his. She stared directly at the camera, at

him, with sheer malevolence in her eyes. It was as if she knew he was watching. The power of her stare seemed hauntingly familiar, and yet he knew he'd never seen this woman before. Surely she didn't know he was watching her. Scorching, prickly heat broke out on the back of his neck.

Breaking the stare, the woman slowly picked up the paper and turned to stand in line. David continued to watch as she moved to the teller and punched the personal code in the keypad on the counter. The teller counted out the bills and the old woman lifted her purse onto the counter. She neatly slid the two fifty dollar bills in next to a pile of embroidered hankies.

She turned, casting a final challenging glance into the camera, and shuffled out the door. The bright afternoon sun quickly swallowed her.

David rewound the tape to the point where the woman entered the bank. Something didn't feel right, and he'd learned to trust his gut long ago.

Once again the old woman shuffled across the floor in her awkward gait. She walked past the forms desk, and David stopped the tape. Slowly, he advanced, frame by frame.

What the hell?

The woman didn't go to the forms counter. She never looked up at the camera. She simply walked to the line and conducted her business.

Again he rewound the tape. Again she walked directly to the line. At the point where she put the bills in her purse, he paused the tape. Two twenties.

Was he going crazy? He'd seen the old woman go to the desk and fill out a withdrawal slip. What had happened to the tape?

He swore and slammed his fist down on the console. The pain came swiftly from the impact, from frustration, and from the curse that he'd almost learned to live with. He stabbed the intercom button. "Send Jackie in here as soon as she finishes with this customer," David instructed the security guard who answered. He saw the guard on the monitor nod even before his words of agreement came through the phone link.

The guard walked over to the teller who had waited on the old lady. She quickly concluded the next transaction before sliding the "Next Window Please" sign in place.

It took only an instant for the teller to tap on the outside door of the observation room since it sat directly behind the teller stations.

"Come in." David didn't look up, but continued to watch the monitor tape of the old lady.

"Jackie? What was this woman's business?" His finger pointed to the frozen image of the old woman.

"I'm sorry, I don't remember."

"She was in here only a few moments ago. How can you not remember?" He spun the chair around and glared at the young woman who stood hidden in the shadows just inside the door.

"I don't know, Mr. Lorde. I've been busy today." Her voice shook, and she didn't venture farther into the room.

"I'm sorry to snap at you, Jackie." David tried to relax. Getting angry with employees wasn't going to help him at all. The foreboding pain in his joints warned him. He fought his anger, tamping it down and shoving it into the empty place where his heart used to be.

"Can you close out and bring your drawer in here? I'd like to look through your day's business."

"Yes, sir." Jackie stopped at the doorway. "I haven't done anything wrong." She slipped from the room quickly, not waiting for his response. David spun the chair back around and watched as she returned to her station. She carefully cleared out the computer before pulling the cash drawer and heading back toward the office.

The light tap of her hand on the door came only an instant after she left the view of monitor six. David stood and opened the door this time, taking the cash drawer from her hands. As he did so, he noticed her hands were trembling.

"Don't worry, Jackie." He meant to be soothing, but he didn't notice any calming in the young woman.

What was she afraid of? Was she in cahoots with the old lady and frightened by the prospect of getting caught? His eyes narrowed suspiciously as he moved to a table in the corner of the room. He set the drawer down and flipped through the deposit and withdrawal slips.

Third down in the stack he found a withdrawal form made out in an uneven scrawl. The arthritic hands.

There was his wife's account number. All the numbers were carefully printed in the same uneven scrawl. On the matching machine receipt were the appropriate I.D. numbers. Whatever code the woman had punched in, it had created the correct number sequence to access the computer.

Rachel was the only person who had known those numbers.

She hadn't even shared with David the fact that the account existed, much less the code numbers. He hadn't known about it until the estate was settled after her death.

He'd planned to close the account—until he'd discovered someone was still making withdrawals.

To make matters worse, no signature was required on any of Rachel's accounts. She'd ranted and raved about how she shouldn't have to identify herself since she was a part of the family who owned the bank. David had finally given in and requested the special adjustment. Her laziness would now be his downfall.

So how had this old woman learned the code? And why?

* * * *

Sunlight slipped down through the trees, splashing across the overflowing produce stands. The peaches, apples and tomatoes all appeared in varied colors in the dappled light.

Clarissa strolled up and down the aisles, her basket dangling from her arm. A wide-brimmed hat shaded her face. Her skirt ruffled against her bare calves in the breeze created as she walked.

She'd hoped to step away from the world today, seeking out the farmer's market for its soothing atmosphere. She picked up a ripe shiny apple. It's crisp, sweet scent wafted up to her and she breathed it in, cleansing her soul.

She felt the tension slipping away and smiled.

Since she'd seen David Lorde at the bank yesterday, the visions hadn't gone away. He was safe now, she was sure of it, now that she'd warned him.

So why hadn't the night returned to normal?

"Can I wrap some of those up for you, dear?" A faded voice startled Clarissa and she dropped the apple. The dull thud it made as it hit the ground sounded somehow ominous and sad.

"Uh, yes." She stooped and picked up the apple, handing it to the old woman standing on the other side of the fruit cart. "I'll take half a dozen."

"All right."

The woman shuffled behind the makeshift counter as Clarissa watched. She reminded her of Granny Clary. Funny, she seldom thought of Granny anymore, her grief having long ago healed. But in the past week her grandmother had come to mind several times.

"That'll be a dollar eighty five." The woman put apples in

a paper bag.

Clarissa dug the money out of her purse and handed it over. As their hands met, the woman smiled and spoke, "Such a good girl. Trust in your instincts."

Clarissa froze and a shiver stole up her spine. She nearly dropped the bag. That same sentence, those same voice tones and accent, had been so distinctly Granny.

"Do I know you?" she asked.

"I don't think so." The woman stared back. "Do you come here frequently?"

"No. I've never been here before." Clarissa took several steps back. The woman watched her, a frown deepening on her brow and Clarissa felt that old fear, that old resistance to her skills as it threatened to overwhelm her.

* * * *

David closed his eyes, fighting the heat that raged through his blood, the frustration that refused to fade. He clenched his fists, feeling the sharp edges of his nails dig into his skin.

He'd gone through all the teller drawers. They all balanced. He'd double-checked every security tape. He found no record or indication of who the elderly woman was or that she'd done anything different than the tape. "Damn," he cursed and raked his fingers through his hair. He took several deep breaths, focusing on the bank of monitors in front of him.

His heart slowed and he felt the changes in his body as he calmed. Relief washed over him, but it was short-lived as the phone rang and shattered the quiet. He picked up the receiver and growled into it, "What?"

"Your three o'clock appointment just cancelled," Melanie informed him.

Suddenly, the afternoon was empty and stretched out before him in blessed freedom. He'd already lost his temper twice today. He wasn't sure that he could regain control if it happened again.

Ever since Clarissa Elgin's visit yesterday, he'd been edgy, and last night he hadn't been able to sleep or escape to the diner. Instead, he'd lain awake, staring at the ceiling, waiting. Waiting for what never came. Today the old woman's appearance on the tape only added to his frustration.

"I'll take some work home. Maybe take off early," he told Melanie. Her surprised silence told him what he didn't need to be told. He, David Lorde, VP of Accounts, never went home early.

Well, today was a different day.

Outside, the fall air was crisp and musty from leaves and the damp. A slight breeze ruffled his hair, and he yanked at his tie and released his collar, recalling his boyhood days when school let out. He remembered strolling down the neighborhood streets, his backpack dragging off his shoulder, the mounds of golden yellow leaves crunching beneath his sneakers.

Life certainly had changed in the years since. He reached his car and pulled open the door. No. He refused to let the past ruin his suddenly good day.

He stripped off his loose tie and suit jacket and tossed them into the backseat. His briefcase followed.

Antsy, he slammed the door closed and instead of climbing in, started walking. God, it felt good to be free.

The heels of his dress shoes clicked on the walk, and he almost convinced himself it sounded like those crackling leaves of old. The late afternoon sun took on a red glow. He felt the sun's pull. The warm fingers of light slipped over the horizon like the whisper of a kiss.

A park across the street teemed with life. People moved about in a mishmash of color and sound. Drawn to the warmth and normality of it, he quickened his step and found a farmer's market sprawled across the lawns.

He joined the moving crowd. A yawn escaped, and he blinked, trying to fight the exhaustion that soaked into his bones. He took a deep breath, dragging the cool afternoon air into his lungs. The urge to throw his head back and cry out nearly overwhelmed him. Instead, he stalked through the crowd, letting the warmth of humanity engulf him. The scents overwhelmed him, and he breathed it all in. Beautiful. His keen senses sharpened, and he took another breath, this time with closed eyes.

Her. He smelled her. All woman, wild and sweet.

He opened his eyes, scanning the pathways until he found the now familiar form. White gold curls tumbled from beneath a straw hat as she bought a bag of apples. He smiled as he watched her talking with the old woman.

A new scent filled the air. A damp, dark scent he recognized all too clearly.

Her fear.

What was she afraid of? The old woman? Was she the same person who had been in the bank earlier today? He didn't think so. He looked closer, but he couldn't really tell. His frustration returned and he knew he'd made a mistake. All afternoon he'd controlled his emotions, controlled the changes. Now he didn't have the strength to stop it.

No, not now. Not here. He balled his hands into fists, struggling against the inevitable transformation. He had to get out of here before anyone saw him change. His steps quickened as he left the park. Bone, sinew and skin shifted, pulling tight and driving pain through every inch of him. A cry broke from his throat, and he ducked behind a stand of lilac bushes, a hedge thick with a leftover green summer coat.

Where smooth skin had been, thick golden fur grew. His fingernails formed claws that he scraped across the bare dirt. Hunched over, he viewed the world from a lower angle.

He no longer walked or jogged, but broke into a full run. The rough dirt trail, sand and stone, bit into the callused pads of his feet. He looked down, saw the light fur-covered paws that he knew were his. Misery swamped him. His pained growl broke the air. This time he gave into the urge to roar that he was here and awake and on the prowl.

His long strides ate up the distance and soon he was far from the park, safe from the prying, misunderstanding eyes. He hunkered down in a bush and dropped his head. His breath came in sharp pants and he waited for his heart to calm

Why did this happen? What made him this...this...man trapped as a beast? A beast he strangely understood. A beast he feared, not because it might harm him, but because what if it one day consumed the man?

As he rested there in the fading glow of the day, the sounds of nature returned. He listened, closing his eyes and praying.

As he calmed, the pain returned, tearing through him with greater ferocity than before. Suddenly, a loud crack broke the quiet. "Scat!" He heard a man's rough voice before the crack sounded again.

New pain tore through his side, burning deep into his body. Once again the world shifted, returning the beast to man.

A man whose blood pooled on the trail and trickled down into the ground.

Four

Clarissa sighed. Three days had passed since her trip to the bank. Three miserable days where she kept thinking about David Lorde, The Infuriating. Three nights where her mind filled with visions of the diner.

The growing night reached out with long shadows across her backyard. The still full trees blocked her view of the neighbor's yard, and she usually liked that. Over the coming winter months, she'd become accustomed to seeing the familiar figure of Mrs. Larson as she washed her dishes each night. She actually looked forward to it, which surprised her.

But right now, she felt isolated and more alone than she had in a long time. In the window glass, she watched herself lift her coffee cup and sip. She was still tired, but in the distorted reflection she couldn't see the dark circles she knew were there. All she saw was the outline of her riotous curls that fell in a tangle down her back. She barely reached five feet. A throwback, Mother had always called her, referring to how she looked like that old tintype of her great grandmother instead of a modern young lady.

She shook her head. She was happy with herself, with her looks. Somehow seeing David Lorde had messed with her thinking.

Why did the memory of the icy coldness in his eyes make her think of heat? So what if he made her heart pound like it hadn't since her first crush? So what if he made her yearn for things like she'd felt back in high school? So what if he made her feel things—and it was obvious she made him feel nothing. Except maybe suspicion.

The straight arrowness of his stance made her feel like melting—and taking him with her. The stiffness of his jaw and the twitch in his cheek told of anger, but it also showed her a man fighting to keep control.

But control of what? Himself? Her? His sanity?

She'd tried to lie down and rest earlier, but her mind filled with the alternating images of David's handsome face and the awful images of the visions. They both overpowered and intimidated her. She wasn't sure which was more disturbing.

She had managed to forget for just a little while at the farmer's market. Until she'd run into that old lady. Even now she shivered as she recalled her words. Trust in your instincts, just like Granny had always said.

She sighed. Her life seemed to have gone haywire lately. Strange visions. Strange people. And David. Clarissa wanted nothing more to do with him, or anyone unusual, for that matter.

She'd done her job. She'd warned him, hadn't she? That had to be good enough. But why didn't it feel good enough?

With another heavy sigh, she flipped the kitchen light off and made her way down the hallway to her bedroom.

She passed the living room and paused. The turmoil and thoughts she couldn't escape seemed to continue. She walked into the darkened room and settled into the old rocking chair by the picture window, recalling the hours she'd spent as a child nestled in it. The heavy wooden arms curled around her in a welcoming hug. The high back hovered protectively overhead. The long, narrow runners had taken her on countless flights of fancy.

She'd longed for this chair when she was away from Granny. As soon as they arrived at Granny's house, she'd grab one of Granny's old musty-smelling books and climb into it.

For hours she flipped the pages, trying to read the old-fashioned handwriting that looked more like curls and art than any letters. She'd woven stories, and sometimes she'd closed her eyes and let the stories play on the inside of her mind. Later she learned she didn't have a normal overactive imagination, but was actually seeing bits and pieces, glimpses, of other people's lives.

She'd stopped looking through the old books then, afraid of what she'd see. When Granny passed away and the books came to her, Clarissa packed them away. She couldn't remember the last time she'd looked at them.

She hadn't been able to pack away the old rocking chair. It was her ground, her lasting connection to the one person she'd loved most.

So the chair remained in her living room and frequently, like now, served in the role of the comforting embrace as Granny had once done. The tension eased and seemed to slip away as she relaxed in the familiar chair.

For the first time in days, she went to bed and slept soundly...

...Until the sudden ring of the phone shattered the quiet.

Fumbling around on the nightstand, she finally located the phone. Though her first inclination was to fling the receiver across the room, she put it to her ear. "Hello," she mumbled.

"Ms. Elgin? My name's Linda. I work at Dove's Place. You, um, were talking to Barbara? She left a note for me to call you when that guy came in."

"Yes. I remember." Clarissa sat up, shoving her hair out of her eyes as she squinted at the digital alarm. Two thirty a.m.

"He just came in. I don't know. Something's not right. He doesn't look good. I think he's hurt."

"Linda, is it?"

"Yes."

Clarissa chewed her lip for a moment before saying, "Don't let him leave, if you can keep him there."

"Oh, once he's here, he never leaves until the sun's up."

After she hung up, Clarissa sat staring at the receiver in her lap. What was she doing? What was *he* doing? She'd warned him. She didn't owe him anything else.

Frightening thoughts slipped into her mind. Should she go to the diner? If she didn't, could she stop the events? What if...No, her visions, especially ones this strong, had never been wrong. She had to convince him she was telling the truth.

Reaching into the nightstand drawer, she pulled out a business card. Mac, the big, burly cop who'd given it to her, was one of her early morning regulars who finished his overnight shift with a strong cup for the drive home. He'd told her to call him if she had problems at her shop. She'd suspected he'd had other motives for giving it to her—complete with his cell phone number, but she wasn't interested in him that way. He was nice enough, but...

Thoughts of David's tall, slim frame came to mind, and she hastily pushed those thoughts away.

Quickly, she dialed the phone number. Scooting to the edge of the bed, she waited for Mac to answer. The deep voice on the other end wasn't inviting in any way. "This is McHenry."

"Uh. Hi, Detective...uh Mac. It's Clarissa Elgin. From The Angry Bean coffee shop?" She spoke fast, before she lost her nerve. "Do you know of a diner called Dove's Place? Do you know where it is?"

At first the line was silent, as if he were trying to get his bearings. "Dove's Place? Yeah. A hellhole just this side of condemned. How do you know about a place like that?"

"I was there yesterday, and I saw something. I think something bad is going to happen."

"Whoa. What do you mean you saw *something* and *think* something might happen? What's going to happen?"

"I'm not sure, but it'll be bad. I think it's going to happen tonight." She tried, and failed, to keep the tremor out of her voice. She knew she sounded like a crackpot, but it was better than being branded as an accomplice.

"That isn't much information."

"I know." She worried her bottom lip between her teeth. "I'm not crazy. Please, just trust me. There was a man there yesterday, really creepy, with blue eyes." She shivered at the coldness in those eyes. "I just got a call from, uh, my friend Linda. She says he's there now." Or would probably be there soon if the vision became reality. She knew lying to the police was probably on some sin list, but she didn't have a choice.

"Is there anyone else involved?"

"I don't know anyone's name except...David Lorde."

A low whistle came through the line. "Lady, you sure can pick 'em." His breath came unevenly, and she knew he was moving around. "Do you know who that guy is?"

"Well, sort of. He works down at the First National Bank."

"He doesn't just work there, he *is* First National. I think his family founded the place. Do you know what you're getting mixed up in?"

She couldn't explain that she didn't have a choice. She'd already been sucked in too deep.

"We'll check it out." She heard a door slam on the other end of the line.

"I'll meet you there."

"No, you won't. We'll handle it. Stay home where it's safe."

"Mac?"

"What?"

"Thanks." She hung up the phone before he could say another word.

She stumbled to the closet and pulled on a pair of jeans and a dark blue sweatshirt over her blue nightgown. Gathering up her keys and shoes, she ran through the house. She had to convince David she wasn't a nut case, that she was telling the truth. She relaxed a little knowing that at least she had back up if that didn't work. *Please, God, don't let me be too late.*

* * * *

David stared at his reflection in the mirror behind the counter. He didn't look any different but he felt different. Inside emotions fought for their place in his mind, struggled to be felt and set free. He grabbed his coffee cup and, with a swallow of the dark brew, he tried to wash them away.

He met his own familiar gaze and saw the triumph there. Once again he felt nothing, a cold, lonely emptiness settled into place. The physical pain in his ribs that had plagued him was duller now, too. But what pleased him most was the lack of emotions he felt.

The door of the old diner opened, accompanied by the faint tinkle of the bell mounted on its frame. He watched in the mirror as the woman stepped into the dimly lit room.

Even in the gloom he recognized the bright riot of curls that cascaded down her back. Her skin looked pale in the dimness, but just as pretty as when she'd walked into his office. While he couldn't quite make out the color of her eyes he knew they were light. And warm.

She stood in the entry as the door slowly closed behind her. She looked around the room as if searching for someone—searching for him?

A frown creased her brow, then their eyes met in the mirror.

The frown vanished, and he thought the color faded in her face. Her shoulders lifted, and she shoved her purse strap up farther on her shoulder. Then, without breaking eye contact, she started toward him.

This time he frowned. What the hell was she doing here? He took another swallow of his coffee and looked away.

He didn't have to see her to know she'd stopped right next to him. A light floral scent reached out to him, daring him to ignore her.

He couldn't resist and turned his head to find her only inches away. Up close she looked beautiful. Her skin no longer looked pale, but light and fair like a soft summer breeze. And her hair fell in those ringlets that tempted him to reach out and touch their softness.

And her eyes were green. Bright and warm, as he'd noticed before, but now he saw something else.

He saw knowledge there and suddenly a reflection of himself.

* * * *

For several long seconds David continued to sip his coffee, staring straight ahead. Then he turned to look at her. Clarissa gasped. Pain marred his handsome features, and the pallor around his lips told her he was hurting.

"You should change your perfume," he said before she could comment. "That scent's a dead giveaway."

She grimaced at his choice of words. "Sorry. I didn't put it on to irritate you. I came here to help you."

"Yeah, like you tried earlier? Sorry to disappoint you, but your warning came a bit too late." He gulped his coffee as if it were laced with something stronger than sugar.

"I'm not trying to pry into your private life. I just don't want the vision I saw to become reality. Just do me a favor and go home."

"Why? Tell me one concrete, believable reason why."

Clarissa bit hard on her lip, controlling the angry retort that nearly sprang from her tongue. "Just humor me. If I didn't have a vision, then you'll be none the worse for wear. If I did, you'll be safe. Is that asking too much?"

"Tonight? Yes, it just might be." He turned then and winced with pain.

"You're hurt." Concerned, she reached out. Rather than accept her touch, he pulled away. Disappointed, she dropped her hand.

"It's no—"

They didn't have time to say more. Suddenly, the door behind them slammed open, the jangle of the bell shattering Clarissa's nerves.

Too late.

"Gimme what's in the register." The frighteningly familiar voice emerged from Clarissa's vision and grew into a terrifying reality. Slowly, she turned to see the masked face. She knew exactly what he look like. The madness in his eyes still shook her.

Linda stood motionless, staring at the robber with a fearful expression.

"Now," he barked, gesturing toward the register with the gun.

At his sharp command, Linda tried to push the correct buttons, but she kept fumbling and missed. Tears formed in her eyes as her fright grew.

Clarissa's heart pounded, and she knew that within a few moments David would be dead. No! She had to do something. But what? She didn't want to get shot either, and this time he could see her.

"Freeze!" The barked command echoed around the room and Clarissa slumped in relief. "Put the gun down. Now."

That wasn't Mac's voice. Turning quickly, Clarissa stared, shocked to see David standing a few feet away, a gun in his hand, aimed and ready. She saw the look of death in his eyes and the responding fright in the other man's. No one could look into David's eyes now and not fear for their very existence.

"Do it." David sounded so calm, but the edge of his voice gave away the intensity of his anger.

"Both of you freeze and drop your weapons." This time it was the officer's voice which resounded through the night. Mac flashed his badge, and the thief hastily put his gun down, his eyes clearly showing his preference for the cops to the angry man before him. David relaxed, his arm falling to his side where the gun dangled between his fingers.

"Lorde. On the floor and kick it over to me."

David's gaze momentarily flickered to the big police officer, as if wondering at the recognition. The sound of the heavy metal pistol scraping across the linoleum filled the air.

Relieved, Clarissa leaned against the counter.

Mac quickly handcuffed the thief's hands behind his back and checked him from head to toe for other weapons. He reached up and ripped the mask off his face. The two men glared at each other for a long minute. Mac broke the silence as he recited the Miranda rights.

Finished, he shoved the punk into a corner booth. "Sit down. There. I'll get someone to haul your lame butt in. You." He pointed at David. "Stay where I can see you. You've got some questions to answer." He glared at Clarissa for an instant and then pulled out his cell phone and punched in the numbers, never once taking his eyes off them except to look at Linda.

"Your cook's out in the back alley. He's okay, but he's got a nasty bump on his head." Linda gasped and made a move to go outside. "He'll be fine." Mac's voice softened. "Stay here. I told him we'd get the EMTs to check him over." Obviously relieved, Linda leaned back against the counter.

Clarissa had barely moved since she'd first heard David's orders. She could only stare at him, at the whole scene.

David moved first, grabbing Linda's arm and guiding her to the seat next to Clarissa. He lifted the coffeepot sitting abandoned on the counter. He poured a full cup and handed it to Linda.

"Drink it." His voice was even and smooth, as if nothing had happened.

Linda automatically did as she was instructed, though the pallor remained on her face.

"You want some?" He lifted the pot toward Clarissa, but she shook her head.

He looked like a totally different man. The anger was still in his eyes, but the mask was back in place. He turned to put the pot back on the burner, after filling his own cup. He took a deep swallow.

And she saw the red stain on his shirt.

"You're hurt." She hurried to his side. She hadn't heard a gunshot. "What happened?"

"Nothing." David pulled away. "I cut myself earlier. I must have bumped it." His features twisted, as if the forgotten injury now hurt.

He wasn't as unfeeling or undisturbed as he wanted her to believe. The muscles in his throat moved convulsively, and she watched his eyelids slip down over his tormented eyes. When they opened again, he'd gained control once more.

Mac pocketed his cell phone. "They'll be here as soon as they can." Turning, he rested his hands on his hips and glared at David.

The two men sized each other up. Clarissa watched the male ritual with fascination. She wasn't sure who would win if it came down to it. Mac was big, muscular and powerful, easily a head taller than David.

But what David lacked in brawn, he more than compensated for in ferocity. The beast often outwitted the hunter. She felt David's strength and sensed that some of it came from the well of anger he carried around with him. She shivered and rubbed her hands up and down her arms, trying to return some warmth to her fright-chilled limbs.

"I'm Bryan McHenry. They call me Mac." The officer extended his hand and David took it. Clarissa saw the tiny muscles in each man's hand move as they gripped each other's fingers. "I hope you got a permit for that." Mac glanced at the gun on the counter.

"David Lorde. Yeah, I do." David continued to meet Mac's gaze, daring him.

"Good." Mac picked up the gun, popped out the clip and then opened the gun and palmed a bullet from the chamber.

He handed the empty weapon to David. "Put it away before there's any more trouble."

David took it and slid it into a shoulder holster under his jacket. His fingers were long and tanned, and as he lifted the side of his coat, she saw the expanse of his T-shirt covered chest. The impression of a warm haven flitted into her mind. All at once, she wanted to snuggle into that haven.

Mac saw the blood stain and pointed at David's shirt. "Care to explain what happened?"

"I fell earlier. On a fence."

Mac seemed to ponder his explanation, and then with a curt nod accepted it. Clarissa wasn't as willing to believe him, but now wasn't the time to question him. Mentally shaking herself, Clarissa tore her gaze away from David's appealing and injured body, forcing herself to look into his anger-filled eyes, to remind herself of the evil that touched this man.

No, warm haven was not a notion she dared associate with David Lorde, and trust was something she couldn't afford to give.

Bright red and blue light strobed through the windows, playing across the dingy walls of the diner and flashing off the metal. In only a few minutes uniformed police officers escorted the punk into the back of a cruiser and Mac prepared to head back to the station.

Linda still sat where David had put her. Clarissa walked up to her and gave the still trembling waitress a hug. "Thank you for calling me."

Looking up, as if startled, Linda tried to smile. "I don't know what would have happened if I hadn't."

"Don't worry about that."

Linda nodded but didn't say anything else. Clarissa followed Mac out of the diner and into the cool night.

"Thanks, Mac." She leaned over, placing a kiss on the big man's cheek. He had the grace to blush beneath his late night beard.

"No problem, just doing my job. Next time, which I certainly hope there isn't, stay home." He smiled at her as if he doubted she'd listen to him. She knew he'd be there the next time she needed him.

The roar of his motorcycle broke the quiet of the empty street long after his taillight disappeared around the block.

"So, why were you here tonight?"

Clarissa stiffened at the sound of David's voice. She hadn't heard him come up behind her. Taking a deep breath, she turned to face him.

The moonlight illuminated his features, while the neon light flickered behind him. Neither light touched the darkness in his eyes. His hands were shoved into his back pockets, exposing the wide expanse of his chest that she had earlier thought of as safe and comforting. He looked casual, but the tightness in his jaw, the narrowing of his eyes told her he was holding back. But holding back what? On his emotions? On his anger?

Whatever it was took strength; she saw it in the tight muscles of his shoulders and arms.

"You know why." Her chin lifted a notch as she met his stare despite her discomfort.

"I called Linda's boss. She's closing up for the night. After I drop her off at home, can we talk?"

Not only did the sudden shift in the conversation surprise her, but she couldn't believe what she'd heard. Now, at nearly three thirty in the morning, he wanted to talk? He hadn't had the time or the understanding to talk to her earlier in broad daylight. Sighing and knowing that tomorrow she'd regret this, she agreed.

* * * *

"Explain to me exactly what you do. What are you?"

Clarissa bristled at David's bluntness. After he'd dropped Linda off at her house, Clarissa had met him at another all-night diner, in a better part of town. She didn't want him near her home, and he didn't invite her to his. She wasn't sure she'd have gone if he had. The fact that a busy street ran nearby comforted her.

Still, they were the only customers in the place, and the silence was disquieting. She stared at him over the rim of her cup. How could she explain to someone who didn't believe? "I'm psychic. I receive images in my mind, usually in my sleep, or just before I fall asleep. Brain patterns are different then."

"What exactly do you see?" He gulped his coffee.

She paused, sliding her finger around the rim of the cup as she tried to figure out how best to explain it. "It's different each time, but usually it's like I'm watching television or a movie. I see what's happening, but the people don't know I'm there. I'm seldom a part of what's happening."

"But?"

"But this time you knew I was there. You talked to me."

His gaze caught and held hers. She couldn't break free from the powerful hold. She felt herself falling into the golden brown depths, saw her own image reflected there. Catching herself as she leaned toward him, she stood and reached for the water carafe the waitress had placed on the next table. Anything to stop the trembling in her hands and the ache in her chest. What was wrong with her? Why did this man affect her so?

Something inside him touched her, filled her with longing, compassion, and fear so deep it chilled her soul. What was even more frightening was the realization that she might not be strong enough to help him.

She turned to face him, pasting a smile on her lips. "All I can do is warn you of what I see. I can't change the events."

"You changed tonight."

"No, *you* did." The waitress delivered their order then, and the unnatural silence of the unfinished conversation stretched out between them.

"How did I change things?" He dug into his pie.

"You heeded my warning, didn't you? That's why you had the gun. You didn't in the vision." Hope hesitantly rose within her. As the moments stretched on and he didn't answer, she let it fade. He stared past her and out the window, as if longing to escape.

The night outside and the lights within bounced their images back at them. What did he see? The sleeping city? Was he watching his own reflection or hers? Clarissa saw herself as she sat at the table and his image beside her. The illusion of distance between them vanished.

"Okay, you have visions. You see things. Can you control what and when you see it?"

She shook her head, her hair tumbling about her shoulders. "I've never been able to, though my grandmother could."

"It's hereditary?"

His surprise made her laugh and the tension ebbed. He looked up, and with the faint traces of a smile trying to fit onto his lips, he took another bite.

"Yes and no. My mother doesn't have the sight. I'm not sure she even believes, and my father's just an Irishman with a big imagination. He's quite willing to believe in leprechauns and that witches really ride around on a broomstick." But not in real magic power. Thinking of her parents twisted a knife in her chest, and she quickly pushed her memories away.

"You're very lucky," he said.

"Why?" She didn't think he was talking about her powers. Recalling the vision she'd seen in his office earlier, she shuddered. His life hadn't been an easy or safe one. She knew violence had somehow been a part of it for a very long time.

Reaching out, she covered his hand with hers, wanting to comfort the grief from him. She wasn't prepared for the warm shock shooting from his fingers to hers. Heat slid up her arm, past her shoulder, and snuggled in against her heart. Though she doubted he even knew it, he reached out to her. Past the darkness, past the pain, past the cold exterior, was a man. She sensed his loneliness as keenly as if it were her own.

"Why do you say that?" she repeated her question, unsure if he'd even answer.

"At least you know your parents."

His revelation shocked her, hurt her with its intensity. She looked into his face again and saw him pull away. A question that had lurked in her mind since that first vision reared its head. She might never get the chance to ask him again. "Who's Rachel?"

The violence with which his emotions snapped shocked her, and she pulled her hand back, clasping it over her chest. His eyes were more than shuttered—iron bars kept her out.

"How do you know about her?"

"You blamed her in the first vision. She wouldn't let you stay home, that's why you were in the diner. Who is she?" She repeated her question, knowing he would avoid answering it.

His anger vibrated around the room, mingling with the pain she already sensed in him. She hesitated to reach out to him on any level, emotional or physical, afraid of the darkness emanating from him.

Suddenly, he stood, his chair scraping against the tile. The echo of the sound slammed against her ears.

"Rachel is—was—my wife."

Without another word, he pulled several bills out of his pocket and tossed them onto the table. He stalked to the door and shoved it open with a force she feared would break the heavy wood. She stood and moved to the windows to watch him walk down the sidewalk toward downtown. At the end of the block, he broke into a jog.

The sun lifted its head, and the dim light in the east backlit his figure as he moved quickly. Like a caged animal finally released, he took off. She sensed he chased freedom, a freedom he wanted with a desperation she couldn't begin to understand. A freedom she realized he might never find.

Suddenly, he bent over. Was his injury bothering him? Worried, she moved a step and then realized he was gone. All she saw was a faint shadow moving into the fading darkness.

She nearly went after him, her heart wanting to ease some of the anguish that gripped him so hard.

Instead, she gathered up her purse and prepared to head home as her thoughts raced. His wife. Rachel had been his wife? Were they divorced?

As she paid her bill, coolness slipped over her skin. A whisper of thought slid through her. Faint images of a woman with long dark hair and warm, friendly eyes wafted through her mind. Rachel. Clarissa knew it was her, knew the images were of his wife. A deep, soul shattering sadness clung to the image.

She knew David felt that pain, that it tormented him.

Was she the woman in the earlier vision?

Had David killed her?

Five

Over the past hour, the sun had vanished and the air in the tiny closet Clarissa generously referred to as her office had grown warm and stale. Outside a soft rain fell, deterring any notion of opening the window or leaving her office and stepping out into the cool fresh air.

The figures on the computer screen before her blurred, and she rubbed the bridge of her nose where a dull ache throbbed. Math had never been her strong suit, and last night's lack of sleep only made the column of numbers look even more like Greek than usual. Bending closer to the neat rows of numbers, she started over. Again.

Halfway through the list, she felt a finger of ice slide down the length of her spine. *What the...*

Turning abruptly, she knocked over her coffee cup. The dark brown liquid soaked into the keyboard and across her papers.

"Damn!" She reached for the box of tissues and hastily dabbed at the mess before it could spread any farther. She tossed the dripping lump toward the trash as a rap sounded at the door. Just what she needed, another interruption.

"Come in." Leaning back, Clarissa closed her eyes, resting them for a moment. She heard the sound of the door opening and waited an instant before opening her eyes. The darkness invited her in. She could sleep right here in this hard chair.

"Clarissa?" Lindsey's face appeared around the door. "There's a man out here who says he needs to talk to you. Says his name is David." The look of pure feminine appreciation on Lindsey's face would have been comical if Clarissa hadn't felt that shiver seconds ago. That must have been the instant David Lorde walked through the front door.

"I'll be right there." She wondered what he wanted, half afraid to ask.

Clarissa sat for several long seconds, taking deep breaths. Her earlier exhaustion had vanished with the sudden adrenaline rush. Shaking her head to clear her thoughts, she tossed her pencil onto the soggy desk and stood. Might as well get this over with.

David sat at a table near the front counter, sipping from a heavy mug. His eyes stared out the window, as if seeing another place and time. She took a second to watch him. He looked so different from the rumpled man in the diner. Today he wore clean, pressed jeans and a black turtleneck that hugged his muscled chest. He'd smoothed his long hair back from his face and secured it at the nape of his neck where a few stray drops from the rain clung. She took a breath and stepped forward.

"Hi." She stopped beside his table, feeling oddly out of place in her own coffee shop, a sensation she didn't like.

He turned and smiled up at her. Like a break in the clouds, his smile was sunshine on a bleak day. Warm reaction seeped through her veins, slowly toasting every nerve ending in her body. She could only stare.

"Got a minute to join me?" He stood, walking around the small table to pull out the opposite chair. The radiance of his smile never wavered.

Clarissa slid into the chair, staring at him when he resumed his seat. Was this the same man? The dark, angry man who'd taken off early this morning as if every demon in hell were at his heels?

"Something wrong?" He lifted his cup, taking a deep drink while she continued to stare at him.

"How's your injury?"

"Fine. See?" He pulled his shirt up, exposing the smooth, tanned skin of his abdomen. Three cuts and a couple deep gouges marred the skin but looked as if they were healing fine.

Forcing herself to come back to earth, Clarissa shook her head and cleared her throat before she could speak clearly. "You...It looks good."

His laughter, rusty though it seemed, sounded warm and sweet in the quiet shop. Clarissa found herself smiling in response. It was a good sound. He should laugh more often.

"Thanks. For the first time in months, I slept. Peacefully. I'm not sure if you're responsible, but thank you, Clarissa."

Letting her gaze take in every detail of him, now that she'd adjusted to the devastation of his smile, Clarissa noticed the other differences. His eyes were light, the shadows, while not gone, were faded and distant. His jaw was scraped clean, looking smooth and strong, tempting her fingers to touch.

He looked rested and at peace with himself and the world.

"I don't know how I could possibly be responsible." She let her gaze drop, her finger tracing a pattern on the smooth table surface, though she realized she wanted to trace the contours of his lips instead.

"I don't either. Maybe just talking and someone else

knowing helped." He reached out and covered her hand, stopping her nervous motion. "But whatever you did, I'd like you to do it again."

His big hand easily covered both of hers. The long fingers felt warm and comfortable across her knuckles. She almost turned her hand to slip her fingers between his, but stopped herself.

She looked into his eyes. "What can I do to help?"

He took a deep breath, his fingers tightening around hers. "I don't know. I don't know how any of this stuff works. Any suggestions?"

"This *stuff?"* She was aware he was talking about her psychic powers, but she knew better than to put her words into his mouth. She'd learned that lesson the hard way a long time ago.

"You know, how you saw the future."

"David, I can't control my visions. They don't ask my permission to mess up my life. I warned you about that last night. There isn't anything else for me to do." The shadows slipped back into the corners of his eyes, and she found herself wanting to shove the darkness away, mourning the loss of his smile.

"There has to be more." The frustration in his voice vibrated through the entire room, bouncing back at her with its intensity. "You know about Rachel." The pain had returned to his eyes, and a responding ache took hold of her chest.

"Y...yes." Why did she feel the trap closing around her? "But what does she have to do with this? Isn't she...dead?" Clarissa dreaded the coming conversation.

"Yes...sort of."

A sick sensation slammed into her gut, leaving a wavering void. She wasn't sure she wanted to know the sordid details of his marriage, especially when realizing she'd just been fantasizing about another woman's husband. Quickly, she stood and walked over to the warmer where a fresh carafe of coffee sat on the burner. Pouring a big cup, she laced it with a heavy dose of chocolate and cream.

She didn't really want the coffee. She'd had enough today to float a battleship, but she had to do something—anything—to occupy her hands and her mind.

Appearing calmer then she ever hoped to feel inside, she turned to face him again and found him staring down into the dark recesses of his cup. What did he see there, in his mind's eye?

"Explain." She didn't dare say any more for fear her emotions would turn her words to mush.

"I can't—not very well anyhow." His head snapped up and his stare pinned her in place. "Will you come with me? I can show you better than I can explain."

As if to punctuate his request, the door opened and several college students came in, their voices shattering the emotion-laden quiet. As two young men and three women seated themselves in a corner booth, Lindsey went to take their order. The illusion of privacy was shattered, and Clarissa knew she couldn't escape, knew she'd have to agree to his suggestion.

Her heart trembled at the thought of being alone with him. If the darkness of his eyes wasn't deterrent enough, the feelings she experienced whenever he was around should be. She had difficulty thinking straight. Even now, her eyes continued to seek his image, and she fought against the desire to feel his skin beneath her fingers. No, she did not want to go anywhere with this man.

"I...I'm sorry, I have to close tonight. I'll be here until late." It wasn't exactly a lie. From the looks of the mess still on her desk, she'd be here half the night trying to get payroll figured out by tomorrow.

"That's all right. I'll wait."

"Not everyone's a night owl like you," she snapped. Why did he make this so difficult? What did he really have in mind?

He sat there for a long time, silence leaden between them in contrast to the students' laughter.

He stood and stepped away from the table. As he pulled his wallet from his back pocket, she felt his anger vibrating through the air. His eyes finally met hers again as he tossed a couple of dollars onto the table. Clarissa cringed in the wake of his heated glare and focused on clearing the table.

Hot coffee from his cup splashed across her hand. Instinctively, she dropped it, and a puddle formed at her feet as it broke. The dream from a couple nights before flashed through her mind. She felt the hot spray of the liquid on her toes and sharp scratches as the pottery shattered and fell across her legs.

"Here, let me help." David's anger evaporated and he moved with agile speed. Taking her burned hand gently into his, he guided her to the sink, shoving the tap on and slipping their joined hands beneath the cold stream.

The sting of the burn faded as the water cascaded over their fingers, but the heat of his palm scorched her in another way. She couldn't speak, though she knew she could do this for herself. She couldn't seem to move away from him, couldn't pull away from the warmth reaching out from him to envelop her.

"Does that feel better?" His voice was soft and low and she lifted her head to look into his face. He tilted his head toward her, bringing his lips so close...so tempting...so real.

"Yes," she whispered, her gaze glued to his enticing lips.

"Why are you afraid of me?"

"I'm not," she said entirely too quickly.

"Then come with me." His whisper brushed over her lips, crept past her hastily erected protections. In that instant, she wanted to go with him, wanted to help ease the hurt she sensed pulsating within him. She longed to see him smile and hear his laughter again.

He was so close, she could almost taste his words. "Yes." The answer slid unheeded from her lips.

He smiled then, sending frissons of warmth all the way to the depths of her soul.

"Thank you. Go ahead and close up. I'll wait."

Bending his head, David's lips met hers in a brief kiss. When he turned and stepped away, Clarissa couldn't move. It was as if her brain ceased to function. Images formed in her mind—images of evil, of pain, of an imprisoned beast.

She trembled. David Lorde equaled danger, but she knew with certainty that she'd just been tied to him. But what frightened her even more was the realization that she didn't want to break those ties.

* * * *

What was wrong with her? For the zillionth time since she'd agreed to go with him, Clarissa questioned her sanity. At twenty-eight years of age she'd been swept off her feet with a simple kiss. If it were physically possible, she'd have kicked herself—hard.

Yet here she stood, hiding in her office. The register was totaled out. Tomorrow's first brew was set to go off at four a.m. She'd even managed to correctly figure the payroll and fill out everyone's checks. Now all she had to do was head to her car, tell David she'd changed her mind and drive home. Simple.

So, why didn't she do it? She didn't know the answer to

that question and that bothered her. All she knew was every time she thought about leaving, she saw David's eyes, felt the warmth of his kiss. All over again, she felt his pull.

A knock sounded on the office door, and she nearly jumped out of her skin. "Clarissa? Are you ready?"

She swallowed hard. She grabbed her jacket and slipped it on. She opened the door, and David stood silhouetted in the hall. He must have been outside. The damp scent of the night air clung to his hair and jacket, and Clarissa breathed deeply, filling her lungs with the essence of David and the dark.

"Ready?" he repeated, his hands shoved into his jean pockets.

He turned and walked down the hall, looking like the caged animal she'd thought of last night. More like an animal pacing behind bars of confinement than a man walking in a room. His hand slid through his hair, much as he'd done in his office.

"I'm ready." She grabbed her purse and turned back to follow him. "Are you?"

He hesitated just a fraction too long. Glancing over his shoulder, he answered. "I don't know." Again he raked his fingers through his hair and resumed his pacing.

All this movement was getting on her nerves. She reached out and touched his arm, halting his progress. "Stop. You're making me seasick."

He didn't smile at her attempt at levity. He scowled and she swallowed the apprehension in her throat.

"Did something change your mind?" What had he wanted her to see? Curiosity almost outweighed her common sense.

"Not changed my mind exactly." His gaze met hers. "This feels a bit odd. I'm used to handling my problems by myself."

She suppressed the smile tugging at her lips. It wouldn't ease his discomfort if he thought she was laughing at him. She wasn't really laughing, but she doubted she could convince him otherwise. Pleasure at his trust flew wild through her. Why did this man affect her so deeply?

"Look." She touched his arm again, this time leaving her fingers on the warm hard muscle near his wrist. "You don't have to say or do anything you're not comfortable with. Maybe you should rethink whatever you were going to tell me."

"No. I can't. I can't go back to the way things were before you knew. Come on." He grabbed her hand and led her outside.

The rain had stopped and a crisp dampness filled the night air. He waited for her to lock the door and then ushered her to his car before either of them had the time to rethink anything.

"I can follow in my car," she offered.

"I'll drive." The coolness in his voice left no room for argument, and yet for some strange reason she didn't feel like running from him. Slipping into the car seat, she only slightly flinched when the door slammed in her wake.

The tone of his voice, and his stiff body language, left no doubt that she would do as he said. If anyone else had spoken to her in such a way she would have railed against it. She would have fervently informed them of her independence and capabilities, but she sensed the reason behind David's insistence. He cared about her safety. She wasn't sure how she knew that, but she did.

A sense of well being, embedded in the feel of rich, soft leather, reached out and held her close. When David opened his door and climbed in, the scent of the leather, his aftershave and the night combined into a heady mixture. The stumbling beat of her heart alerted her to its spell. Straightening, she moved closer to the door, as far away from him as physically possible in the small space.

Bright headlights reflected back at them from the picture window as David backed the car out. The loud rumble of the powerful engine was muffled by the luxurious interior, but Clarissa felt the vibration beneath her feet.

The night quickly swallowed them, and Clarissa watched the last of the city lights grow distant in the side mirror.

As David shifted gears, a surge of power and raw machine vibrations shot through her. That same power emanated from every pore in David's body.

"Have you heard the story of my family?" His words came out clipped and cold.

"No. Mac—the cop last night—hinted at something, but he didn't explain."

David's cold laughter chilled the car's warm interior. "He would know."

As they turned onto a narrow paved track, David fell silent again, and she couldn't help wondering if he was unable or unwilling to share more.

A large white sign, faded by years of harsh winters, dangled from a weatherworn post, telling Clarissa they were on private property.

The air grew cooler as they ascended into the mountains. The road wound back and forth, nearly on top of itself, climbing the hillside. She could feel the height, and just as she gathered her nerve to turn and look at David, he pulled around the final curve.

She gasped. Before her stood the most beautiful yet eerie mansion she'd ever seen. Thirty-foot trees with their heavy branches hanging into the night gloom stood like sentries around the house. The mountainside's thick forestry held the night in a tight grasp, tucking it in around the house as if to protect it from unwanted visitors.

David slowed the car as they approached black iron gates at the top of the road. He pushed a button on the car's dashboard, and the gates slowly swung open until she clearly saw the mansion.

Built in the Georgian style, its tall white columns soared from the expansive porch up toward the sky and the second floor roof. Dried leaves from the soon forgotten autumn lay helplessly around the steps and veranda, evidence that no one had been here in a long time. Overgrown hedges, vines and a rundown lawn failed to mask the grandeur and wealth emanating from the entire building.

She wasn't aware of David getting out of the car, until he opened her door. Recovering from the house's impact, she looked up at him.

Every muscle in his body was as tight as a bowstring. His eyes stared coldly at the house, his hatred floating thick on the night air.

Taking a deep breath, Clarissa stepped from the car. The air was still, with none of the usual rustling night sounds. The night birds didn't sing. The crickets didn't chirp their mating call. Not even a breeze filtered through the thick tree branches. Was it possible for all of nature's beauties to know they weren't welcome here?

Where did that thought come from? Clarissa turned to David, forcing a smile she didn't feel. "Well?"

"Do you feel anything?" Faint hope filled his eyes. "Anything?"

Did he mean emotionally? If he did, her whole body responded to his tension and wanted to wrap itself around him. She didn't think that's what he meant. Disappointed, she met his gaze, trying to keep the sympathy out of her eyes. "It's not that simple." She watched the shadows fill his eyes. "May we go in?"

David stood frozen for a moment, and then nodded. He

reached out and grasped her elbow, guiding her to the wide front entrance.

The double doors creaked open. Clarissa shivered, sensing that whatever lay beyond the threshold was enough to make her quake and long to run away.

She hesitated to walk into the darkness, but the wind, absent only moments ago, pushed against her back, propelling her forward. As she stepped inside, the breeze twisted and turned around her. Then it vanished as quickly as it had come.

The moon offered little light inside, but it reflected in silver shards off the mirror on the wall. Silhouettes of David's form fell against the white walls.

With a simple flick of his wrist, David illuminated the foyer. Crystal light from the chandelier hanging from the second floor ceiling scattered across the white marble floor. The wallpaper, the gold trim encasing the mirror, and even the brass door handles had faded with grime and time. Dust covered everything—except the chandelier—which gleamed as if it had just recently been hung.

Clarissa sensed how beautiful this house had once been, and she felt the love someone had put into building it.

"It's lovely," she whispered.

David didn't reply, but led the way through the foyer to a set of doors on the left. He paused and then turned the handle, his hesitation not lost on Clarissa. She knew before he opened the door that this was the room where the man and woman in the vision had been.

She swallowed the sudden gripping fear that threatened to overwhelm her and took a step back, unable and unwilling to look beyond the few feet the light reached into the room. The shadows were thick and harbored secrets she didn't want to know.

David moved slowly, his hand searching the wall for the light switch.

"Not yet," Clarissa whispered.

The suddenly new vibration coming from the room surprised her. Slowly, she moved past him, barely brushing his arm with hers. A spark of awareness arced between them.

She hurried past him, leaving him standing on the threshold.

"This room was a happy place for you once, wasn't it?" She didn't wait for an answer. The wood floor creaked beneath her feet as she circled the dim room. Images of Christmas trees and toy trains flitted through her mind.

Tracing her finger along the delicate edge of a serving tray sitting on a side table, she saw glasses filled with champagne, heard voices raised not in anger but laughter. She responded with a smile. "Yes, this room was happy once."

She felt David's pain stab through her. Pain so piercing it reached across the room to her, pushing her away while simultaneously tugging at her heart. Wanting to see his face, she said, "Okay, you can turn on the lights."

Light blazed from another overhead chandelier. The décor used in the foyer echoed in this room. An Aubusson rug covered the middle of the floor, and two white leather couches were accented with brass and glass tables.

Over the white marble fireplace hung a large oil painting of a man and a woman. As she stepped closer to the portrait, Clarissa found herself lost in the depths of the woman's deep brown eyes. They were so alive. So beautiful. So happy with love, and she wore a grin that was so full of life.

Clarissa turned and looked at David, looked into those same eyes, but found darkness and pain where the happiness should be. His cold stare seemed to cool the warmth of the room. He couldn't see the joy that had once been. He'd lost those memories long ago.

"Do you feel anything?" he demanded, his teeth clenched tight as if afraid to ask the words.

"Yes and no." What could she say to him? Instead, she turned away and examined the rest of the room. A tall wooden cabinet caught her eye, and she moved toward it. It towered over her head, the doors and top ornately carved. A jester's head provided the corner piece on each side, like a gargoyle she'd seen once on an old church. Fascinated, she reached out to feel the rich wood.

"Careful," he warned.

She wasn't sure if he meant for her to be cautious because of the value of the piece, or if there was something dangerous lurking inside. Before she could ask, David was there beside her, slowly opening the doors.

He took a deep breath and then spoke very softly. "My...my father brought that back from his last business trip to Germany."

Slowly, reverently, David pulled open the doors. Surprised and delighted, she watched as he exposed a huge mechanical device. A silver disk nearly a foot and a half across with holes and bumps on it rested on a spindle.

"What is it?"

"A music box."

"A music box?" Something cold slipped into the room and down her spine. "This big?"

He laughed—actually laughed—at her surprise. Some of his tension faded. "They used them at carnivals and fairs. They're like the calliopes we hear now on a carousel."

"It's...it's beautiful. Does it work?"

He nodded slowly, reluctantly. He opened another, smaller door on the side to reveal a large crank bar. He turned it several times before stepping back in front of her and pushing a small lever.

The disk spun slowly, and the sounds of bells and waterfalls filled the room. It was beautiful...and suddenly too familiar.

She took several steps back, her fear of the visions too strong to avoid. It returned, all too real in her mind, only this time she saw everything clearly. *They were in this room arguing. Their voices echoed from the past. "Please. No. David. I...I love you."*

The man's voice was clearer now, too. "No, my dear, treacherous wife, you don't love me. You just love my money and position and everything it gives you."

"No, David. No." The woman's screams exploded through the room. A gunshot was followed by cold, empty silence.

"Now, my sweet, you can't hurt me anymore."

Clarissa looked over at the white rug. A different rug had been there then, forever ruined by tragedy. She looked at David and then up at the painting. "Your father's name was David, too?"

"Yes." The single word tore from his throat. The music stopped and the silence returned.

"What happened here?" She knew but didn't want to believe it.

He looked at her and must have seen the knowledge in her face. He grabbed her, his fingers hard on her arms. She shivered, not out of fear, but from the intensity of his pain. "You know already, don't you?"

"No, not really. Just what I saw in the vision the other day."

"Tell me. Tell me what you saw."

"They..." She tilted her head toward the picture. "They were arguing. Here in this room. I don't know what about, but it was bad. He killed her."

David's face paled, and his hands dropped to his side. Slowly, he closed the side door on the music box.

"And the music box was playing," she whispered.

David stopped. Not a muscle moved. She wasn't even sure if he breathed. Then he spoke. "No, it wasn't."

"How do you know? I heard it in the vision."

"I know because I was here." His anger exploded, and he slammed the final door, the bells inside crashing against each other with the impact. "I was hiding inside this music box."

"How old were you?" she whispered, afraid to touch off his anger again.

"Five."

She looked over at the picture. The murder had happened not long after the portrait had been painted.

Suddenly, David threw back his head. Agony gripped his features, and he curled his hands into fists. "Get out." He ground out the words as he fell to his knees.

"David, what's wrong?"

"No!" he screamed as his body twitched, and he writhed against whatever took hold of him. His fists curled even more as they became wicked claws. He seemed to turn inward, shrinking before her eyes. Black feathers burst from his skin, and suddenly David was no longer there.

A black raven, its eyes amber and brooding, stared at her from where David had been. It screeched, then lifted its wings and rose into the air.

Soaring once around the room, the bird headed for the painting. Reaching out a clawed foot, the bird scraped the fragile canvas leaving deep gouges across the woman's face. And then it flew out through the foyer and into the night.

"David! David!" she screamed into the night as the black bird flew higher and higher, as if headed straight into the moon's bright face.

Six

Clarissa ran. Out of the room. Out of the house, away from whatever lurked inside. She ran into the dark shadows of the surrounding forest, and fear pushed her deeper into the darkness.

What had happened back there? Was this a vision? A dream? Was she going insane? Nothing made sense and the pounding of her heart made it nearly impossible to think straight. People didn't turn into animals. They didn't vanish into thin air, either. Where was he?

"David?" she called. Still there was no answer.

Hidden in the safety of the trees, she took several deep breaths, bringing the calming scent of pine into her lungs. A soft bed of pine needles crunched beneath her feet, and patches of white moonlight sifted through the branches. She focused on the calm of nature. She'd seen many strange things in her life and in her visions, but nothing like this.

A thought flitted through her mind and she tried to catch it. *Think.* She recalled hearing about Native American legends where animals represented emotions. There was something in her books at home but she didn't know enough to help her now.

The quiet night closed around her as the moon rose higher in the sky, slipping behind a stray cloud and momentarily plunging her into darkness.

"David?" she called again, expecting no answer but hoping, maybe.

"Yes?"

He startled her as he stepped out from a clump of pines. The shadows clung to him, the darkness reluctant to let him go, though the moon came back out just then. Her gaze swept upward over his fitted jeans, to the dark turtleneck that seemed none the worse for wear. The only physical difference seemed to be his hair that now hung loose instead of pulled back.

Until she looked into his eyes. She sucked in a breath, knowing she was staring into the eyes of danger.

"What are you doing here?" he demanded.

"Looking for you. That was you, wasn't it?"

"Where?"

"The bird."

He didn't say anything more, simply passed her and headed back to the house. Where the night had been silent, a cacophony of crickets and breezes and the crunch of his shoes on the forest floor erupted. He kept walking, and she hurried to keep up.

Now that he was safe, she let her curiosity step in. "Please, tell me what happened." Fear and excitement bubbled inside her.

"Nothing." His voice was even and cold, all emotion now gone.

"I'm not crazy, David. Even though you think I am. I know what I saw." Old tales that Granny had told her as a child returned to frighten her anew. Her thoughts clearer now, she recalled one of her favorites. A story of beasts in the forest that had cloaked themselves as men seemed suddenly all too possible.

The moon slid out fully from behind the cloud, its silver rays reaching down to caress the long stands of his hair. A part of her ached to reach out and touch him as well, to ease the pain she saw in his eyes, to soothe away the sadness she felt in him.

"Let's get you home," he said, an order in his voice.

"I'm not going anywhere until you explain." She stopped, waiting for him to do the same.

He kept going for several feet and then stopped mid-stride to glare back at her. "You're going home, and you're going to forget I was foolish enough to bring you here."

"Don't count on it." She wanted to provoke him, wanted to crack that cool demeanor he fought so hard to keep up. No man—no human—was as empty as David Lorde pretended to be.

Lightning split the heavens, and on its tail a roar of thunder shook the ground beneath her feet. Clouds she hadn't noticed moved quickly across the sky. Even in the pale light, she saw growing emotions in David's eyes. She stepped closer to him, resting her hand on his arm. The skin was warm beneath her fingers, and his muscles tightened as he clenched his fist.

A breeze whipped up with the coming storm, and the scents of the forest danced around them. That and the warm scent of him. She breathed in, taking him inside, settling him in the empty place in her soul.

The night grew even darker and she looked up. Clouds

nearly covered the sky, eating up the last of the stars.

"Do you ever make wishes?" she asked.

"Don't be silly." He pulled away and resumed walking.

"I do," she called after him.

He stopped and turned back, as if curiosity was too much for him. "And what do you wish for?"

She hesitated only an instant before moving toward him. When nothing more than a breath's distance separated them, she reached up and placed a finger against his jaw.

"For this." She stood on tiptoe and pressed her lips to his, pleading silently for him to feel— to *let* himself feel—something besides anger.

A growl escaped from his throat as his arms enveloped her and pulled her tightly to him. The hard, hot length of his body pressed against hers took her breath away.

This was madness. She willingly reached out to him, and he responded with a heady sensuality that turned her knees to water and jumbled her remaining sanity. He was too dangerous. She couldn't trust him.

Then why did she ache so? Why did it feel safe and right when his arms held her? Drained and slightly out of touch with reality, she let him kiss her, let him touch her, let her body melt into his. She slid her arms up over the muscles of his chest and held on tight.

His strong, firm jaw sported a heavy five o'clock shadow that felt rough beneath her fingers. She recalled that day in his office when he had rubbed his fingers over his chin, sending a soft scraping sound around the room. She'd wondered then how it would feel beneath her fingers. Now she wondered how it would taste against her lips and tongue and proceeded to find out.

She slipped her hands into his hair, relishing the softness of the thick strands twining around her fingers.

"What are you doing to me?" he whispered, lifting his head only a fraction of an inch.

"Nothing," she said, parroting his earlier words and pulled his lips back to her.

He returned to devour her with his kiss, engulf her with his arms. She let herself experience him, giving back as much passion as he did. Suddenly, the feel of his hair between her fingers changed. It was courser, stiffer. Different.

She pulled back, looking into his shadowed face. "What's

happening?"

"Between us or to me?" The thick gravel of his voice surprised her. "Don't ask questions you can't handle the answers to." He stepped back and she followed. "No," he whispered deep and low.

"Why? Tell me what's going on."

"No. Go home. Take my car. The keys are in the ignition. Take it and get the hell out of here. Now."

The dark night soon swallowed him, though she heard his footsteps long after he'd left her. She wanted to go after him, to find out what tore him apart inside and away from her.

He couldn't keep walking away, but she couldn't force him to stay, either. Frustrated, she kicked the ground, enjoying a brief sense of satisfaction as the dirt flew into the air around her. "You *will* talk to me," she called out to the night, knowing from the echo that he heard her.

A distant growl of a mountain lion came back to her and she shivered, realizing she wasn't safe out here alone. She headed back to the house, defeated and disappointed.

Every light in the mansion still blazed. She stood at the edge of the yard looking at it. It was so beautiful and such a waste sitting empty out here in the middle of the woods.

David's car sat in the drive just where they'd left it and the keys dangled from the ignition. As she stood there, raindrops fell around her, kicking up dust before the dry ground succumbed to its seduction. The uneven beat rat-tatted on the car.

She didn't want to go home. Not yet, not until she understood what was happening. With a glance at the keys, she hurried into the house's empty foyer before she changed her mind. The crystals of the chandelier chimed together in the breeze that came in with her.

"David, are you here?" she called, but no answer came back to her. Was he still out roaming the woods? Surely not.

He was somewhere on the property. He couldn't have gone far. He'd come back to the house soon enough, especially as the rain increased.

She couldn't leave him, not until she got some answers, and not until she helped him. She didn't know how, but she knew she had to do it.

Pushing a matching set of doors open on the other side of the hall from the parlor, she found a book-filled library. The dark wood was a striking contrast to the light airy decor of the rest of the house.

She experienced no lingering emotions, didn't feel anything. No visions or images stole into her mind. No David, either. She went from room to room on the ground floor. Nothing appeared out of the ordinary, but something kept drawing her mind back to the portrait of his parents. She knew David's mind must be filled with memories of them, memories that for him were real and painful.

As she reached the curved staircase, she called out again, hoping he'd answer her. The silence emphasized that she was alone, but instead of giving in to the dark emotions, she moved on. Grasping the brass handrail, she took the first step, then the next, slowly climbing to the top. A single step creaked, the third one up, the only sign of her ascent.

Once on the landing at the top, she glanced down at the foyer. A strange sense of vertigo gripped her as she stared at the hard tiles below. Nothing stood between her and the drop but the gleaming rail. She stepped back toward the wall and away from the edge.

A short distance into the hall, a door stood partially open. Taking the initiative with more confidence than she actually felt, Clarissa walked to it and went inside.

She fumbled for the light switch, but as her eyes adjusted to the dark, she realized she didn't need any light. The entire east wall of the room was made of glass with no curtains to impede the view.

The city of Boulder, with Denver off in the distance, lay at her feet. Like a toppled Christmas tree, the forest fell away and the city lights gleamed up at her, reaching out across the prairie. The beauty took her breath away as she walked toward it.

She felt David's warmth behind her, sensed his love for the view, for the room itself. "You love this room." Relieved that he'd returned, she waited for him to answer.

He did after several long, silent minutes. "This was the nursery when I was a child. I have no idea why Mother would put so many windows in a baby's room, but, yes, I loved it."

He fell silent and she waited, not questioning his use of the past tense in regard to his feelings. She sensed his pain and knew he needed to escape, even if it was simply by refusing to say the words forming in his mind.

"After my parent's deaths, my aunt and uncle moved in and I moved down the hall. After we married, Rachel turned this room into her study." His voice faded. "She spent most of her spare time here."

Clarissa turned to look at him. His face was illuminated by the city lights, and the play of shadows added depth to his already severe features and darkness to his troubled eyes. Instinctively, she reached out and caressed his now familiar and dear face.

He took a step back, away from her touch. She didn't question her disappointment. "Thank you for showing me your home. I understand you and your past a little more."

"It's not my home. It hasn't been for a long time. I wanted you to see—to feel—what's here."

Clarissa frowned. She'd picked up on some old memories and was now attuned to the emotions roiling within him. But other than that, she'd only experienced the curiosity of visiting a beautiful house. "The strangeness here," she said, and then paused to carefully choose her words, "is the change in you, and I can see you're not going to explain any more now than before. I don't feel anything unusual about the house. Am I supposed to?"

"Damn!" He stepped farther away, leaning his back against the thick glass. "I knew she'd do this."

"She?" Why did Clarissa suddenly not want to know the answer to that question?

"Rachel. She's here. That's one of the many reasons I can't live here."

He was serious. She felt it in the air, heard it in his voice and knew in her own heart that he was being completely honest with her.

"I'm confused. What happened?"

He was silent too long, but she didn't push him, not yet.

Finally he spoke. "She died three years ago." The grief was strong in his voice. "She had cancer. It went so fast. I couldn't do anything to save her."

"You believe her spirit is here?" She spoke softly, afraid to shatter the fragile confidences. He simply nodded.

He believed Rachel was here. But was she? Really?

Moving away from him, Clarissa cleared her mind of his emotions and her own reactions to him. She'd told him she couldn't force the visions, but Granny Cleary had been able to seek them out, maybe Clarissa could, too. She closed her eyes and opened herself to the possibilities as she'd seen Granny do.

Wandering through the room, she touched objects, feeling nothing but texture and shape, warm or cool.

Had she sensed anything else in the house? Running her thoughts back, she stepped out into the hallway. The vertigo she'd experienced earlier was still there, and the undercurrents grew stronger and more intense as she stood here.

"David?"

He joined her, coming to stand a few inches away from her. Suddenly, a breeze whipped in through the front door. The chandelier tinkled again, sounding like the notes of the music box. Just as quickly as it had begun, the air stilled.

Clarissa closed her eyes, and the image of a woman came into her mind. The woman was shadowy, her features vague. Her arms were raised, palms out in front of her as she moved closer.

As Clarissa watched the woman, her image grew clearer. Her dark auburn hair fluttered as she moved. The smooth, aristocratic features would have been beautiful, if they hadn't been contorted with malice and pain.

Wanting to help the woman, Clarissa reached out, but before she could communicate with her, the woman rushed forward. The impact of her force caused Clarissa to stumble back.

"David!" Clarissa cried, her voice mingling with the woman's sobs. She opened her eyes just in time to see the brass banister. She was falling over it and toward the hard, cold marble tile.

Head over heels she tumbled, her screams echoing through the foyer. Thankfully, darkness reached out to buffer her. She never felt the impact she knew would break every bone in her body.

Seven

Warm, sweet leather pillowed her head, mingling with the scent of spicy aftershave. Vaguely, she heard rain beating on the outside of the car. Clarissa's eyelids felt heavy, and she didn't fight the comforting drowsiness holding her in its grip. Safety and warmth. She clung to them.

"Clarissa." David's voice invaded the cocoon she hovered in, pulling at her senses and forcing her to rouse to near consciousness. "Clarissa?"

Fighting the desire to sleep, she forced her eyes open. She saw nothing but darkness, just as she had seen behind her closed lids. After an instant the darkness changed. She saw the faint silhouette of David's head. As she continued to search within the shadows for a clearer image, her eyes adjusted and she saw David's face only a few inches away from hers.

"David? Wh...what happened?" As she tried to move, every muscle in her body protested. A low groan slipped from between her lips. She'd fallen, hadn't she? Her memory was vague.

"You fainted." Concern thickened his voice, and suddenly she felt his arms around her. That explained the warmth. Was that also why she felt safe?

Suddenly regaining her strength and memory, she struggled against him. How could she feel safe in the arms of the man who'd put her at such risk? He let her slip away, and while she tasted the sweetness of freedom, she immediately missed the comfort of his embrace.

"Where is she?" Clarissa gazed out the car window at the mansion.

"She?" David turned abruptly in his seat, spearing her with an intense gaze.

"The woman who pushed me."

"Pushed you?"

"Yes. I was standing there, and suddenly she came out of nowhere and pushed me over the banister." Clarissa moved carefully, testing each bone and muscle and finding nothing but a dull achiness. She'd lived through that horrid fall.

"I don't know what you're talking about. You were standing there on the landing, looking at me. You screamed and an instant later you crumpled to the floor. That scream's going to stick in my head for a long time."

David turned away, his fingers curling around the steering wheel. His knuckles turned white enough for her to see them in the faint light. "What did she look like?" The tightness gripped his voice.

"Auburn hair, about to here." Clarissa touched her own shoulder with a trembling finger. "She was dressed in white, I think, and her face—she was in pain. The poor thing."

"Rachel." The single word spoke volumes. It held recognition of his wife and the emotions he still felt for her. Clarissa detected love, pity and anger all rolled together. A twinge of envy stung her heart.

"Do you have a picture of her? Then I could tell for sure."

"In there." He indicated the house with a tilt of his head. "But I'm not going back in tonight." Without warning, he twisted the key in the ignition and sped down the driveway, leaving a spray of damp gravel in their wake as the tires ground the pavement.

Every light in the house still blazed.

* * * *

For nearly an hour they drove around the city. Familiar sights gave way to unfamiliar, and Clarissa wondered where David was taking her. She wasn't afraid exactly, but exhaustion took its toll. His emotions, which she now felt inside herself, were jumbled. But despite the confusion, she felt oddly safe.

When he pulled up in front of Dove's Place, she wasn't even surprised. The small diner was his haven, and while she was tired and longed to go home to bed, she recognized his need for company. She didn't bother analyzing why that need made her glow inside.

"Care for a cup of coffee you don't have to fix yourself?" David's words were warm, but that warmth didn't reach his eyes. She nodded and climbed out of the car. The same neon fizzle filled the air, and the fluttering blue light pooled around them. She wondered vaguely how long the sign had been broken and if the owner ever planned to fix it.

Inside the diner, the air hung heavy and a new waitress worked behind the counter. Linda had resigned, she explained. Clarissa made a mental note to get in touch with Linda tomorrow. Maybe she could find a place for her at the coffee shop.

"She's in your head," David said after they were seated,

and they both knew he didn't mean Linda. His words echoed through the small diner and into Clarissa's soul.

"What do you mean she's in my head?" Clarissa asked, a shiver crawling up her spine. Did she really want to know the answer?

"She's in yours just like she's been in mine for months. She's why I can't sleep, why I can barely function." He hadn't yet sipped his coffee, and now he took a hefty gulp. He frowned, as if needing more than caffeine could give him. "Do you know anything about this type of thing?"

Clarissa needed and wanted to offer him solace for his loss, for all the pain he'd experienced in his life. She reached across the scarred tabletop, covering his strong hand with her own smaller one. His skin felt warm and rough as he turned his hand to twine his fingers between hers.

"She doesn't have any connection with me," she said. "I think I'm picking up on your emotions and the connection she has with you. I'll be fine, but what about you?"

"I'm a big boy," he teased, a genuine smile tugging at his lips. "So what now?"

He wanted reassurance, and she tried to give him some. "Just like anything else, I believe there are answers. We have to work to find them. There's some research I'd like to do."

"Research? Can I help?"

He needed to help, needed to help himself. Clarissa saw that need painted all over his handsome face. "Yes, but let's try to get some rest tonight and tackle it tomorrow. I'm not used to running on so few hours of sleep."

Grit filled her eyes, and the weights on her eyelids returned. Nodding, he paid the bill and escorted her out to the car. In only a few minutes, she stood at her own front door. The familiarity of home wrapped around her heart.

David stood nearby in the shadows as she unlocked her door. His tall frame dwarfed her and made her think of the days when a boy had walked her home from a date. This time, though, her father wasn't standing on the other side of the door, waiting.

"Good night. I'll take you to your car in the morning." He turned to leave.

"That's fine. Not too early, though. I'm sleeping in. Lindsey's opening the shop."

He stood looking at her for a long minute, and then he

moved to the steps. She took a step forward. "David?" He stopped a step below her, and she found their eyes level.

Only inches separated them, and a knowing tingle formed on her lips. Should she? As if an invisible silken thread wrapped around her and tugged her toward him, she leaned that last little distance. Their lips met. He didn't pull away and she leaned even closer. Telling him more clearly than she ever could with words what she felt growing between them.

He was strong and sweet against her. His arms slid around her, pulling her to the edge of the step, where she leaned against him. Her arms fit perfectly across his shoulders and around his neck. They were both reluctant to move away.

"I told you to get away while you could." He gently pushed a lock of hair out of her eyes.

"I don't do what I'm told very often."

He laughed, then winced as if in pain.

"Are you okay?" She touched his face.

"Yeah." He set her firmly on her feet and hastily moved down the steps away from her.

"Good night, David." She backed up to her door, turning only when she felt the solidness behind her. Pushing it open, she cast him one last wistful glance before disappearing.

She was tired. More than tired. She was bone weary. The sheets on the bed invited her. Her pillow called to her like a mirage to a desert traveler.

Stripping off her clothes, she didn't bother with a nightgown. That would have taken the effort of going to the closet, which was beyond her capacity right now.

The night claimed her quickly, and she sighed in complete surrender as the pillow hugged her head, cradling her in sweet slumber. For awhile, at least, she could leave the world and problems of David Lorde far behind.

If only it were that simple. Some small part of her wouldn't leave him alone. The compulsion to help him was strong.

David was a part of her, just as the other visions had become ingrained in her psyche. And when Clarissa found herself gazing up at his dream image, she wasn't afraid.

There was something different about him now, here in the confines of her mind. For several long moments, she stared up at him as he stood there beside her bed. He shouldn't be here. She didn't remember leaving the door open, but a shiver of excitement that he was here crept over her.

How handsome he looked in the moonlight filtering through the open window. The breeze was cool, but it did little to ease the heat inside her body.

He wore no shirt, and in the dim light, Clarissa saw the rigid outline of each muscle on his chest and smooth, flat stomach. She could see the bulge in his upper arms and realized he clenched his fists, making the tendons in his forearms tense and push tight against his skin.

The thick mane of his hair hung loose about his face and shoulders. At work and during the day, he pulled it back, but she liked it better this way. She thought perhaps it was more like the true David. Wild and free.

Her fingers ached to touch the thick strands, to weave them around her fingers. She wanted to bind him to her.

And then it hit her. It was his eyes. They were the difference. The pain, the anger, the burning remorse were still there, but dimmed, dimmed so that she had to search for them. Instead, she saw a passion for living, a warmth and excitement for experience—and desire for her.

With careful movements, she rose on the mattress to kneel before him. Their eyes were nearly level, just like on the step, and while hot desire melted her, he looked as rigid as newly forged steel. If it hadn't been for the fire in his eyes, she'd have doubted his desire.

"God, you're beautiful," he whispered, his eyes breaking loose from gazing into hers and glanced over the rest of her body.

Too late Clarissa remembered she wore nothing. A warm flush moved quickly over her skin, but she didn't try to hide herself. His gaze sent shock waves coursing through her. He couldn't have affected her more if his hands had actually done the caressing.

"Why are you here?" he whispered, his eyes meeting hers again.

"I live here."

David's eyebrow arched upward. "Since when?"

Taking a moment to tear her gaze away from his, Clarissa looked around and realized she was no longer in her room. A shudder of surprise shot through her. Where was she, and how had she gotten here?

He read her questioning gaze and a smile tugged at his lips. "We're in Lorde Manor."

"I don't remember this room." The room was less austere than the rest of the house, though the four poster bed, carved highboy, and velvet drapes were no less expensive than the rest she'd seen.

"I didn't show you. This used to be my room."

David's room. The room he'd grown up in. The room he'd spent his teenage years in. The room he'd taken Rachel to as his bride?

Foolish pride sent Clarissa climbing off the bed. She didn't want to share a bed with him here, not with Rachel's memory near. Not with the possibility her spirit could be watching.

He must have sensed her reaction. Before she could move away, his strong hand shot out to close around her arm. She felt small as his long fingers completely closed around her wrist. His strength was greater than hers. His hands could probably snap a bone with little effort.

"Don't run away." Was that pleading in his voice? "Don't leave me now." He turned to face her and loosened his hold. He gently gripped her shoulders, turning her to face him. "I need you. I need your beauty, your strength, your understanding."

There was that word. *Need.* It had always been the key to her heart. Her need to be needed was as strong as ever. Tentatively, she reached out to touch his chin. She wasn't disappointed to feel the roughness against the tender pads of her fingers.

She couldn't stop there. She cupped his jaw, feeling the roughness against her palm and the smoothness of his cheekbone against her thumb. He was a contradiction in texture as well as emotion.

His fingers moved slowly, enticingly, over her bare shoulders. His thumbs moved in circles that were an ancient rhythm, an echo of her heartbeat. Her pulse quickened, shoving the desire through her veins until it reached every inch of her body. She longed for him to quench the fire, even while he stoked the inferno.

How many times in the past few days had she thought about the taste of his lips? Now she knew what could be. The same knowledge stared back at her. As his head moved closer, she knew she was going to find more than a gentle kiss. A thrill shot through her. Her fingers slipped to the nape of his neck, her impatience growing as she urged him closer.

Warmth. Sweetness. Tenderness. Not emotions Clarissa had previously associated with this man, but emotions that poured from his lips into hers. She was drowning and thanking every god and saint for the experience.

David's arms gathered her close, fitting her against the curves and planes of his body, filling the empty places with bonding heat. He gave her all he had to give and took nothing more than what she wanted him to have.

"Love me." She sighed against his lips, wanting to belong to this man as she'd never wanted a man before. The fire he'd built within her blazed with an intensity she knew was consuming. She offered more.

As if she weighed nothing, he slid his arms beneath her knees and lifted her. She knew he'd carried her like this twice before, but she didn't remember either time. The sensation was familiar, as if his arms had left their mark.

She slipped her arms around his neck, encircling him in her embrace. As David stepped across the floor, Clarissa's lips moved to the warm column of his neck, seeking the hot beat just beneath his skin. When her lips found it, her tongue slipped out, seeking his taste.

His breath faltered at her intimate touch and his arms tightened as his steps quickened. It was only seconds until he laid her back on the sheets. The cotton had cooled in her absence, but it did nothing to cool her ardor.

"I want you. I've wanted you since that first day. You had me on fire before we even met." His voice was soft and words became obsolete as his lips found hers again. No language had yet captured what he wanted her to know, to feel, to be.

David's touch was tentative and gentle as his fingers explored every inch of her. His feather-light touch tickled at the ridge of her collarbone and teased at the slope of her breasts. He found the aroused tip of her nipple, and his hand trembled just before he covered her, filling his palm. Moving slowly, enticingly, his hands moved in perfect harmony, creating magic. He generated a hot whirlwind within her.

Arching her back, she offered him more. Her breathing grew quick and hard as she fought the vortex of passion threatening to swallow her. His lips replaced his fingers, and she nearly cried out. She wanted more. Much more.

Just when she was sure she'd lose control, David moved away, leaving her swollen and hot. He trailed his hand down across the sensitive skin of her abdomen.

His long fingers splayed across her hips, seeking each inch of her, teasing her, until she couldn't stand the restraint any longer. His fingers slipped between her thighs where he found her warm and ready, tight and welcoming.

She wanted to touch him. Her fingers ached, and she slid her hand over the broad expanse of his shoulders and back, helping remove the last of his clothing. Rippling muscles moved beneath her touch, setting fire to the nerve endings. She was trapped by the desire coursing over every inch of her skin.

Suddenly, David's face hovered above hers. His gaze probed hers, seeking and finding her responding desire. He kept his weight off her with his arms, and Clarissa sensed the restraint in his muscles. He rested just on top of her, his skin barely brushing hers.

With one swift movement, he settled deep within her. At first he didn't move. Eyes closed, head thrown back, he paused as if relishing the hot, wet feel of her.

Slowly, enticingly, he moved again, and Clarissa arched against him, pressing her swollen breasts against the taut muscles of his chest. There wasn't room in her desire for any distance between them.

When the tenderness faded, she didn't know or care. The urgency grew with each step of the dance, and just as she was sure she could take no more, she felt herself falling.

She welcomed the hot fire searing her and ached for the bright shimmering stars that shattered in her mind. His name tore from her throat, echoing in the room and through her mind in an endless caress.

Her cry broke the air. Together they fell into the blissful heat, then landed in the quiet of the night.

The room grew silent except for the sound of their rushed breaths. Louder and louder it grew despite her desire to remain with her eyes closed. Relishing the sweetness thrumming through her body, Clarissa slid her eyes open.

David's eyes were open and staring down into hers. Gone was the warmth and tenderness. Gone was the sweet longing that had bound her to him from the beginning.

The darkness had stolen back in. The evil had slipped through when their barriers were down.

"No!" she cried, wanting to get away but knowing she could never escape his strength. She was still beneath him, and the heat that had enticed her earlier now scorched her skin.

"Let me go." Looking into his eyes, she knew this wasn't David. Not really. Not the David she knew.

"I can't." His voice was no longer soft but had returned to that growl she had come to associate with him. She trembled as the sound of his voice filled the room, growing strong with each resounding echo.

What was happening? Struggling, she fought to escape his embrace. He was big and strong, though their energetic lovemaking must have weakened him some. Clarissa knew she would have done better against him without the throbbing protest of her still trembling limbs. What had he done to her?

He rose, and she watched his silhouette in the moonlight. Hastily, she pushed away. She stood beside the bed. She had to run, but where? There was no door. All she saw was the single window where the moonlight crept in.

The growl came again, this time a mighty roar. She spun around to find a mammoth lion crouched in the corner.

Its eyes glowed in the darkness. A scream escaped from her throat, but the lion appeared not to hear it. With one mighty lunge, it came at her. Long, sharp teeth surrounded the roar and stinging pain scraped across her throat.

Darkness settled around her, and she struggled against the heaviness of the air that wouldn't allow her to breathe. She was dying. She was sure of it. She didn't want to die, but pain and blackness like this could be nothing else.

Suddenly, her eyes opened and she jerked up in bed. She stared at the familiar walls of her room. The air was cool, and the only sound was the slamming beat of her heart.

She pushed her hair out of her eyes, feeling the tangles and sweaty dampness. Her eyes darted around the room, finding nothing out of the ordinary. But she didn't trust her own eyes. She turned on the bedside lamp and looked around again. She stopped short of peeking under the bed.

She tried to still the pounding of her heart, tried breathing slowly, but to no avail. Her heart was still reacting to the intimacy with David's dream image and the fear of the lion's attack.

Had it been a dream? Was it a vision? Or had it been real? No, it couldn't be real. But it had felt so real. She threw the covers back and climbed out of bed. As she did so, she caught her reflection in the mirror over the dresser.

Her eyes were wide with fright and her skin pale. She moved closer and couldn't stop staring. Looking down, she noticed her swollen breasts with a light rash running across her skin. She'd had few lovers, but she knew whisker burn when she saw it.

Her body told her the truth. Every muscle screamed to her that she'd experienced reality.

She shoved her hair back and stared at her neck. A bright red scrape cut across the tender skin. Touching it, she winced. The pain was real.

She stared at the bed, here in her room. The truth was confusing, but she knew that somewhere in the darkness she'd been made love to, but by whom...or what?

Eight

When the doorbell rang, a few minutes before ten the next morning, Clarissa nearly jumped out of her skin. Since she'd awakened from that horrid dream—or whatever it was—she hadn't slept again. Every time she tried to close her eyes, the frighteningly sensual image of David reappeared.

She wasn't sure what scared her most. The vision dream—or the reality of knowing he could actually change into an animal. Did the fact that he'd changed into a bird mean he *could* become a lion? Or was that just her mind playing tricks on her? Or was it Rachel? A dozen questions swirled around in her mind. Like why and how this could happen.

As she went to answer the door, she rubbed her burning eyes. She had no idea how she was going to make it through the day.

Through the peephole in the door, she saw the all too familiar shape of David's head. The bright morning sun glinted off the dark strands of his hair, and her knees trembled.

But who—what—was really on the other side of the door? The bird ready to take flight? The man with the gentle kiss? The angry lion from the dream? The lover who'd caressed her body with sweet expertise?

Last night's haunting images were too real. What if she opened the door and that horrid beast was there, ready to lunge at her? Putting a protective hand to her throat, she shivered. Even the soft fleece of the turtleneck she wore provided little comfort.

She could still see the gnashing teeth, still feel the throbbing pain of the gash along her throat. Backing up, she bumped against the wall.

Time stretched on, and after a few more minutes, David rapped on the door. "Clarissa? Are you awake?"

His voice echoed around the front porch. She knew she had to answer it, but she also knew she didn't have the nerve. She had to know before she opened the door what she'd be facing.

Slowly, she slid down the wall, huddling on the floor. She put her hands over her ears and breathed deep and slow. Like she had as a child, just as Granny had tried to teach her, she worked on clearing her mind of the negative images and her own fears that clung tightly to her sanity. She breathed slowly. In. Out.

That's it, child. She heard her grandmother's remembered voice soothing and encouraging her. *Trust your instincts.* This was Granny's technique for reaching past the concrete and pulling the elusive to her mind. It had worked for Granny, and it had to work for Clarissa now. It just had to.

Softly, the world slid away. Clarissa's rough nerves soothed, and in a short while she drifted away from the worries that plagued her.

She could feel the vibrations coming around the door's solidness. They were strong, which wasn't unexpected with David's strength of being. Sorting them out proved more difficult than she'd anticipated. Slowly, she again breathed out, cleansing her own confusion away. Sensing his emotions, she found concern and worry. Those feelings buoyed her flagging spirits.

But deep beyond that, she felt fear and a healthy dose of complete terror. Once she picked up on that emotion, it seemed to bombard her, assaulting every emotion she held dear.

It wasn't just David. He was strong, yes, but this was beyond him. Something dark and evil clung to him. She couldn't discern its origin, but she knew it was there, holding on to him. Trying to control him. And whatever it was had failed so far.

David was still in control.

For now. But for how long?

Lifting her head, Clarissa stared at the closed door. It hurt to deny him, hurt to turn away from him and the feelings she felt growing for him. It didn't hurt to turn away from the beast, though.

She stood and turned and walked into the kitchen. The silence pressed in on her as she strained to hear the sound of him leaving. When an engine roared, her eyes misted, and with the fading sound as he drove away, the tears slid down her cheeks.

The phone rang, which didn't surprise her. She stared at it, certain it was David calling. She let it ring. Let the machine answer. When his voice reached out and filled the room, she slammed her hands over her ears. She wasn't ready to connect with him yet.

Instead, she waited until the machine had stopped. Then she picked up the phone. After dialing Faith and asking her for a ride to work, she laid the receiver on the counter beside the phone.

* * * *

Faith had been gone for less than a week, yet Clarissa felt as if she hadn't talked to her friend in years. After climbing into the car, Clarissa stared silently out the window as the city passed by.

Faith managed to stay quiet for half a block. "Okay, what's up?"

Clarissa almost laughed out loud. "You don't even want to know."

"Yes, I do. Especially when you look like you haven't slept in a week."

Clarissa probably hadn't had a decent night's sleep since the last time they'd talked. Faith twisted the rearview mirror toward her. "See?"

Clarissa pushed the mirror back. She knew how bad she looked.

"Does this have anything to do with that guy you were looking for? Did you find him?"

"That's an understatement," Clarissa mumbled, then cleared her throat. "Yeah, I found him."

"Really?" Faith's excitement brightened the car. "Who is he? Is he okay?"

"Yes, he's fine. We, uh..." What should she say? "His name is David Lorde. I went to the bank where he works and told him about the visions."

"*The* David Lorde? As in the gorgeous bank owner? The one rolling in dough? The one people think killed his wife? Holy shit."

"Thanks so much for your help." Clarissa leaned her head back and closed her eyes. She was exhausted, and her eyes ached. Heck, her whole body ached from the exhaustion. But instead of peace and rest behind her closed eyes, she saw David's tormented face.

Was there no escape?

She felt the car come to a halt. She knew Faith was in curious reporter mode, but Clarissa didn't need or want that right now. "I just need a friend," she whispered.

The silence was heavy, and Clarissa knew the decision was tough for Faith. She'd been a reporter too long to let go of her training.

"You got it," Faith said softly. "I won't say a thing if you don't want me to."

The offer was tempting, but Clarissa knew her thoughts were too mixed up, her emotions too raw to be able to judge what to do. There were too many variables to the whole situation. Visions. Ghosts. Shapeshifting. Passion. She needed Faith's impartiality to help her decide what to do.

"No. I need to talk to someone. Let's head to the shop. Lindsey needs to go home. Do you have time for a cup?"

"Twist my arm and I'll take that triple mocha you're famous for."

"Deal."

They accomplished the remainder of the drive in silence, though Clarissa knew Faith's mind spun a mile a minute. She could almost see the gears turning in her friend's head. Faith managed to hold off the questions, though, and that meant a lot to Clarissa.

As it turned out, Lindsey had to wait for a ride, so she agreed to stay awhile longer as Clarissa and Faith sat and talked. By the time they settled into the privacy of Clarissa's office with their coffee, Faith was ready to burst.

But now that she had to talk, Clarissa wasn't sure what to say, where to begin, or even if she should.

Faith had other plans. "You can't fink out on me now. You have my curiosity going, but that's not the worst of it. You look like hell, Clarissa. What did he do to you?"

Clarissa liked the protective sound in her friend's voice. It comforted her, made her feel like she hadn't lost quite all of her mind. "He hasn't done anything bad. Not yet."

Clarissa felt herself relax and would have laughed at herself if her vision last night hadn't been so vivid and frightening. She couldn't seem to get it—or David Lorde—out of her mind. Everything made her think of him.

Heck, what *didn't* make her think of him? His eyes were the color of her morning coffee. His hair was the same shade as the rich imported chocolate she loved. The way the long strands fell just past his shoulder when they were freed and rippled in the wind as if beckoning to her...

Faith snapped her fingers in front of Clarissa's face. "Where are you off to?"

"Oh, nowhere." Clarissa reached out and picked up her drink. The rich mocha scent filled the air before they spoke again.

"Have you ever done any para-photography?'

"As in trying to take pictures of ghosts?

How simple she made it sound. "Yeah. Sorta."

"What are you involved with? Does this have something to do with Lorde?"

Clarissa hesitated. She wasn't sure if Faith, who focused on facts as a photojournalist, would believe her or not, but she needed to talk to someone she trusted.

"Don't get mixed up with him." Faith stirred her drink with more force than was necessary. "They never cleared him of his wife's death, though the autopsy report said she died of cancer."

The image of Rachel as Clarissa had seen her in the mansion came to mind. He'd told her about the cancer, but had he hastened her death?

"Her cancer was treatable, if caught early enough. She wasn't getting treatment from any doctors here," Faith said.

"That doesn't mean she wasn't getting any treatment." Once again she heard David's remorse about trying to help her.

Faith didn't look convinced. "It wouldn't be so suspicious, I suppose, if David Senior hadn't killed his wife."

"What do you know about that?" All of a sudden Clarissa felt as if she were nosing around in David's life. He'd asked for her help, but did that mean prying into his past? Did it have anything to do with what was going on now? "No, don't tell me. I don't want to know."

"There isn't much to know." Faith took a deep swallow of her drink and smiled. "Yum. I don't know what you put in this, but it's heaven." After another sip, she grew serious again. "There were no witnesses in the first Lorde case, and all the evidence showed it was a murder-suicide."

No witnesses? But David had told her he'd seen it all. That he'd been hiding in the music box. Had he lied? Had he seen it and never told anyone? Was that part of why he kept his emotions so tightly controlled? Or had the papers simply chosen to protect him and not report the entire story?

The only person who knew was David, and she wasn't sure if asking him was a good idea. Not only might she be putting herself in physical danger, but emotionally it was too risky.

"So, how did you keep your vision from coming true?"

Faith interrupted her thoughts. "Did he believe you?"

"Not really. Not at first." Clarissa explained what had happened that night at the diner. Was it really only a couple of days ago?

"There you are."

The sound of David's voice startled both of them, and Clarissa nearly spilled her drink. She swore and hastily set the cup down.

He filled the entire doorway, making the office suddenly seem even smaller than usual. "H...hello, David.

"I was worried." His smile was bright, but there were dark smudges under his eyes that marred the effect. "I stopped by your house this morning to give you a ride."

"Uh, David, this is my friend, Faith Burke. Faith, David Lorde. Sorry about this morning. I had things to do, so Faith gave me a ride." Faith nodded but didn't speak.

David turned to face Clarissa. "Could we talk?" he glanced at Faith. "In private?"

"I'm pretty busy right now. Can it wait?" Clarissa picked up their empty dishes and carried them out to the sink. Anything to escape the close confines of the office and Faith's too interested gaze. David followed. Clarissa noticed Faith stayed in the office, though she knew her friend could hear every word they said from where she sat.

David's steps sounded heavy and loud in the sparsely filled coffeehouse. Lindsey sat at one of the tables by the door, rolling silverware in napkins, not paying them any attention.

Clarissa's mind kept seeking conversation starters, but all she came up with seemed so inane that she gave up. She didn't want him to see how nervous she was. She didn't want to alert whatever seemed to be shadowing him to the instability of her emotions.

"So, how did you sleep last night?"

She nearly stumbled. "Not bad," she lied, again unsure how much she should tell him. "You know how it is when you're too tired. It's almost worse than being wide awake." She walked to the sink and immersed her hands in the hot soapy water. "Want a cup of coffee? You look like you could use it. Help yourself." Normal everyday activities helped keep her grounded.

"So, how did you really sleep?" He filled a cup and took a deep swallow of the black coffee, never looking away from her.

"What do you mean?"

He laughed, but it wasn't a humorous sound. "I can see you hardly slept at all. It's not worth lying to me. I've been living in the land of insomnia too long not to know the signs."

"Okay." She shrugged and turned to lean against the counter as she dried her hands. She wasn't about to get any closer to him then she had to. She wished he wasn't here, but short of throwing him out, she couldn't avoid him. "I didn't sleep well at all. Does that satisfy you?"

"No. I'm sorry I got you involved in this."

"Sorry? Why?"

"She's in your head now." He rubbed his eyes with the heel of his hand in a gesture of exhaustion.

"You said that last night. What exactly do you mean by that?"

"In your head." He pointed to his own temple, stabbing at it with an angry finger. "She's already manipulating your thoughts. Soon you'll be sure you're going crazy. If the dreams don't do you in, the lack of sleep will."

Clarissa didn't miss the dejected slump of his shoulders. He looked as if he'd been through a war. And lost. "I did have a dream last night that was frightening. But it was just a dream." Who was she really trying to convince? Him or herself?

"Are you sure?"

"Y...yes. It has to be." She was trying to convince herself.

"Tell me about it."

"No!" There was no way she was going to tell him about the intimacy of the lovemaking she'd experienced, even if it was with him. Sort of. Heat scattered throughout her body, and she could feel his hands and lips moving over her skin again. Suddenly, the dream was all too real.

He set his coffee cup down with deliberate care and stepped closer to her. "Then let me tell you." He placed an arm on each side or her, trapping her between the counter and his body.

Leaning on his palms, he moved even closer but didn't touch her. His dark eyes grew cold and empty as they stared into hers. "We made love. Hot, passionate love...didn't we?" he whispered. She felt his body heat reach out and engulf her. "She knows I want you, knows how much. So she put you in my arms, then ripped you away."

Nine

David's voice broke, and he turned his back to her and stalked away. "I haven't been with a woman since long before Rachel died." He looked over his shoulder at her. "You're the first one I've wanted."

Clarissa felt the pain emanating from him. She knew it took so much for him to admit this to himself, let alone to her. He wanted her. A warm rush slid through her. He wanted to make love to her. A smile tugged at her lips, but it quickly faded away.

The only way he could know about her dream...was if he'd dreamed it, too. Every move, every touch returned. Her cheeks burned with the memory. Suddenly hot, Clarissa reached out and snagged the counter chair. She had to sit down. This was entirely too overwhelming.

He'd shared her dream. In a warped sort of way, they *had* made love. Hadn't they? She remembered every sordid detail, felt every sweet, warm kiss he'd given her. The heat of longing coursed through her, and her heart raced. Dear God, she still wanted him.

She didn't dare look at him. If she did, he might see the hot longing in her eyes. She wasn't sure she could resist him, and right now he was the last thing she needed.

David's silence set her on edge, and she knew she had to turn and face him. With a deep fortifying breath, she turned and faced him again. He'd been running his fingers through his hair. She could see the tracks he'd left. His actions had also loosened the groomed locks, and his hair hung about his shoulders, just like in last night's dream.

She gasped, surprised and intrigued by the wild passion she saw in his eyes. There was no way she could ignore the longing that reached out to her, pulling her into his web of desire. She was trapped and though she fought it, she knew it was inevitable. The dream had been real in some twisted way, and it would be again.

"No!" David roared loudly and angrily, startling Clarissa. In the distance she heard silverware clatter to the floor. Lindsey was listening.

He moved quickly away from her, putting space and rational thought between them. "I want you, God and Rachel know how much. But I won't mislead you. I want it real, not some damned vision she puts in our heads."

He turned away and Clarissa felt his absence as if the sun had vanished from the sky. An ache formed in the region of her heart, and she felt a tightness grow in her chest. What was that warmth on her cheeks? Reaching up, she was astonished to find the tears on her fingertips.

Was she crazy? She wanted more than a dream lover as well, but she wasn't sure how to separate the two. She ached deep in her soul. Until they found those answers, what choice did they have? She didn't know how to explain that to him.

The door of the coffee shop slammed against the wall as he left.

Faith came racing out of the office. "What happened?" Worry filled her eyes.

"Nothing." Clarissa whispered. "I'm fine." She wasn't sure which was the bigger lie. "You need to get back to work, don't you?"

Faith glanced at her watch and then back at Clarissa. "Yeah, but I can call and tell them something came up if you need me."

"No. I'm okay." She had to be.

Lindsey's ride arrived just then and she was also reluctant to leave her. She assured both Faith and Lindsey that she was fine and needed only silence and a chance to be alone for a few minutes. The heavens complied with her hopes as no customers came in.

Pulling herself together, Clarissa reached for the dirty dishes. Noticing David's unfinished coffee cup on the counter, she picked it up and took it to the sink. It still held something of him, and for a long minute she stood looking at the liquid in the cup.

Taste it. The words were so soft, little more than a passing thought. Suddenly, her mouth grew dry and her tongue slid over her parched lips. She saw the faint smudge where David's lips had been.

Lifting the mug, she sipped the brew. Her eyes closed. She saw him as he'd been only moments before. His hair loose about his face, his eyes filled with desire. As the drink slid down her throat, she tasted him and longed for more.

Dear God. She *was* going crazy! Dropping the cup, she watched it hit the porcelain sink. It shattered in a clatter of noise.

Touch it. The words whispered in her mind, louder than the last command.

As if of their own accord, her fingers reached toward the sharp pieces. Bright red blood swirled in the sink. Looking down, Clarissa saw it dripping from her fingertips. Why didn't she feel pain? Why didn't she feel her life's force flowing from her? Surely that much blood would leave some sort of impression.

"No," she screamed, turning away from the sink and running for the door. The bright sunshine bit into her tired eyes. She couldn't leave, but she couldn't stay either.

Strong arms closed around her. She recognized him immediately and didn't struggle. She couldn't. David was the only thing that seemed real and solid in this mixed-up world. His gaze met hers, reflecting back her fear. Then his concern crowded out her fear. Her heart slowed and she dared to look down at her hands again.

The blood was gone.

It had been an illusion.

Collapsing, she fell against his broad, warm chest, seeking anything and everything he could give her. He held her, his hands moving smoothly and slowly over her back. Yet even while he held her, he stood rigid and silent.

He didn't ask her why she'd screamed. She didn't ask him why he hadn't really left. It was as if neither of them wanted to speak for fear their words would trigger the return of the vision. Instead, he reached up and tilted her chin until she looked into his eyes. He didn't speak. He simply lowered his head and gently kissed her.

The tenderness astounded her. Tears of reaction burned in her eyes and she melted into him. She leaned into the strength he so willingly shared, wanting to draw some of it into herself.

Suddenly, he pulled away, a grimace of pain on his face. "I...we can't," he whispered, pulling away.

She wasn't letting him go without an explanation. The last time he'd experienced this pain, he'd changed into that bird. No, this time she needed answers. "David, tell me what's happening."

"I can't explain."

"You have to. This involves me now. She's in my head. Am I going to start changing into animals, too?" Fear tore through her, and she grabbed his arm, knowing her fingernails dug into his skin. But she was unable to stop the urgency raging inside her.

"I don't know. I don't know why it happens." Despair cloaked his voice even as he took several deep breaths. Sweat stood out on his forehead, plastering his shirt to his skin as he fought whatever it was that threatened to overtake him.

The long minutes passed and he slowly relaxed. "Let's go back inside," he suggested and took her arm.

The interior of the shop seemed dim after the bright sunshine, but warm and welcoming, like home. She relaxed and slowly turned back to the sink, forcing herself to look into it.

No blood.

It had never really existed.

She poured them both an icy glass of water. She had to do something, had to help him fight this torment that threatened to tear them both apart.

"Please explain. I need to know what's happening."

He slumped into the nearest chair, the heavy wood slamming into the wall from the impact of his weight. "It all started about a year ago. I think that strong emotions trigger it. Whenever I'm angry or feel passionate about something—" He looked up at her. "—or someone. If I can stay calm, it doesn't happen. That's why we can't..." He left his sentence unfinished.

She knew what he meant. That's why they couldn't make love. Why he couldn't let himself feel anything for her. Because then the dream would come true.

"I can go to Dove's Place," he said. "It doesn't happen there."

"Why there?"

He frowned. "I have an idea, but I'm not positive. Rachel grew up in Dove's Hollow. That's the town that used to be there. She hated it, swore she'd never go back. The dreams and the...what do you call it? The change? It doesn't happen there."

"She can't reach you there? How did you figure that out?"

"By accident." He leaned back and drank the rest of the water. "We used to go there a lot before her parents died. I liked the place, and after her death I found I could relax there."

"She can't go there. That's why she sent that kid to kill

you."

David shrugged. "Probably. I don't know anymore. I have a hard time believing she'd want to kill me."

Clarissa paced. Her thoughts raced. "She might, if she thought you'd be with her."

He looked up then, his surprise evident on his face. "What type of screwy logic is that?"

"Who said any of this had to be logical?" She tried to smile, to ease the tension and help them concentrate without the emotional distraction.

The phone rang then, breaking the tension better than she ever could, bringing the real world back into place. She answered it, knowing she still had a job to do. Her livelihood depended on it.

"Clarissa?" Lindsey's voice came over the line. "I forgot to tell you that a lady named Linda called earlier. Sorry. She wanted to know if we had any job openings, said she knew you."

Linda. Thank goodness. Clarissa was so glad to hear she was all right and already looking for a job. Clarissa's fears eased. "Did she leave a number?"

"I put it on your desk on a yellow sticky."

"Thanks."

"See you tomorrow." Lindsey hung up and the silence returned. David didn't say a word, just sat staring out the window, lost in thought.

"Lindsey," she explained. "She said Linda called looking for a job."

He turned to face her then, his eyes troubled. He tried to smile. "I'd hire her. Tell her to put me down as a reference." The monotone of his voice hurt her heart. He was back in control again, unfeeling, uncaring, unliving.

She didn't say anymore as customers came in, jangling the bell over the door. Two young women stood discussing what they'd order. Clarissa knew she had a couple of minutes, but not much more.

He stood and paused at the door. Obviously she'd given him some things to think about. "I'm working late tonight. I can't get to certain files until after hours. Can I see you afterward?"

She looked at him, her hopes rising at the thought of going out with him.

"We could talk more," he said.

Disappointed, she chose to ignore her feelings about the fact that he wasn't really asking her out on a date. Emotion flickered and then faded in his eyes before she could identify it. "Yeah. We can do that."

He stepped closer. "Don't be alone if you can help it." His tone grew even more serious, if that were possible. "And don't believe anything you hear or see."

She nodded. "I'm going to call Linda. I'll see if she can come over today." She glanced at her watch. "The evening rush will start soon. I'll be busy."

He seemed reluctant to leave. She didn't want him to go, but she knew he couldn't stay. Even now the temptation to reach out and pull him close was strong.

He closed the distance between them in an instant, kissing her hard and deep and fast. "Definitely worth the risk," he whispered before he hurried away.

She stood there for a few minutes, savoring his kiss and wishing—

"Excuse me," one of the girls called, and Clarissa turned back to business. That kept her busy for awhile. It was several minutes before she could get back to the office to look for Linda's phone number.

After searching through several piles of papers, Clarissa found the yellow sticky note with the woman's name and number on it. After several rings, she was ready to give up, but then the phone picked up and she heard Linda's warm hello.

"I was just heading over there. The waitress this morning said you'd probably be in around lunch."

"How soon can you start?" Clarissa didn't stop to think how she'd fit another employee into her already tight budget. She had to take time off, and Lindsey was already stretched to the limit.

"How soon do you need me?"

"Now?" Clarissa had never hired anyone without first checking all their references. She didn't believe in hiring anyone to replace herself, but she'd never been in quite this type of position before.

"I'll be there in—" She paused. "Half an hour?"

"You're hired." Clarissa laughed as she hung up the phone and reached into her desk drawer. Pulling out a time sheet, she filled it out and stuck it on the bulletin board outside her office before she could change her mind.

She slumped against the wall, resting before the rush began. So much had happened. She'd seen so many emotions warring in David's eyes, none of which gave her any comfort. Fear. Anxiety. Exhaustion. They were all there, tangled up and confused. If *he* couldn't sort them out, she'd never get a handle on them. Those same emotions battled within her. He'd answered some of her questions, but so many more came to mind.

Slowly, she moved away from the wall and headed back out front. She had to keep busy or risk falling asleep.

Several minutes later the familiar voice came from the doorway and her spirits lifted. "Clarissa?"

"Linda? In here."

The sound of Linda's footsteps was normal and reassuring. As the woman poked her head inside and smiled, Clarissa felt herself relax. Linda looked good. She wore a thick sweater and formfitting pants that made her look much younger than she had in the diner's retro uniform.

"I didn't know what to wear, a uniform or what." Her smile was hesitant.

"You look great. It looks like you're recovering."

"Yeah. The robbery just made my decision for me. I hated working there."

"Well, you're more than welcome here. I'd appreciate the help."

"I appreciate the job. I'd go nuts sitting at home." Clarissa returned Linda's smile, knowing how she hated to be idle herself.

Linda sat in the wooden chair at an empty table. After they finished the paperwork, Linda's eyes watered. "Thank you," she whispered.

"We're both going to benefit from this," Clarissa admitted and realized she spoke the truth. She liked Linda and her instincts told her she'd made a good choice.

A few minutes later, Clarissa slipped back into the office while Linda filled out the employment paperwork. She couldn't remember if she'd ever been this tired. She needed sleep; she knew that. David had told her that she'd go crazy with the lack of sleep. Maybe he was right.

She sank into her chair for just a second. Just a brief second. Sleep wasn't long in coming and she fought against it, but she didn't have the strength to hold it at bay.

Before she could take more than a few breaths of peace, the visions appeared. She was inside a room she'd never seen before. This was different. Usually she knew where she was.

She found herself drifting, watching what transpired. The room looked cold and sterile, the walls lined with file cabinets. David came in and pulled open two drawers, removing several files before he sat at a computer terminal and booted it up. Soon, boring ledger pages appeared on the screen.

What was he looking at? She couldn't tell from where she was, and she couldn't move closer. Suddenly, the room brightened, and flames shot out of a box on the table. Books and ledgers blazed. Smoke billowed into the air, filling the small room.

David stood, searching for something to put out the fire. There wasn't anything to use. Not even a fire extinguisher near the exit.

He coughed, bending nearly double as the smoke thickened and filled the room. He fell to his knees, gasping for air, then tumbled to the floor, his eyes closed.

"No!" she cried. "David, get out!" But he couldn't hear her. She wasn't there.

She opened her eyes to stare at her office walls. Everything looked so blessedly familiar and safe. She had to warn him. She picked up the phone, then realized it was after hours for the bank as it rang. No one picked up. He'd said he'd be working late, but she hadn't thought about him being alone.

She dug through all the papers stacked on the desk. David's business card was here somewhere. She had to find it. There had been a direct number for his office. Had there been a cell phone number on it? She shoved papers aside, scattering them over the desk and onto the floor.

Finally she found it. There was no answer in his office and no cell phone number. *Damn*. She had to get in touch with him, warn him.

The bank wasn't far. Linda was out front waiting to be trained. Good Lord, she was actually thinking of leaving the woman, untrained, in her shop. It was the worst thing she could do to someone new.

Yet when she stepped out front, Linda had made a fresh pot of coffee and was in the middle of making a cappuccino for a customer.

"I can't believe I'm doing this," Clarissa mumbled to herself, then explained to Linda that she needed to leave. After showing her where everything was, giving her the cell phone number and a key, Clarissa left the shop. She might be putting her business at risk, but David's life was far more important.

Moments later, she parked along the curb near the closed bank. She hurried to the front door and peered in. No one was inside. She leaned against the thick glass, staring in. She banged on it, hoping maybe someone would hear her.

Someone did. A night watchman came to the door. "I'm sorry. The bank's closed. What do you need?"

"Is David Lorde still here? We—uh have a date." She'd pay for these lies later, she was sure of it.

"Oh, yeah. He mentioned somethin' about that. Sorry I forgot. I didn't know he ever dated." Then as if regretting his words, he gave her a sheepish grin. "Mr. Lorde's down in the basement, looking through files. Come on in." He stepped aside and let her in.

"Thank you. Can I go down?"

"Sure. Elevator's that way." He pointed the beam of light toward the shiny doors. She pushed the button and impatiently waited for the elevator to open.

She heard the clank and whir of the machinery in the shaft echoing down the chamber. The sudden swish of the doors startled her.

Anxious to see David, to make sure he was okay, she stepped quickly into the elevator. Stabbing the down button on the panel, she watched it light up. A gentle ding filled the air as the doors slid shut.

The sudden, gentle lurch of the car as it moved had always unnerved her and was no different this time. Her stomach hovered around her knees for an instant then righted itself. The soft hum of the machinery was comforting and familiar.

The hum slowed. Seconds later the entire car stopped with a sudden jolt. The light overhead blinked, and she reached out to steady herself against the steel walls. The metal felt cold and hard beneath her touch. Its solidity offered little reassurance when the elevator stopped between floors and the door didn't open.

Silence pushed against her ears, painfully and nearly deafening as she leaned into the corner of the car. She wasn't normally prone to claustrophobia or hysteria but the events of today combined with being stuck in the elevator were different stories.

Then she saw the phone. Reaching out she shoved against the panel as the written instructions told her to do. It didn't budge. Banging on it, the glass gave, breaking into pieces that fell to the floor. Lifting out the handset, she put the cold black receiver to her ear. The comforting sound of the dial tone soothed some of her fear. Pushing the buttons, she heard the musical tones of the numbers. Another familiarity that eased her discomfort, and she breathed a little easier.

The line connected and rang. One ring. Two. Three. By the fourth, her palms were damp against the plastic receiver. On the fifth ring, a click echoed in her ear and an artificial voice answered. It took several seconds before she realized she wasn't talking to a person but to a machine.

"We're sorry. The number you have reached is temporarily out of service. Please hang up and try again."

"No." Clarissa cried as much from frustration as fear, the sound bouncing off the metal walls in a tinny tone that grated on her nerves. Her fingers trembled and she dropped the phone, letting it hang from its cord, loose and useless as it banged against the steel wall.

She dug for her cell phone and barely resisted the urge to throw it when the tiny screen read, "No Service." She screamed again, her frustration growing.

A loud pop exploded over her head. As if in slow motion, she looked up. Before she could brace herself, the elevator car fell.

She tumbled back against the wall, the metal handrail catching her in the back. She cried out in pain as it bit into her ribs and she sank to her knees.

Anticipating the coming impact, tensing, she closed her eyes, hoping it would be quick and painless. Hoping she'd die instead of becoming a useless body with no mind, or vice versa.

She lost sense of time, of falling, almost as if she tumbled head over heels, as if the car spun through the air instead of falling straight down to earth, like she knew it was.

Seconds became hours as she huddled in the corner of the car. Her mind filled with images she hadn't thought of in a long time. Her childhood in Boston. Her father's warm laughter. His hot anger. Granny Cleary's warm hugs and encouragement. She missed them. Missed them desperately. And now she'd never see them again.

But what she'd miss most was David's warm touch. She wanted his love to be real. The images they'd shared last night and today's kiss had only been a prelude to something that could be wonderful. Once they beat Rachel.

Even the thought of Rachel shot green jealousy through Clarissa. An emotion she hadn't had time for in the past, but which she had time for *now?* Her mind refused to function, but she forced it to.

Was this fall for real? David had said not to believe everything she saw. Would she die any second now, or would she only be hurt? Or would the thought that she might die cause her to? What was going on?

Closing her eyes, she shut out the sensation of falling, forcing her mind to focus on David. On the image of his strong features. On his smile.

Loud crunching and the grinding sounds of metal hitting pavement shattered the quiet in her mind and searing pain shot through her back, to every inch of her body. Warm blood flowed from the cuts on her legs and pooled around her. She felt it curl around her legs and arms, slowly cooling as it crept across the metal floor of the elevator car.

Was this real? She couldn't tell, and right now she hurt too much to care.

Ten

The sound of the doors swishing open managed to break through the dense fog filling Clarissa's brain. Pain radiated from her back and through every inch of her body. She felt cold, so very cold. She shivered.

"Clarissa?" David's voice sounded tinny and distant, as if he were a long way off, through one of those telephones she remembered making as a child with a can and string.

Slowly, she pried her eyes open. She slammed them shut again as bright overhead light stabbed at her. Her entire head felt like it could explode. She almost wished she had died.

Feather light touches skimmed her cheek and chin, and she turned her head toward it. David's hand felt so good, so right, so gentle.

"Clarissa, open your eyes."

Slowly, carefully, she did as he instructed, blinking rapidly as tears of pain formed in her eyes. Where was she anyway? Looking around, shock shot through her.

The smooth, steel sides of the elevator car rose up above her, seeming taller than they had when she'd been standing. She could see the metal handrail just above her head. The cool tile of the floor pushed hard against her pained muscles and something soft was beneath her head.

"Hey, you scared me." David's smile was forced, and she realized he held her loosely in his arms, as if afraid he'd hurt her if he held too tight.

"What happened?" she whispered through her painful throat.

"I'm not sure. When the elevator opened, you were lying there, looking as pale as death." His voice shook as he uttered that last word.

"No. I mean..." She struggled for words. "The elevator. It fell." Turning her head slowly, she looked around. The elevator looked normal, not crushed. There was no blood anywhere around her. Hesitantly, she moved one leg, then the other. No pain, just the soft whisper of her nylons against the floor.

Closing her eyes, she felt every tight, painful muscle in her body relax. It hadn't been real.

Her breathing was shallow, and she struggled to slow her

pounding heart. Frightened was a mild version of what she felt.

"She did it again," Clarissa whispered. She sensed rather than saw David lean closer to catch her words.

He hesitated before he asked. "She?"

She looked at him in disbelief. He knew who, but she repeated it anyway. "Rachel." Carefully, Clarissa slipped her hand from David's and planted a palm on each side of her body. She pushed against the cold tile. Her head spun as she sat up. Taking several deep breaths, her strength slowly returned. She leaned against the cold metal wall. David sat where she'd left him, looking at her with apology in his eyes.

"Don't feel guilty," she admonished. "You warned me, and I guess I didn't really believe you." She tried to smile, to comfort him, to ease the pain she sensed in him.

"*Now* we're going to Dove's Hollow." He didn't ask her, but he didn't immediately usher her away either. She couldn't speak, but she nodded. She had to get away. Already she felt the weakness fading, but she knew it wouldn't go away completely. It was just as he'd said. The dreams were the frontal attack, but the lack of sleep was the secret weapon. If they didn't shore up their defenses, and soon, the battle would be lost.

They would be lost.

"Let's get you out of here." He stood, extending a hand and gently pulling her to her feet. For a long moment she leaned against him, regaining her equilibrium.

"Can we, uh, take the stairs?" She gripped his arm as they stepped from the elevator. He pulled a key ring from the main panel, and the doors swished closed behind them. She'd never be able to get on an elevator again, and the sound of the doors would always set her teeth on edge.

"I only have a couple more things to tie up. Then we'll head to your place and get your stuff."

She nodded in agreement. After she'd settled into a worn vinyl desk chair, her mind registered why she'd been headed here in the first place.

"Those papers." She leaned forward, her exhaustion momentarily forgotten. "That's why I came early. I saw them. Burning."

He looked up at her, a self-satisfied smile on his lips. "And here I thought you were just anxious to see me." He winked, surprising her with his upbeat mood. She'd never seen that side of him before and she wanted more. Much more. She shook her head to dispel her fascination.

"That must mean there's some information in here," he said.

"Take them with us." Urgency tinged her voice as the scent of the smoke from her vision seemed almost too real.

"We can't. This is bank property. It has to be kept secure."

"It isn't safe here. Tell whoever you need to that you're taking them to study. Maybe without Rachel's interference, we can see what's really there."

He hesitated and she felt her panic return. The visions were too strong. She knew they needed to get out of here. She wanted to help him, but she knew they would be ineffectual if they remained where Rachel could influence their thoughts. A sense of urgency told her time was running out. They had to find the answers.

She felt as if there was so much more she could—she *should*—do for him.

A heavy sigh rumbled from his chest. "All right." He gathered the heavy book that bound the computer sheets.

Something nagged at her memory. "Is there a red three ring binder?"

David's face registered surprise. "Yes, but why would that be involved?" he said almost to himself.

"I don't know. I just see stuff. It's like puzzle pieces. The picture isn't complete until they're all together. I know there's another book, too."

"There is. But it's in my uncle's special files."

"Your uncle? What does he have to do with this?"

"He's the other partner in the bank. He and Dad started it and now he and I are working together."

"Could he be the embezzler?"

"No!" David was defensive, but she didn't get the impression he was hiding anything. "He's the one who alerted me to it. If he was the guilty party, he wouldn't do that."

"Still...there's something important in it."

"All right. We'll go get it. Anything else?"

She sat quietly for a minute, trying to remember anything else in the image. Nothing seemed important. "Not right now. But I'll try to remember." She smiled up at him and was rewarded with one of his rare and devastating smiles. Her heart flip-flopped, and she felt a tug in the same general region.

"Just before I experienced the—fall—I was thinking about you." She tore her gaze from his, focusing on the top button of his shirt instead. It was safer than his mesmerizing gaze.

"What did you think about?" he whispered.

"About the images last night. I want to know how much was real."

His long, callused index finger reached out and slid beneath her chin. Gently he pushed until her face tipped up toward his.

"Not enough."

There was no time to resist, and no wish to. His lips were hard and warm against hers. Initially, the kiss was gentle and probing, but as she responded, he pulled her against him with urgent, longing arms.

She felt small against him, fitting perfectly, her curves soft against his hard planes. She wound her arms around his neck and knew she was lost. She was drowning in a sweet pool of longing and had no desire to come up for air.

Clarissa felt herself falling again, only this time she anxiously anticipated the landing impact. It would be in the center of a wonderful and sweet love.

Slowly, subtly, the texture of his skin changed beneath her fingers. Disappointed, she pulled away carefully so he wouldn't think she didn't want to stay in his arms. Then she stepped back and turned away from him. She immediately missed the warmth and nearly turned back into his arms.

"We've got lots to do." Her voice was soft and still shaky from the impact of his lips and her experience in the elevator. Turning back to face him, she silently pleaded with him to understand. After...yes, after...they'd have time for this.

He ran his fingers through his hair in that familiar and endearing gesture. After several deep breaths, he said, "Yes, you're right. I'll get the book and we can go."

He rummaged through a couple of drawers and then walked down the hallway. For a long minute, she watched him, wishing she could read his mind. Her emotions were somehow attuned to his, but while she felt some comfort in that thought, she knew he shut them off quickly and easily. In contrast, desire, fear and frustration ran rampant through her, each vying for the forefront, and she had no control over them. She wasn't sure which would win.

He returned and together they headed to the stairwell.

Pushing the door open, they climbed the stone steps. The sound of their heels echoed up the shaft, loud and hollow. It was a lonely sound, and she shivered as she hurried ahead of him.

Shadows leapt out around each corner as they reached each landing. With each turn, she half expected something to jump out at her. She hesitated, afraid of what would be ahead. Even more afraid of what was reality—and what wasn't.

When they reached the ground level, she stopped, listening for David's footsteps behind her. The silence startled her. Where was he? "David?"

There was no answering call. She shivered and hurried into the lobby where a few lights still burned.

Normal. It looked so normal. So why did a cool chill seem to have enveloped her? As she turned her head, she felt the stiffness of abused muscles. How real had that fall been?

After the "dream" of David making love to her, she'd found the scratch across her neck. After "falling" over the banister at the mansion, every muscle in her body had ached. What telltale sign would she find this time? Her back tingled and she knew there would be a bruise there.

The stairwell door opened and David strode out. There was an urgency in his step, and she met his gaze with a questioning stare. He shook his head and tilted it toward the side door.

Silently, they walked through the lobby, her stride shorter than his, but she managed to keep up—barely. Under his arm he carried the files and the red notebook. She shivered, suddenly afraid of what they might find in them.

His car was parked in the reserved lot, and she followed close at his heels. When he unlocked the door and held it open for her, she hesitated.

"I need to take my car home." She was reluctant to leave him, even if it was only for the few minutes that it would take to drive through town. She wanted him to reassure her. Wanted him to lie, if he must, and tell her that everything would be fine.

"I'm in control," he pronounced, almost too loudly, as if he were telling her as well as someone else.

Reaching out, she touched his arm. "What happened? Was there a problem when we came upstairs?"

He paused, as if weighing whether to tell her. "I almost shifted in there."

"Almost? You can tell when it's going to happen?" He

nodded. "How much can you control it?"

"Not enough. We'll talk. Let's get going." Tearing his gaze from hers, he moved away. Popping the trunk, he threw the files in and then walked her to her car.

In a matter of minutes, he was seated behind the wheel of his car and she pulled away from the curb.

His headlights followed her home. When her house came into view, it seemed so normal and familiar. Familiar meant safe. She glanced back at David's headlights.

At least she'd thought it had meant safe until last night's dream.

* * * *

This time she didn't have to ask where they were going. He'd told her about Dove's Hollow, but was it real? Were they actually going to be safe there? As they drove past the diner and into the old city limits she felt safer, though she couldn't explain why.

Leaning her head back against the rest, she let her eyelids slip down. She fought sleep, fought against the possibility of another vision. The gritty feeling in her eyes that had plagued her for so long increased. She stared out the window, fighting to stay awake.

The familiar buildings of Dove's Hollow surrounded them, and even in the dim night, the town looked dark and uninviting. David drove past the garage and turned another corner. This time she saw the remnants of a once tree-line avenue that sat huddled against the foothills.

Overgrown with weeds, the buildings were ramshackle and as they drew closer, she realized nearly every window was boarded up. It was a dead town, waiting for time and the elements to wipe it away. At the thought, she felt sadness settle around her heart. These homes were nothing more than the outer shells of what used to be.

He pulled to a stop, gravel crunching beneath the tires. Looking out his window, past his silhouette, she saw a house that at least had the boards taken off the windows. All except one, in the far upper right. The shattered glass was covered with what looked like cardboard.

"This is where Rachel grew up. It's the only place she can't reach us."

"Are you sure she can't?" Clarissa didn't think there was any place the horrid visions and sensations couldn't follow her, but anything was worth a try at this point.

"It's where I've stayed a few times since she started driving me crazy, and it's worked. Come on."

He climbed out and rounded the car before she could do more than turn and grasp the door handle. He had the door open in the same instant she lifted the latch. She slid out and stood within the protective haven between the car and the door. She found herself hesitant to leave it.

"If she can't reach you here, why don't you stay here all the time?"

"I've considered it, but it would become a prison."

He stood on the other side of the door, his gaze meeting hers. He was asking for her trust, asking her to help him. She couldn't deny that look any more than she could deny the urge to breathe. Stepping out from behind the door, she slammed it with a decisive wham and slipped her fingers between his.

Hand in hand they made their way across the cracked cement sidewalk. It was difficult, as the tree roots had shoved several sections upward, allowing weeds to grow through.

The front step sagged and David helped her up, making sure her foot landed on the strongest part of the board. Taking a key out of his pocket, he stepped to the door. The lock moved easily, as if he'd oiled it recently, and he shoved the door open. Taking her hand in his, he guided her into the small foyer.

Despite the dust and cobwebs, she thought it must have once been a nice house. Quaint. Modest.

What disturbed her was the fact that she felt nothing. No vibrations, no impressions that anyone had ever lived here. It was truly an empty house. A sadly lonely house.

Moonlight streamed in the grime-coated front window. Its milky white color illuminated a few dust motes as they danced in the breeze the open door created.

David flipped a light switch, and a small lamp in the corner came on. Shadows and dust cloaked the room, and in the center of what had once been the living room, sat a huge brass bed. A familiar brass bed. The one in last night's vision.

The scratch on her throat throbbed in response to the memory. She took a couple steps back. "Were you here last night?" she asked him.

"No. I was at my apartment."

Relieved, she relaxed a little. "That bed..."

"Yeah, I know." He swallowed. "It was in the dream. It

used to be in my room in the big house." Rumpled sheets and a tattered old quilt lay haphazardly across the mattress.

The evidence of his stay here, of his tossing and turning beneath those sheets, shot hot sparks through her bloodstream. She saw him in her mind's eye, as he'd been last night, nude and beautiful. Heat fused every cell in her face, and she turned so he wouldn't see. "Interesting place for a bed." She fought for normal ground.

"It was the easiest place to move it into. I'm not planning on this being a permanent arrangement."

The soft hum of a small refrigerator in the corner startled her. She watched as David walked over to it and pulled out two beers.

"I don't suppose this is your usual fare, but right now I need something." He twisted off the top of one bottle and handed it to her. After opening the other, he tilted it to his lips.

She saw the muscles in his throat work as he drank, and hot desire came alive in the pit of her stomach. He sat down on the edge of the bed, and she slowly walked across the room to sit on the dust-covered window seat. The beer tasted good and soothing and all too normal in this strange place. The silence actually felt good.

"The heater doesn't work, so we're stuck with the fireplace. I'll get some wood." He finished his beer and tossed the empty bottle into a basket in the corner.

The house was silent. No sounds of settling, no appliances except the small refrigerator. Nothing gave her any reassurances that this was a good place. She shivered and walked over to the couch where she settled down. This was probably the best place for her to sleep. She glanced back at the unmade bed.

There was no way she'd sleep there. Not with David's scent there, not *that* bed.

David came in then, a load of wood in his arms. In a few minutes the fire blazed, and he turned around to face her. He'd said they'd talk, but suddenly she wasn't sure she really wanted to do that.

Instead, she sat on the couch and stared into the struggling fire. Instead of sitting in the wingback chair, he pulled the blanket off the back of the couch and moved to stand beside her.

"Here," he whispered and settled next to her. The strength of his arms, and the solid wall of his chest against her back, eased her fears a little.

"I'm afraid to go to sleep," she admitted, though with the fire, the alcohol in her system, and the lack of any recent sleep, she doubted she'd be strong enough to resist.

"The visions shouldn't come back." She noticed he didn't promise.

The fire popped and sizzled in the silence. For a long moment, she watched the dance of shadows and light on the faded wallpaper. Almost pretty, in a macabre sort of way.

"Tell me," David said.

"Tell you what?"

"About what scares you. What inside that pretty head sees these horrid images?"

"You think I'm pretty?"

"Don't change the subject."

They laughed, and she breathed a sigh of relief and resignation. She didn't speak, though.

"Come on," he softly prompted.

She swallowed the lump in her throat. "I grew up in Boston. My family had migrated from Salem a couple centuries ago, so the stories of witches have always been tied to us."

"Are you?"

"What? A witch? Not unless I'm having a really bad day." Again she paused, and he nudged her. "In the summer before my senior year in college, I had a dream like that first one of you. Very vivid—a little boy was trapped in a dark place. I could see his face but nothing else."

Even the distant memory made her shiver, and David's arms tightened. She leaned her cheek against his shoulder, as if she could hide from him and the memories that made her long to weep.

"I tried to find him. I lost my job because I'd see someone I thought was in the vision. I tried to find out who the boy was. Finally, I went to the police."

David groaned, as if he knew what was coming.

"As soon as they found the bodies of two little boys in the woods, I was arrested."

"You're kidding."

"No." The memories of that time in jail made her voice tremble. "I spent two weeks in jail and months as a suspect."

"You're not in jail now. What happened?"

"They finally used modern techniques and caught the real

killer." She fell silent.

"But?"

"But not until halfway through my trial. While they were more than willing to use the information I gave them to help solve the case, they weren't willing to really believe I had psychic powers. The press fried me."

"I can understand that." He didn't elaborate, but she recalled Faith's comments about his past. How bad had it been when his parents had died? Did he remember that? What about after Rachel's death? She snuggled closer to him. They'd blamed him for her death. She didn't ask him to explain. She didn't have to.

"Is that why you moved clear out here to Colorado?"

She shook her head, hiding behind the gold curls that fell across her face. "No," she cleared her throat. "I left because of my family."

"What did they do?"

She watched the shadows again, watching as they seemed to form into her father's angry form and her mother's shocked and appalled face. "They accused me of ruining the family name. Of putting us back into the days of Salem."

"Surely they knew better."

She laughed, a mirthless laugh that hurt. "No. The only person who ever understood me was Granny Cleary, and she'd died just that summer."

"You miss her."

"Yeah, a lot. Funny, I've thought about her several times in the past week. There was a woman at a farmer's market I went to who reminded me too much of her. Scary."

His arms tightened and she felt his lips press against the top of her head. She closed her eyes, not inviting sleep this time, but to take the memory closer inside.

She wasn't at all surprised when he turned her around and kissed her. She kissed him back, letting herself feel the freedom of it without the fear of what would happen to him. The blanket slipped away, and he pulled her close, his warmth engulfing her.

"I don't think I should stay," he whispered, slowly moving away from her. "I can come back in the morning. You'll sleep better that way."

"Why?" Was he nuts? She'd never sleep out here in this isolated place alone. "Don't you need to rest too? What's the matter?"

David closed his eyes and then opened them to stare at her, his gaze full of hot desire. "I want you. That's not a good thing."

She almost agreed with him. Almost. "I thought we were safe here."

"You are, I'm pretty sure. I...I haven't tested the limits of my shifting. I haven't had anything emotional happen when I've been here."

She stared at him. Then her gaze darted to the bed. The images and feelings were too close to ignore. "I'm not sleeping in that bed anyway. You might as well use it.

"You might be at risk."

"Okay." She sat up straighter, pulling the blanket back up. "You said earlier we'd talk. I think we need to. Now." She wasn't even sure what she wanted to ask, what she wanted to know. "Can you explain exactly what happens to you?"

He didn't say anything for a long time.

His voice was soft and yet intense when he finally spoke. "So far it's happened half a dozen times. Usually it's the bird, but there are others."

"What else?" She forced herself to ask, seeing the beast from her dream.

"Once a cat. That's how I got those cuts on my stomach. Some idiot shot at me to scare me away."

She frowned. He could have been killed. What would happen to him if he were hurt or killed while he was an animal? She shivered and curled her fingers into the blanket.

"In my dream last night, you turned into a lion."

"I what?" He sat up straighter. "I didn't dream that. Are you sure?"

"Yes, I'm sure. See." She reached up and pulled the high collar back. She didn't know how the marks looked now, though they still stung a little.

"I did that?" He leaned closer, his breath fanning across the tender skin. Suddenly, he stood and paced in front of the fire. "You shouldn't have come here with me." He reached for his jacket. "I'm leaving."

"No." She stood, grabbing his arm to stop him. He couldn't leave her here, and she couldn't face going anywhere right now. "Please, stay. I know how you feel about me. I know that what I feel for you is stronger than anything I've ever experienced before. I can't believe you'd hurt me. Ever."

He groaned and sat back down, pulling her tight against him. "God, you shouldn't believe in me. No one else ever has." His voice came out muffled as he buried his face in her hair. She felt his lips against the first scratch, soft, gentle and soothing.

His touch felt so right, so wonderful. She knew he'd never intentionally hurt her, but what about unintentionally?

Dare she test him, herself, and this place?

Before she could change her mind, she turned into his embrace and slipped him into one of her own. Burying her fingers deep in his hair, she brought his lips to hers and opened up to him. He responded with a kiss that erased all her previous memories and created new ones.

The fire popped, the sound filling the quiet as he lifted her and carried her to the bed.

Eleven

The flickering light of the fire had been bright near the couch, but the bed sat farther away. As the flames danced, so did the shadows on the wall, across the bed, and over David. He gently settled her against the pillows and sat beside her on the edge of the bed.

"I love your hair," he whispered, as he combed his fingers through the long strands.

Clarissa smiled, watching the wonder as it covered his face and reflected in his eyes. She touched him, rubbing her hands up and down his solid arms.

There was no pain, no threat, to this time they had. Not here. Not now. The worry she'd carried with her drifted away, and she knew tonight that things were real. So very real.

"Kiss me," she whispered, the words a soft plea.

He slowly leaned down, his shadow covering her first and his lips following.

He tasted faintly of beer and strongly of man. A man who had held back too long and was still trying to. His lips were warm and hard, and she kissed him back, wanting him to let go and feel. To let himself experience this with her.

She unbuttoned his shirt and slid her hands inside to feel his warm skin. A sigh escaped her and vanished into the kiss.

She pulled his shirt off as his hands slipped beneath her blouse. The feel of his fingers on her skin was nearly too much. Hot desire sifted through her blood. She leaned back and pulled the turtleneck over her head. He didn't wait for her to take off her bra, but instead released it himself.

"I want to see all of you." He leaned back and quickly removed the rest of her clothes. When she was naked before him, he stood and removed the last of his own clothes, never taking his gaze from her.

She'd barely had time to feel the ache of his absence before he returned and settled close to her, his hands on her waist and his lips hungrily feasting at her breasts.

Molten heat flowed through her, melting any doubts or questions or coherent thoughts she had. All she knew was he was here with her, warm and alive and loving her. She gave into his skilled seduction and let him bring her body to aching life.

"I want you. I want it real," he said, as much a command as a plea.

Poised above her, his arms taught with restraint, he waited for her reply. She paused only an instant, only long enough for her mind to fill with anticipation and desire. Finally, she whispered, "Yes."

And then he was there, where she wanted him most. She cried out with ecstasy and surprise as he thrust into her.

He filled her, swiftly and deeply, again and again, until she was no longer aware of where she was and no longer cared. All she wanted was to remain one with him. To love him. To hold him. To keep him.

Higher and faster they climbed until she shattered into a million pieces of joy. He trembled in her arms, and her cry mingled with his.

She didn't open her eyes, didn't move for fear of breaking the spell. She listened as their breath mingled in the cool air. Neither of them spoke for a long time, and the air cooled as the firelight dimmed.

Softly David kissed her, and she let herself relax. She realized she'd been waiting, fearing what would come next.

She opened her eyes and gazed at the smooth expanse of his bare back over his shoulder. Shadows danced across his skin and she smiled against him.

As if the movement alerted him, he moved away, rolling to the side and taking her with him. He wrapped the blankets around them.

Still they didn't speak, as if afraid words would break the spell. Clarissa just wanted to savor the feel of him and the normality of the moment.

As the last flicker of flame winked out, exhaustion finally caught up with her, and she let her eyes drift closed. For the first time in what seemed like ages, she felt safe enough to sleep.

* * * *

David leaned against the doorjamb watching Clarissa as she laid there, cuddled under the patchwork quilt. The moonlight stole through the front bay window, almost as if it couldn't resist touching her either.

The lamp beside the bed was turned down low. Clarissa had fallen into a deep, sated sleep. Her hair tumbled across the pillow, shimmering in the soft lamplight.

The hardwood frame felt cool against his bare skin. The entire house, for that matter, was cool, but he didn't move to put on his shirt.

He'd slipped his jeans back on when he'd first decided it was time to leave her. But now, he couldn't seem to continue dressing or leave.

He simply stood there, watching the slow, even rise and fall of her bare shoulder as she breathed.

So alive. And beautiful.

She'd done so much for him. Warning him of her visions and staying with him, even when she realized what he became when the emotions overcame him.

And what had he done for her? Exposed her to danger. Brought the evilness of Rachel into her mind.

And worst of all, let her believe that he could love her.

David had given up on being able to love too damn long ago. It was an illusion he'd let have too much control over his life. And that control had nearly killed him.

No, he couldn't really love her. He no longer had the capacity to love.

But he did feel as if he owed her something. He owed her his life at least, not that it was worth much right now. But it was the one thing he possessed that he could call his own.

With it, he could protect her from the world, from herself, and from harm. He could support her through this and then let her go back to the life she'd worked so hard to build. He'd give her the freedom she deserved by banishing the visions.

Taking a long pull on the beer in his hand, he smiled. What had ever made him think he'd get sleep with her around? But this lack of sleep wasn't nearly as disturbing. This was good old hormones—something he could deal with, not fearful thoughts and dreams.

He continued to watch Clarissa sleep, so peaceful, so innocent in her belief that they were safe—that she was safe here alone with him.

He felt the beast of desire race through his bloodstream. The "dream" they'd shared last night had been the flint to his steel. Ever since the embers had been sparked, he'd felt the consuming heat. But he'd held back. He'd leashed the animal fire. Tonight's lovemaking had only fueled his desire.

But he didn't know how much longer he could hold the shift back. He didn't know how much longer he'd be in total control of his life and of his soul.

Closing his eyes, he leaned his head back against the wall. He abandoned the idea of easing back into the bed next to her, though his body screamed for him to do just that.

He was exhausted and sleep nearly overtook him as he leaned against the wall's solid support. But he fought it, fought the dreams that lulled him into safe havens only to turn into horrific nightmares.

In the beginning, he'd dreamed Rachel was alive again, alive and living with him in the mansion. There were no shadows in his dreams then. But always it ended the same—him reliving the prolonged horror of her death. How many nights had he lain in the bed alone, weeping for the woman in his arms, the woman he'd never hold again, the woman who would never love him again? He'd lost count.

He didn't know when the dreams changed. When he'd begun to rebuild his life, he supposed. He'd started to date and every woman he went out with appeared in his dreams—and died in them. Just as Rachel had.

Then Rachel returned to his dreams. Angry. Hurt. Vengeful. His guilt had nearly done him in. And then the shifting began.

And after that he'd avoided sleep. Without sleep, without control, he felt the insanity breathing down his neck. When he knew he needed it, he'd drowned the dreams in a bottle of whiskey. Finally, even that hadn't worked. So he tried to stay awake. Stupid, but when he operated with only half the needed sleep, logic took a hike.

Shaking himself out of his reverie, he opened his eyes and once again found his gaze drawn to the form on the bed.

Clarissa murmured in her sleep. A sound much like those she'd made earlier, when he'd held her close. She rolled over and slid her hand beneath the empty pillow where he'd been lying only a short time ago.

A frown came and went on her brow as she settled back into the sleep of the exhausted.

* * * *

Clarissa sat behind the hard wooden table. Her attorney, an older man her father had hired, didn't care about her as much as he cared about his paycheck sat beside her. His crisp shirt practically crackled with starch, and the red power tie he kept straightening made her want to grab it and strangle him with it.

Not good thoughts, she admitted, and turned her gaze down to her clasped hands. She was, after all, on trial as an accomplice for murder—a crime she didn't commit.

Why was this happening to her? Why was she trapped in this nightmare? She longed to lay her head down on her arms and close her eyes. She didn't remember even a single wink of sleep last night.

She didn't bend down, but she did close her eyes and forced her mind to clear, thinking instead of a bright sunlit garden. Anything to ease the tension. Taking a deep breath, she opened her eyes and focused on the witness now on the stand.

Elizabeth Riley was eleven. Clarissa knew that from the documents her attorney had given her to review. So much time had been wasted before they found the bodies. The girl had been nine at the time Mike and Stevie had disappeared. Right now she looked like that frightened nine-year-old must have.

The prosecutor paced, his polished shoes making loud clicking sounds as he walked in front of Clarissa.

"Tell the jury, Elizabeth, what you saw that night."

"I...I saw someone on the corner by our apartment building."

"Do you know who that person was?"

"No."

"Are you sure?"

"Yes."

The prosecutor turned and gazed over his shoulder, spearing Clarissa with an accusing stare. "What happened next?"

"The boys came down the stairs. They were playing cops and robbers. Mike was chasing Stevie."

"What was the other person doing?"

"Watching, leaning against the basketball hoop."

"Did the person do anything?"

"He waved at the boys, and they laughed and all three of them disappeared down the street."

"Did the boys go with that person?"

"Uh-huh."

"Your witness." The prosecutor smirked and sat back down. Clarissa's attorney sat silent for a long minute.

"Mr. West," the judge spoke from the bench. "Do you have any questions?"

The attorney nodded slowly. "Just one." He stood with much show and straightened his tie and coat. "You said something there that surprised me, Miss Riley."

"I did?"

"You said, 'he.' Was the person by the basketball hoop a man or a woman?"

The little girl stared at the prosecutor. Her eyes teared and her face flushed red. "I...I don't know."

"No further questions," the attorney sat back down. This time he smirked.

A smile that still sent chills up Clarissa's spine. She looked up then, and watched in horror as the attorney's face changed and she found herself staring into a familiar face.

David's face.

Outside the courtroom, the sound of horse's hooves broke the air. Suddenly she was in the dark, safe and away from the trial that had threatened to destroy her life.

Clarissa opened her eyes. Where was she? Shadows from the fire danced on the walls, reminding her how they'd danced on David's skin. She reached out and was surprised to find the other side of the bed empty. Relief washed over her as she realized the trial had been a dream. David hadn't been there. Her old fears were returning to torment her, but nothing more.

Where had David gone? She crawled out of bed. The nearest piece of clothing was his T-shirt and she pulled it on. The hem fell nearly to her knees and she smiled, feeling as if he somehow engulfed her.

The house was silent. Looking out the window, she saw his car in the drive where they'd left it. He was still here somewhere. The fire was low. Had he gone out to get more wood? The basket was only half empty.

The full moon hid its face behind a veil of clouds. Clarissa stared up at it, feeling its pull in her blood, knowing that the creatures of the night scurried just beyond the window. In her mind's eyes, she saw yet another creature. One that caught her breath and teased her soul.

The visions were distant, but those she'd already experienced were strong memories. She smiled when she recalled the last one. It hadn't come true—not all of it anyway. David hadn't changed into a beast after they'd made love.

She still felt exhausted and wanted to give into it, but someone—or something—out there didn't want her to rest. And she didn't want to rest until David returned. Edgy, she opened the door, hoping to find him sitting on the front porch.

The short rest she'd taken had cleared her mind, strengthened her. As she stepped outside, a flash of movement broke the darkness of the forest behind the house. What was that? She leaned closer to the railing. Her breath fogged in the air for an instant and then vanished.

There it was again. Moving between the trees at the edge of the lawn. A feathery flutter followed and then it, too, vanished into the night.

Slowly, quietly, she stepped out onto the lawn. Another flash appeared and then vanished. The curve of a shoulder barely visible.

She walked across the grass. The dew dampened her toes and muffled her steps. She moved closer to the woods. Then at the edge of the yard, she rested her hand on a tree. Its rough pine bark felt reassuringly solid against her palm.

She waited. Would it come again? What was it? Why did she want to see it so badly?

She didn't have time to answer her own questions before a thundering noise startled her. A great black horse cantered out of the shadows, stopping only a few feet away from her. He rose up on his hind legs, his front hooves pawing the air. A pained whinny cut the night air.

His coat glistened in the moonlight with the sheen of perspiration. His sides heaved with deep breaths. How long had the animal been running, and how far?

"Shh, boy," she said softly, hoping to soothe the wildness in his eyes. He was a beautiful animal, and she hated seeing him distressed. "It's okay." She took a step closer.

The horse landed hard on his hooves and paced back and forth across the edge of the lawn. White plumes of his breath rose in the air.

"I won't hurt you," she crooned, reaching out to touch his slick dark coat.

He stopped, staring down at her with big dark eyes. He blew out what sounded like a disgruntled sigh before stamping his foot. He shook his head, lowering it to the ground, and then turned quickly away. He trotted off, the cool air fingering through his mane and tail.

The shadows devoured him quickly, and the black night and the dark horse soon became one.

And then she looked down. Bright moonlight pooled on the trampled grass. Something dark glistened on the ground. She bent down, gingerly reaching out, only to pull her hand back.

A similar wet darkness covered her hand.

Blood. The horse's blood.

She swallowed her reactive scream.

David had said the dreams couldn't reach her here. This couldn't be a dream. It didn't feel like a dream. Swallowing hard, she fought the rising panic.

She stared back at the dark woods. The horse was hurt, and badly. Was the horse David? Or was he the beast that had injured the animal? Frightened, she backed away from the bloodstain.

"David," she screamed into the night, hoping, praying he'd appear in the doorway of the house, or come strolling out of the woods like he had the night he'd transformed into the bird.

The only response she received was the echo of her own voice.

An echo the dark woods swallowed whole.

Twelve

She wasn't frightened. Okay. She stared at the front door where she'd wedged one of the wingback chairs. She was a little scared, but she realized some of that fear had turned into anger.

She paced the living room rug. The fire had faded, but she no longer needed the heat. Her anger and the pacing kept her plenty warm.

David had lied to her. He'd said they were safe here, that the dreams couldn't reach her. While she admitted she hadn't had any dreams or visions, and she'd gotten a decent sleep, he hadn't.

And now she was fairly sure he was out in the woods, possibly hurt. Making her worry. What should she do? Should she go looking for him? Should she wait for him to come back? What if he never came back? What if even now he was dead or dying, alone and out in the cold night?

She couldn't call the police. She wouldn't even know what to tell them. Mac had accepted her explanations that fit into some semblance of reality. She wouldn't even know what to tell him to look for—a horse or a man? Or something else?

What if he'd simply gone over to Dove's Place for a cup of coffee and her imagination was in overdrive?

The hollow thud of footsteps startled her. She ran to the door and nearly yanked it open. She stopped herself just before she turned the doorknob. What if it wasn't David?

Who else would it be?

The cold metal turned against her palm, and she squealed, pulling her hand back and shuffling behind the chair. Thankfully, she'd locked the deadbolt before shoving the chair in front of the door.

Silence stretched tight, and then several sharp raps broke it. "Clarissa," David called, his voice sounding strained.

"David?" Was it really him? Or someone—something—else? She didn't have a window or peephole to look out.

"It's me. Honest."

A loud thud rattled the door. She heard something scrape down the length of the wood, landing with a muffled thump on the floor.

He was hurt. She thought for an instant that she felt his

pain and she remembered the horse's blood. What was happening to her? She hurried to the fireplace and grabbed the metal poker he'd used to stir the fire earlier. It slid in her damp palm and she wiped her hand down the cotton shirt before grabbing it again. She had to see if it really was him, but she was prepared to fight if he or anyone else meant to hurt her.

She returned to the door and pushed the chair back far enough to open the door a crack. At first she didn't see anything. But then she looked down and saw him sitting against the doorframe.

His feet were bare and looked blue in the pale light. He wore only jeans, no shirt—obviously, she realized, since she wore it. His breath was shallow and rough. The long strands of his hair hung loose, almost to his shoulders. His eyes were closed, but he opened them slowly when she stepped into the doorway. "I—" He licked his dry lips. "Sorry."

She knelt beside him, looking at the pain masking his face. "What happened?"

He laughed, a sound that abruptly changed into a groan. "Guess I shouldn't have believed I was safe. I tried to stop it." He tried to get up, groaning as he did. "Damned barbed wire." He nearly pitched forward, but caught himself on the edge of the doorframe.

"What happ—" Words failed her when he turned, exposing his back to the light. A bloody gash ran from his right shoulder to the top of his left hip. Blood smeared across his back and continued to trickle down his skin. The jeans were blood-soaked in back.

He tried to go inside, but stumbled. The back of the chair caught him and though the air rushed out of his lungs, he didn't fall.

"You're going to the hospital," she ordered, her voice only shaking a little.

"Not a chance. I was stupid to leave the grounds once. I'm not doing that again."

"What do you mean?"

"Help me to the sink and I'll explain. Grab the flashlight."

The struggle to get him into the tiny bathroom took longer than either of them expected. He slipped an arm around her shoulders and leaned on her. While she knew she wasn't carrying his full weight, his height and weakness made it nearly impossible for them to walk. It took several tries before they figured out the rhythm. "I never was good at the three-legged race," he admitted as he finally rested against the counter by the sink.

Clarissa set the flashlight on the vanity, the light bouncing off the ceiling barely bright enough to see. "What do you want me to do?"

"Just clean it. The water's ice cold but it will have to do."

"Shouldn't we heat it?"

"Probably, but I'm not up to waiting. It'll do for now."

The old pipes moaned and groaned as he twisted the spigot. "There are some towels on those shelves over there."

She fumbled around in the semi-light. She found the towels and turned back to the sink. She soaked one, her fingers aching with the icy water. He leaned on the counter, his arms straight, his eyes closed.

"This is gonna hurt," she warned him.

"It already does. Go ahead." He swallowed hard.

She felt him resist the urge to jerk away as she put the freezing towel on his skin. The cold seemed to help numb the pain and slow the bleeding. It made cleaning it harder, but she took her time, trying not to hurt him any more than necessary. Soon they were both shivering, but at least his breathing had returned to normal and his skin wasn't as pale.

"So when were you going to tell me all you had was cold water? That I would have to take an ice cold shower tomorrow?" she asked to break the tension.

He laughed softly. "I hadn't really thought about it. Sorry."

"Are you going to fill me in on what happened?"

He was silent for so long she thought he wasn't going to answer her. "I couldn't sleep so I went out for a walk. I wasn't really paying attention where I was going."

"How far did you go?"

"Not far, but Dove's Hollow doesn't extend too far west."

"How far does it go?"

"About half a mile. Then it butts up against the back of my estate."

"What?" She stepped back and leaned around to look at him. Despite the shadows, she could see the pain on his features and it tore at her heart. "I'm sorry. Did I hurt you?"

"No." He shook his head, his hair falling down to hide his face. "Is it still bleeding?"

"A little. We need to bandage it."

"I don't think we have anything."

"You need stitches. Why don't we run over to the emergency room? It won't take long."

"No!" He stood up straight, grimacing with pain. The only thing keeping her from looking to see if he'd started bleeding again was his anger. "I was fine walking around, I could control the shift. But the instant I stepped over the line, it hit me. I couldn't stop the change."

Relief shot through her and she smiled at him. He hadn't lied to her. They were safe here. "Okay. We'll stay here, but I'm calling for some help. You have to have that looked at."

He didn't argue, which was probably as close as he'd get to agreeing.

Carrying the flashlight, she followed him out to the living room. His steps were slow, but at least he was able to walk under his own power. He turned a metal chair around and sat leaning his arms across the back.

The room had cooled, and she fed the dying flames with a fresh log. The dry wood caught quickly, and soon the room was bright enough that she could see his wound better. It wasn't as deep as she'd thought, though it still looked painful. "Did you say something about barbed wire?"

"Yeah. I guess horses need to know about those things. I hadn't a clue."

"So, you do know what's going on after you've changed? Your thoughts are the same?"

"Sort of. They're simpler. It's hard to explain. I remember seeing you outside. What were you doing out there, anyway?"

"Looking for you." She settled onto the couch and watched him. "Don't change the subject. You still think like David when you're in a different form? Is that why you came back here?"

He nodded. "I thought if I could, I'd change back sooner.

His logic made sense. "Okay. I'm going to call Faith and see if she can bring us some bandages."

He frowned. "What'll you tell her?"

She hesitated. "Enough. She knows about my abilities. She won't be as suspicious as other people might be."

He nodded and turned to stare into the fire. Clarissa paused to watch him as she called Faith and woke her out of a sound sleep. She only briefly wondered what excuse Faith would give her husband for running out in the middle of the night. She knew curiosity, if nothing else, would ensure Faith came to help them.

* * * *

David sat silent as Clarissa and the pretty redhead who'd just arrived discussed his injury. He felt like a specimen under a microscope as they verbally dissected him.

He shivered at the thought. If anyone found out about his changing, the medical community would want to dissect him for real. With the shiver came a spasm of pain. Damn, it stung. The cut wasn't as severe as he'd first thought, but now that his skin had warmed, the stinging had returned.

"So, am I going to live?" he asked, gritting his teeth, more from frustration than pain.

"I'm sorry." Clarissa quickly moved to his side, and he resisted the urge to touch her and smile. That would kill her concern, and he was definitely enjoying her sweet ministrations. Despite the pain, the touch of her hands on his skin tormented him. It hadn't been that long ago that they'd made love, and his body was telling him he wanted her again in no uncertain terms.

Why do I still need her so badly? With an effort, he shut those thoughts off. Not good. Not good at all. Her dream hadn't come true last time. He wasn't sure if he could guarantee it again.

"I brought antibiotic cream," Faith said. She rummaged around in the sack she'd brought and handed a wicked-looking tube to Clarissa.

"That should help." Clarissa leaned over his shoulder, her hair brushing his bare skin.

He gritted his teeth again, sure she was trying to drive him crazy.

"This might hurt." She moved back, and he heard her rummaging through the bag.

At least the pain took his mind off her nearness. He closed his eyes and nodded, not trusting himself to speak. She'd think he was dying from the wound, when it was actually desire that threatened his sanity.

He felt the soft edge of cotton rub along the cut. He flinched and heard her gasp. He vowed to keep his reactions to himself after that, even when she gave up on the cotton and used her fingertips to smooth out the cream. It almost felt like her touch when she'd been in his arms and he'd been inside her.

"Hell," he cursed and abruptly stood up. "Just put the bandages on."

"I will," she crooned. "Just sit back down."

Thankfully, she stopped touching him, and he heard the sound of tearing paper. The two women had decided on the butterfly bandages so he presumed that was what she opened. He sat rigid as her hands returned to his skin, her touch soft and gentle as she put the bandages in place.

"Finished," she whispered.

He didn't turn around to look at her. He didn't dare. Instead, he stood and strode to his bag to pull out a clean shirt. He struggled to put it on without pulling the bandages loose.

Finally dressed again, he turned around to face them as he sat carefully on the edge of the bed.

The fire was bright and lit the room. Clarissa finished cleaning up, and Faith sat in the wingback chair. After a long minute, she fidgeted, her feet crossing and uncrossing.

Still no one spoke. The fire popped, and Clarissa dropped the bag. Its plastic rustle sounded incredibly loud in the following silence.

Faith broke the silence first. "Do I get to know what's going on, or should I just let my imagination fill in the blanks?"

Clarissa groaned. She turned and looked at him before she spoke. "You know who David is, don't you?"

Faith nodded. "I know."

The silence returned.

"And Clarissa says you know about her visions," he said.

Again, she nodded. "Yeah. Including the one about you getting shot. That's not a bullet wound, so what happened?"

Her gaze was direct, and David sighed, feeling the tendrils of exhaustion reach out for him. He didn't have the time or the inclination for all this. He didn't owe her anything; he didn't owe anyone explanations. He'd stopped doing that years ago. Clarissa, on the other hand... He looked over at her again and his heart twisted.

"Before you say anything, you should know Faith is a reporter." Clarissa's words sounded rushed, and she rolled up the bag slowly, carefully, as if to stretch out time. She moved over to stand by the fire. "But I trust her."

He looked hard at Faith who returned his stare. "Should I? The press doesn't exactly trust me."

"I don't necessarily agree or disagree with my colleagues. Clarissa is my friend."

He noted that she didn't extend that friendship to him. He knew he had to explain something, but he had to be careful.

"On the record, or off?"

"Off," she assured him. "This is personal. I know what the press did to Clarissa."

"You do?" Clarissa turned suddenly, clearly surprised.

"The whole country heard about those little boys. I know what it must have been like. I read the wire stories of your trial. I work with those sharks, remember?"

Clarissa turned away, and David fought the urge to go to her. She'd been through too much. Damn but he couldn't lie to her and say he'd protect her, but...he wanted to. Even if he didn't say the words, his actions would imply it. He knew he couldn't protect her when what he needed to protect her from the most was himself.

"I didn't think anyone out here knew about that," Clarissa whispered.

"Not many people do anymore," Faith said, her eyes meeting David's as if to ask him for help.

"No, they've been too busy worrying about my family's dirty laundry." He pointed the finger at himself to take some of the pressure off her.

"Unfortunately, he's right." Faith stood and walked over to her friend. "Look, I don't need to know anything. I just want to know you're safe." Her gaze returned to David, warning him. "And you'll stay that way."

"I'll be fine here." Clarissa smiled and hugged her friend. "It's late. Thank you for your help. I promise I'll keep in touch."

"I'll hold you to that. If you don't, I'll...I'll write something scandalous and sell it to the tabloids." Even to his unfamiliar ears the threat sounded like a friendly tease.

"You can't write fiction," Clarissa teased back and led Faith to the door. "Go home and get some sleep. I'm sure Cord's wondering where you are. I'll call you. Soon. I promise."

Faith hesitated, as if deciding if she really should leave. "Yeah, I'm sure he's sound asleep, but you have a point." Faith grabbed her purse and then hastily left.

David admired their friendship. It was comfortable and easy, something he'd never had with anyone. Not with his family. Never with a friend. Certainly not in his marriage.

Keeping her back to him, Clarissa stood in the open doorway until Faith's taillights vanished around the block. "You can trust her. She won't say anything to anyone."

"If you trust her, I do." It was hard for him to say it, but once the words were out, he realized they were true.

She turned to face him then, staring with eyes that looked suspiciously damp. "Thank you."

"For what? Putting you in danger? Bringing you close to insanity? Taking away your life?

She laughed and shook her head. "You really don't know, do you?"

He shook his head. She walked toward him, stopping just inches away from him. "Since my trial, no one has trusted me or my judgment." Her voice shook and she took a deep breath. "You came to me when you were hurt. You let me take care of you. Now you believe me about Faith. Thank you."

She'd sucker-punched him. He stared at her, shocked by the power she had over him. The intensity of what he felt for her surprised him. He'd shut his emotions off for so long, and now they all rushed forward, swamping him. He couldn't sort them out. All he knew was the taste of her lips as she leaned close and kissed him.

He pulled her into his arms, barely noticing how carefully she touched him. The pain faded, and he held her tight, never wanting to let her go.

And knowing he had to.

But not quite yet.

Thirteen

It was just after nine thirty a.m. when Clarissa opened her eyes. Sunlight fell across the room, giving her a view of the big-faced alarm clock beside the bed. She hadn't noticed it last night, but then looking around the house hadn't been a top priority since she'd gotten here.

She stretched and snuggled back under the covers. It felt good to be lazy. A vaguely familiar clicking sound broke the quiet, and she opened her eyes again.

David sat on the couch, his back bare except for the bandages she'd applied last night. Broad shoulders tapered down to a narrow waist—a waist she distinctly remembered circling with her legs last night.

Heat shot through her body, and she felt her cheeks warm. She turned her face into the pillow. What had he done to her? She smiled at the images that flashed through her mind. Maybe a better question was, what hadn't he done?

This time her whole body blushed.

The clicking continued, bringing reality back. He must have a laptop with him. She wondered briefly what he was doing, and then decided she didn't care right now. She nearly laughed out loud at the carefree person she'd become overnight.

The scent of coffee wafted in the air, teasing and taunting her. She knew she drank too much of it, but she loved it. Besides there were worse vices. She thought she could probably become just as addicted to David's lovemaking. She swallowed the laugh and buried her face in the covers. She'd never felt so alive.

"Hey, sleepyhead." David's soft, warm voice reached out.

She peeked out from under the covers. Her heart skipped a beat or two at the sight of him standing at the end of the bed, leaning on the tall brass footboard. "Hi yourself."

"How are you feeling?"

"Fine. How about you?" She struggled to sit up, fighting a growing sense of unease. What would he think about her, about her wantonness last night, in the light of day? "How's your back?"

"No problems." He failed to hide a smile behind his coffee cup as he took a sip. "I'll recover. You and Faith did a great job. Thanks."

"You're welcome." She sniffed in a not so subtle hint. "Do I smell coffee?"

"Yeah. I'll get you some." The soft sound of his chuckle remained in the room after he'd disappeared into the kitchen. While he was gone, she grabbed his discarded T-shirt from the end of the bed and slipped it on. The neckline gaped and it nearly engulfed her, but at least she was covered.

David came back with a steaming cup in each hand. "I went over to Dove's Place before you woke up," he explained as he handed her the cup.

She sipped it tentatively, expecting the bitter brew she'd had there before, but realized that the person who had made it knew what they were doing. She sighed in contentment after the first swallow and looked up. David was watching her, his eyes dark with desire. A responding warmth settled deep in her chest—and other places, too. Perhaps iced coffee would have been a better choice.

"What are you working on?" She tilted her head toward the computer, hoping, reluctantly, to break the spell he'd cast over her.

After a brief hesitation, David went back to the couch. "Same old thing." He turned to face her again. "That first day in my office, you said I'd never find the embezzler. What did you mean by that?"

She thought a minute, taking several sips of her coffee as she tried to figure it out. Where had it come from? It seemed so long ago, and the thoughts were so vague compared to the visions. "I'm not sure." When he frowned in response, she said, "The thought just popped into my head complete, almost as if someone had put it there."

"Damn." He snapped the computer screen down. "Rachel."

"What does she have to do with that?"

David leaned back and drank before speaking. "All the missing money is coming out of her accounts."

"That's strange. Why don't you just close her accounts? You can do that, can't you?"

"I can, but—" He paused. "I hate the idea of anyone getting away with it."

His words said a lot about him. Clarissa filed away that knowledge, mentally applauding his sense of justice.

Realizing his feelings for Rachel must have been strong,

Clarissa swallowed back a sudden pang of jealousy. No one had ever loved her enough to care about her after she died. She wanted to know more about a woman who could attract him so strongly. "Maybe you should tell me about Rachel," she said softly, moving to sit on the couch and faced him.

"What do you mean?"

"How did you meet her?"

He paused as if letting the memories sift in slowly. "In college. My aunt and uncle took an automatic dislike to her, just because of where she came from." He looked around at the small house they were sitting in. "They thought she was a gold digger."

He fell silent and she waited for him to continue. When he didn't, she asked softly, "And was she?"

"Yes and no. She didn't want money. I guess you could say she was an emotional gold digger."

"I don't understand."

"Rachel was beautiful." His voice softened. "Growing up she was the perfect child, beautiful and adored. In the outside world, anyway. At home, her mother was distant and her father..." David paused again. "I think he'd be considered abusive by today's standards. He was a harsh, demanding man. I think Rachel wanted to bring that outside adoration into her home life. She thought she'd found it in me."

The sunlight seemed to dim just a little as his voice softened.

"You loved her," she said, not really needing to.

"I guess in a way, yes. I look back now—" He set his empty cup on the table beside the computer. "We were too young, both looking to fill empty places in our lives with each other. Toward the end we both knew it wasn't working. She changed. I probably did, too."

"How?"

He thought for a moment before answering. "The cancer scared her. Scared us both. She flew into jealous rages, accused me of wanting her dead." Sadness filled his face, and Clarissa felt her throat tighten in response to his pain.

"I didn't want her to die, though at that point I did wish she was out of my life."

"Did she know that?"

"I think so." His eyes grew distant and troubled. "We kept up appearances, but the passion was gone long before she died."

He looked at Clarissa then, and the fire in his eyes sent familiar heat through her body. "She never looked as good in my shirt as you do right now."

Clarissa blushed and felt the warmth stain her cheeks. She looked away from him and sipped her now cold coffee.

David reached out and took her cup, setting it on the table beside his. He scooted closer to her. "It's incredible to *feel* again," he said in a soft, rough voice. "For so long I've kept my emotions in check."

"So you are safe here? No shifting?"

"No shifting. Only if I step over the line." He leaned close. "Is this over the line?"

She thought he was going to kiss her, but instead he ran the tip of his tongue over her lips in a slow, sensual tease. "Mmm...I love the taste of coffee on you," he whispered. Then he did kiss her and she returned it, joining him in tasting the passion growing between them.

The computer beeped, its insistence worse than an alarm clock at dawn. He pulled back reluctantly. "Hopefully that's the file I've been waiting for."

"Mmm." Words? What good were words right now? He opened the computer and she snuggled against him, her head resting on his uninjured shoulder.

"Is that about the embezzlement?"

"I hope so." He tapped in the commands, and a long file in tiny print leapt to the screen. He read as he scrolled down. "Damn. Nothing."

"Wait. What's that?"

"What?"

Clarissa reached out and turned the tiny screen more clearly toward her. "There. That paragraph." She pointed at the screen.

He leaned closer. "I don't see what you're talking about."

"That's my name."

"Where?"

"There." She pointed at the screen

He read the paragraph aloud. "It's nothing but a bunch of statistics. It's all numbers." He didn't mention her name.

Except she saw her name as it blinked wildly within the text. "My name is there. I can see it." She couldn't tear her gaze from the screen, almost mesmerized by the rhythm.

David cursed and hit the keys so hard she thought they might break. He yanked the phone cord out of the machine and then stood to pull it out of the wall.

"She knows we're here," Clarissa said, realizing what she'd seen hadn't been real.

"She's known." The defeat was strong in his voice. "Now she's trying to find a way to get here. She's manipulating the other end." He wound the cord up as he spoke and threw the coil into the computer case.

Despite her own unsettled feelings, she watched him, observing the changes. While his anger made him clench his jaw, curl his hands into fists and pace, there was no sign he was on the verge of shifting. She breathed more easily, realizing she'd been holding her breath.

"This past year has been hell," he growled.

Clarissa frowned. There was some piece of the answer in his words. She knew it, but which piece? "A year? Why this year? What's different than before?"

He shrugged and slumped back to the couch. "I'm not sure exactly. The first time I shifted was right after I'd started dating again, right after the first anniversary of Rachel's death. Scared the hell out of me."

"What did you become?"

"A snake." He shivered and laughed. "I hate those things. I felt so guilty and low for dating again. After that, I've been all kinds of things. It's like someone cast a spell on me or something."

A spell? Dread crept over Clarissa. Her mind spun with sudden memories and a longing for comforting answers. She looked at David. An image of her own past came to mind.

If it was a spell, she might actually have the means to break it. Reluctant to tell him what she thought, she hesitated too long. He looked at her, a curious frown on his brow. Fear reared its head. What would he think of her now? She squashed those old feelings. "Remember those legends of the witches I told you about?"

"Yeah?"

"They're not totally false." It was her turn to get up and pace. "Granny told me her mother and the women before her in our family practiced magic. She said she knew some as well."

"I thought she was dead. That's helpful how?"

She bit her lip, trying to decide how best to tell him. Better to plunge ahead without thinking. "If a spell's been cast, we have to break it."

He looked at her with skeptical eyes, but at least he was listening. "And how do we do that?"

The silence was heavy. Too heavy. "I have Granny's old book." Old book. She almost laughed at the simple description. She saw the grimoire in her mind's eye. There was a reason she'd put it where she had. To keep it safe and herself from the temptation. The irony almost made her laugh aloud.

"Then let's get it. Where is it?" He was on his feet and headed to the door when she grabbed his arm.

"You can't go."

"Why not?" She resisted the urge to roll her eyes. "The shifting, for one." She recalled some of what she'd read in the book long ago. Old stories that had been visions came back too clearly. "It may be a progressive spell. It's possible you might stop changing back to human form at some point." She watched the color drain from his face.

"You can't go either. She'll get you with the visions," he countered. "Can Faith bring it?"

"No." Clarissa wrung her hands. This was *not* a good development. "Not unless the staff at your bank can let her into my safe deposit box."

He stared at her as if he wanted to spit out a litany of curses. He settled for a fiercely whispered, "Hell." He clenched his teeth, fighting to stay calm. "Where's your key?"

"In my purse, on my key ring. Where else?" She dropped back down to the couch. Hysterical laughter bubbled in her throat. They couldn't leave. Not without putting themselves at risk. She'd only felt this trapped one other time in her life. The day they'd shut her in a jail cell.

* * * *

David saw the distress in her eyes and slumped onto the couch beside her. Together they stared at the ash-filled fireplace. Even if Faith were willing and had the key, the bank wouldn't let her into the safe deposit box unless her signature matched Clarissa's—which it didn't. He scrubbed his hand over his face. He couldn't believe he was considering trying to hoodwink his own bank. "This is nuts."

She laughed, telling him he must have spoken aloud. "I have to go to the bank, you know," she said.

"You can't."

"What other choice do we have? Can you get it?"

"No." The vault key stayed at the bank and it took two keys to open the box. He could get the bank's and he'd have Clarissa's key. Except the damned security system he'd insisted on being installed would record his every move in the vault—on tape for everyone to see. They'd wonder why he was alone opening a box that wasn't his. Unless he had a court order to drill the damned lock, there was no other choice.

Damn it.

She was right. What other choice did they have? None that he could see. She was the only one who could go get the book. He watched her stand, helpless to think of any other way. He stood too, following her to her purse. The jangle of her keys was too loud in the quiet room. He reached into his pocket and handed her his car keys. Before he let go, he said, "Don't believe anything she shows you."

"I know."

She looked up at him for a long silent moment. She shook her head and stood on tiptoe to kiss him.

"Not enough." He folded her into a tight embrace.

* * * *

Clarissa stopped at the edge of Dove's Hollow. The faded city limit sign sat inches in front of the car's bumper. Her hands sweated against the warm steering wheel and her heart pounded in her chest. With a deep breath, she pushed the accelerator to the floor, feeling as if she could outrun the visions. When no odd images appeared, she let out her breath and laughed nervously.

She drove back the route they'd taken the day before. Only hours had passed since she was at the bank, yet it felt like years. As she walked in through the wide glass doors, a different security guard nodded and smiled at her from his perch. Sweat reappeared in her palms. What was she nervous about? It was her stuff in her deposit box. Another deep breath helped.

She stood in line, impatiently waiting her turn. Was everything moving in slow motion or was it just her impatience? She tapped her foot and fought the urge to pace.

Finally, the clerk smiled at her. They'd just stepped inside the vault room when loud heels clicked on the tile floor.

"I thought that was you."

At first Clarissa didn't recognize the voice. David's secretary stepped further into the small room. "Oh...hello?"

"I'll take care of everything." Melanie smiled at the teller, who nodded and handed the key ring to Melanie.

"I'll only be a minute." Clarissa sensed something wasn't right here, but couldn't quite tell what it was. Why would a secretary help her with the safe deposit box? The teller hesitated in the doorway, as if she felt something was amiss also.

"Of course." Melanie's expression was too bright, but she opened the lock without another word. After she stepped back, Clarissa took out her key. She noticed Melanie didn't leave, as was the usual procedure. She turned and frowned at the woman.

Melanie didn't take the silent hint. She actually stepped closer. "Do you know where Mr. Lorde is?" she finally blurted out.

Clarissa stared at her. She wasn't sure what to say. David had been on the computer this morning, and he'd been in contact with the bank.

"It's just not like him." The woman paced and wrung her hands. "He never misses work. Never. He has been acting strange lately." Melanie seemed to be talking as much to herself as Clarissa.

When the woman paced away, Clarissa quickly pulled the box open and felt the familiar cover of the book. The timeworn indentations fit in the palm of her hand. She curled her fingers around it and hastily pulled it out. She shoved it into her bag just as Melanie turned back around.

She wasn't sure why she didn't want Melanie to see the book, but she knew it wasn't a good idea. She pulled out the other papers she kept there and pretended to read them.

"I'm sure something's happened to him," Melanie said. "He's been acting even stranger since you came in that day."

"I'm sure he's fine." Clarissa wanted to reassure the woman, but if David had wanted her to know where he was, he'd have told her.

"If you hear from him..."

"If I see him, I'll let him know you're worried."

Melanie's features relaxed a little. "Thank you." Impulsively, she reached out and gave Clarissa a hug.

The warm human contact felt wonderful. For an instant, Clarissa was tempted to confide in Melanie, who obviously cared about David.

Pulling away from the embrace, she bid the woman farewell and hurried to the car.

Climbing in, she headed back to the house. She only stopped long enough to pick up a few groceries and fill up with gas. The closer she got to Dove's Hollow, the more she let herself relax. As she drove the now familiar route, she let herself believe that maybe—just maybe—this nightmare would be over soon.

And then what? Would she and David go their separate ways? Would he return to the stuffy old bank, and she to her struggling coffee shop? Or was this the beginning of something new and wonderful—and for her, frightening?

All of a sudden the radio blared. She reached over to turn it off. At first she couldn't find the button, and when she did twist it, nothing happened. The music continued.

She looked up from the dial and saw a tree appear from out of nowhere. She slammed on the brakes. The car skidded, the back end swerving on a paved road that had turned to gravel. She didn't remember turning off the highway.

She knew this road. This wasn't in Boulder. The thick overhead branches. The tall roadside grasses. Around the next bend she'd find her grandmother's house. A house that still stood in Massachusetts.

The car came to a halt at the edge of the road, a cloud of dust rising up into the air, clogging her throat.

She realized it was a vision. She watched the sun sink low in the sky, setting the treetops on fire with its fading light. Where the sounds of nature normally soothed her, the high pitched music continued. It grew louder with each second. She slammed her hands over her ears to shut it out, but it didn't work.

Finally, the music started to fade, growing softer and more tolerable. It reached a point where she could stand it—and recognize it for what it was.

A music box. A soft, sweet sound. As the music faded, the sunlight brightened and the dense trees vanished. The open highway reappeared, and instead of being parked on the shoulder of the road, she realized she was stopped in the middle of the left lane of traffic.

Car horns blared around her. She tried to shift the car into drive, but it stalled. The deep throaty roar of a truck's horn broke the quiet. She looked in the rearview mirror just in time to see a semi barreling toward her.

Fourteen

The car finally responded. Clarissa rammed the gas pedal to the floor and jerked the wheel to the left. Thank heavens for the wide grassy median.

The truck's passing blast of air shook the entire car as she slammed on the brakes again. An ear-shattering crash made her scream. A large black rock that the truck's tires had spun up from the road hit the safety glass and spiderwebbed the windshield.

For several long seconds the car rocked back and forth, with almost the same rhythm as her heart pounding in her chest.

She took several deep breaths. Resting her forehead against the steering wheel, she clung to the wheel with a knuckle-whitening grip.

Traffic passed, but she ignored it, hoping and praying no more rocks would fly up. She wasn't able to make her body move yet.

She thought over the vision that had nearly gotten her killed. All of her visions were different, but this one had been unusual. Was she missing Granny so much she'd hallucinated her house? Or was there a clue there?

Then she remembered the music. Granny had never owned a music box. It wasn't something Clarissa could even imagine the old woman being interested in. So why had she heard one?

She grabbed her cell phone, and after three tries with her trembling fingers, she punched in David's number. She waited while the phone rang...and rang.

* * * *

Fresh from the shower, wearing nothing but a towel, David stared at his reflection in the old bathroom mirror. He stared, memorizing his own features and praying they wouldn't be lost forever. He examined the edge of his jaw that was so often obliterated by fur or feather. The straight line of his shoulders that frequently bowed and curled...

His cell phone rang and he nearly didn't answer it. Was this how a dying person felt when they reached that final moment? Hungry to see and experience everything they could? Grasping at straws? Avoiding the things they didn't want? He reached for the phone and left his thoughts behind.

"Hello," he said.

"Do you recall another music box?" Between Clarissa's lack of pleasantries and the breathlessness in her voice, he knew something was wrong. It also did strange things to his nerves. Nerves that clearly remembered making love to her.

"Where are you?" He didn't like the sound of her panic or the roar in the background.

"On the highway. I'll explain later. The music box. It's important."

She was one of the things in life he wanted to experience more of, and her fear echoing over the line hinted that he might not get the chance. "I don't have a clue."

"It's important." Her voice rose, almost in hysteria. "A music box?"

"You saw the one in the living room."

"No. No. Not that one. Another one. A small one. I didn't see it clearly enough in the vision, but I heard it."

Where was she? And what was she doing? Standing in the middle of the highway? He straightened as her words registered over the roar. The towel slipped, and he hitched it up to a more comfortable place. "You had another vision?"

"Yes. Just now. It was foggier than usual, but I'm sure it's a vision."

"What happened?"

The silence on the line told him she didn't want to tell him. "I was at my grandmother's house for just a moment. I heard a music box clearly in the background."

"Heard? Did you see it?"

"No." Her desperation came through the phone line. "But I heard it. That's all."

"Are you sure it wasn't Mother's music box?"

"Yes!" She snapped out the word. "It was a tiny sound. Faint and small. Like one I remember from when I was a little girl."

"Maybe it was yours. The vision might not be connected to me."

"No. I'm sure this is a sign. We've got to find that music box."

"Why?"

"It's somehow the key to all this. I know it."

He wanted to ask her how she knew it, but he stopped himself. "Rachel might have had one." Before she could ask anything more, he turned away from the mirror and ordered,

"Get back here."

"Why? What do you have in mind?"

"Nothing specific. Just get back here where you're safe." He cleared his throat, trying to banish the emotions that swamped him. He didn't think he was going to shift. But the ache to hold her and assure himself she was safe suddenly seemed too overwhelming. He might not be psychic like her, but he knew she was in danger where she was now.

"David?" Her voice echoed in the small room.

"I'm fine. But hurry."

* * * *

Clarissa shoved open the door of the old house. The hinge's soft squeal seemed too loud.

"David?" She let the door close. The silence engulfed her. She set her purse and the bag of groceries on the small table by the couch. Where was he? She'd tried calling his cell twice more on the way back but he hadn't answered.

"Hello?" Still no answer. She shivered and, picking up the groceries, headed to the kitchen. Maybe he was there. But he wasn't. No note. Nothing.

Where was he? Maybe he'd gone over to the diner. She relaxed a little at the thought and looked around the small, cramped kitchen. Except for a couple pots and pans and some odd dishes that filled one shelf, the cupboards were empty.

A wide wooden door on the other side of the table caught her eye. Painted the same color as the wall, she hadn't noticed it right away. It was open a fraction of an inch.

Where did that go? Outside? Into another room? David must be in there. What had he said just before hanging up? Rachel must have had a music box. She'd grown up here. Would it be in there?

She moved around the table and felt a cold draft slipping under the door. She shivered as she reached for the handle.

Blackness greeted her when she opened it. Thick, inky blackness. The light from the kitchen fell only a few feet inside, illuminating a couple of wooden steps and a rough stone wall on either side of the stairs.

The air smelled of stale, dry dirt. Where the rail was supposed to be, a two-by-four had been bolted at an odd slant along the wall. She leaned forward trying to see. Only darkness. Where did the stairs lead? How far down did they go? What was at the bottom?

"David?" He didn't respond, and she realized she hadn't really expected him to.

Curiosity nagged at the back of her brain even as common sense told her it was unsafe and unwise to go looking in dark, unknown places. Common sense won, and she stepped back into the kitchen and closed the door. She had enough to deal with without wasting time searching an old basement. She needed to find David.

She realized she wasn't used to worrying about anyone but herself. It was an odd feeling—one that, she reluctantly admitted, felt good. Well, having someone to worry about felt good. She could do without the worry.

She pulled her cell phone out and dialed David's number again and heard the distant chime of a phone. He'd left it here. She found it in the living room on the table next to his computer.

At least she knew he hadn't gone to the bank. His computer and briefcase were still here. Along with several dishes from the night before. She gathered them up and took them back into the kitchen. Anything to distract her from her worry.

Immediately, her attention turned to the door.

What *was* down there? Surely, David knew. It was his wife's house, wasn't it? Even before Rachel's death he'd visited here. She'd ask him when he got back.

"This is nuts," she said out loud, as much to reassure herself as break the ridiculous spell the door and stairway had cast over her.

There's probably nothing down there except old dust, furniture and maybe a few stray spiders. Junk stored away...

What if the music box is down there? Grabbing the flashlight, she pulled open the door again. This time she took a step. It wasn't bad with the pool of light and the daylight coming in from the kitchen.

She stepped down, her gaze following the curve of the wall once, then twice, and again where the beam of light shone. She leaned her hand on the makeshift railing, hoping the creak of the first step only meant it was old, not rotten. The air grew icier as she descended.

She moved slowly, cautiously, down the stairs until her foot met the hard-packed dirt. Taking a few steps, she let her eyes adjust to the dimness. Across the room, she saw a single milky beam of light that crept in through a far window and fell on the unfinished floor.

She saw vague shapes and forms. Boxes probably, stacked against the far wall. She headed toward them.

Something brushed her face. She screamed and pulled back. The feathery cotton of a spider's web dangled before her. She choked back another scream, shuddering. She hated bugs.

She almost turned around and went back upstairs. Determined, she headed toward the stack on the far wall.

Several chairs lay in pieces to the right. A broken headboard sat next to a cracked mirror. She looked at her distorted reflection through the numerous fissures, then quickly looked away from the broken image.

Three boxes were stacked precariously. The top one was full of filthy children's clothing. The next held a set of old dishes. She'd keep those in mind in case they ended up here for awhile. Then she reached the third box. One side had caved in from the weight of the dish box on top of it.

It didn't matter. The old photos lying on top were intact, even though some were wrinkled and bent. She looked around for a place to sit. She pulled the box over to the stairs and sat on the bottom step.

She propped the flashlight on a higher step and let its beam reflect off the wood. Whispers of memories barely broke through her thoughts as she opened the box. The forgotten past made her eyes mist with tears.

Dust coated the top few photos. She gently, reverently, picked up the first one and held it up in the dim light. She nearly dropped it when she saw who was in it. David's parents. The resemblance was strong, and she recognized them from the visions and the painting in the mansion. They stood together, their hands clasped. The smiles they directed at each other showed love, desire, and deep warm passion.

David Senior had most definitely been in love with his wife, and she had at one time been devoted to him.

So what had happened that made him pick up a gun and end her life? Why had these two people left their son to deal with a lonely world?

She picked up the next photo. A small child stared up at her. A familiar child. So innocent and trusting. Too familiar.

Clarissa's hand trembled and she dropped picture. It wafted down to mingle with the others.

"Oh, my God!"

She jumped to her feet. The box tipped over, scattering pictures and dust across the dirt floor. She didn't care.

Her stomach knotted in fear and confusion. No answers came to her from the silent pictures. Just smile after smile and beautiful scene after beautiful scene. Those eyes. That boy's face. She'd seen it before, too many times. Shaking her head, she tried to cleanse her mind of the painful visions from her own past. She'd been looking for the wrong boy.

A cool breeze slipped over her and she shivered. She spun around, looking up at the square of light in the open doorway above her. It seemed so very far away.

The light at the top of the stairs vanished. "Who's there?"

* * * *

Brain cells slammed into each other, shifting and morphing. David cringed and then cried out as the pain increased and his body changed. He'd stepped over the property line.

He found it difficult to even think. All he saw was a blinding haze of color—first red, then blue, and finally a soft gold.

He looked around, the world at a lower height than his normal six feet two inches. Each time it was like this. Those lost minutes of thought, those moments of adjusting to discover what he'd become.

Glancing down, he saw four light brown toes edged in thick black, curled claws. Heavily muscled legs, four of them, came into sight as he turned a heavy head to look around. His hair was thick and his beard itched around his face.

Fear snapped through him. Clarissa had dreamed about a lion that attacked her. Was her dream—and his worst nightmare—finally coming true?

Fighting the instincts that came with each shift, he forced himself to keep walking, forced his new body to move.

Finally, the mansion loomed ahead. It was silent as he entered through the already open front door. There were a few lights that hadn't burned out. The daylight muted their brilliance, but his mind's eye still saw them as they'd appeared in the rearview mirror when he and Clarissa had sped down the driveway.

His feet clicked on the tile floor, and he felt their echo in the air all around him. He had to find the music box. If there was any chance the spell could be broken, he'd take it.

Even as he thought it, he shivered. Then he dismissed his

own hopes as masked fears. He'd have to try, but he doubted he'd accomplish much else.

He looked around. A frightening déjà vu settled over him. He'd once seen the world from this height. When he'd been five. When he'd watched his parents die.

His grief returned and pain engulfed him. He fell to his knees, and a loud, excruciating roar burst from him.

Before the agony consumed him, it was over. He stared down at the tile floor, seeing not claws, but his own human hands, his own arms supporting him as he knelt on the floor.

"So, where do we go from here?" He didn't expect an answer and sat down, staring at the beautiful carved staircase.

He nearly jumped out of his skin when he raised his head and looked directly into the ethereal eyes of his dead wife. A cry of shock escaped him.

"It's okay," Rachel's voice soothed him, though her lips didn't move. The words simply appeared whole in his mind.

David gulped, forcing himself to let go of his fear and face Rachel's ghost head on. "Rachel?"

"Yes, it's me." The image hovered a few feet above the floor and he couldn't help staring. She wore a gossamer gown of white nearly too bright to look at. He wanted to shield his eyes but didn't. Her beauty was too entrancing to look away.

He'd loved her once. So long ago.

Somewhere near where her image hovered, he heard the faint sound of a music box. And then he remembered. He had heard that song so many times. His father had also brought the small music box back from Germany years earlier. His mother had dearly loved it and played it often. After her death, it had been put it away. He hadn't seen it since. Hadn't ever wanted to.

It wasn't Rachel's music box.

The forgotten memories returned full force, tumbling over themselves to fill his mind. The strains of the music brought back memories—poignant, painful memories of his parents.

"Stop it," he screamed.

He covered his ears with his hands, wanting to shut out the sound, but realized it echoed inside his head, not in the room.

How had Rachel found that box? *When* had she found it? Anger, strong and painful, filled him. He'd experienced so much of that emotion in his life—after his parents' deaths, right after

Rachel's death. Anger at himself, at the world, at everything. He'd spent an entire year traveling the world, trying to find a cure for Rachel only to return home with nothing.

Not even his wife.

He'd hidden his anger deep inside. Anger at her for leaving him. Anger at the fates or God or whoever was responsible for being so cruel. Anger at the unfairness.

His anger had dimmed, but as he looked at this unreal image hovering before his eyes, he realized Rachel had been angry, too. And her anger was alive.

Her unspoken threat vibrated on the air. He realized that threat went well beyond himself. Clarissa, and anyone in his life, was at risk as well.

"What's going on?" Could a ghost be reasoned with? He didn't have any choice, he had to do something.

"What do you mean?" She still played the innocent.

"Aren't you supposed to have crossed to the other side or something?"

"I don't know." Her eyes stared in confusion at him. *"I can't leave you. You need me."*

Was that why she was still here? Because of some misguided eternal bond? Was she trying to take care of him? If so, how? And why? In life she'd never been overly interested in nurturing him or his life.

"Damn it, Rachel. This doesn't make sense." David surged to his feet. "Let go and leave."

The image moved closer without appearing to even move. Suddenly, David felt coolness glide along his arm. He shivered and took a step back.

"Dance with me," she whispered.

Her translucent arms lifted and her hands gently caressed his arms. He shivered at the cold that seeped through his skin and settled deep in his bones.

He wanted to move away, wanted to turn and run screaming from the house. The image of doing so flitted through his mind, but he found himself rooted in place.

As her unearthly hands moved over him, he let his mind drift back to the warm arms that had held him last night. To Clarissa's hot response to his touch.

Sudden blinding pain shot through his head, and he stumbled away from Rachel's cold touch. He backed into the newel post and sidestepped to keep from falling.

"No!" Her voice echoed through his mind. The crystals in the chandelier tinkled and the entire fixture shook. *"No!"* she cried again.

Her eyes, or what he believed were her eyes, filled with red and a single crimson tear slid down her cheek. The tear burned as it fell, leaving a black sooty trail in its wake.

"You're mine. Yet you think of another when you're with me?"

"You can read minds?" He was almost as astounded as he was frightened.

She laughed, the wicked sound notching his fear deeper. *"You don't know the half of it, of the power I have."*

"Power? What kind of power?" He needed answers. He *wanted* answers. Why was she driving him crazy? "Like the dreams you put in my head?"

"Dreams? What dreams?"

"The dreams you've been sending to my mind for the last month."

"I don't know anything about dreams."

He knew she was lying. She'd never been good at it. A gust of hot air blew in from the parlor door, and David felt the heat push against him.

"Dance with me," she repeated. The words were whispered in his ear, and he spun around to find Rachel's frigid, ghostly arms slipping around him. The soft tinkling sound of the music box grew louder and louder until he not only heard it but felt it in his head.

They twirled around the room. He couldn't stop his body, and didn't feel his feet moving, but he saw in the mirror that they spun higher and higher into the air. The music vibrated around and through him. No matter how hard he tried, he couldn't break free.

He saw his own arms lift and encircle her unsubstantial form. He saw the solidness of his forearm through her waist. Was this another dream? For the first time, he hoped so.

The only woman he'd held since Rachel's death had been Clarissa, and her very alive image came to mind. Once again the blinding pain shot through his head, sending sparks behind his eyes that radiated down his entire body.

He felt himself falling. Then he landed with a bone-jarring thump on the floor. The clatter of his boots against the tile seemed unusually loud in the sudden silence.

He looked around. Nothing. No image. No music. No warm air. Nothing. He shivered, and his entire body shook with the impact.

"No."

He heard the soft voice and spun around to see if Rachel's image was behind him. It wasn't, but he was certain she hadn't gone far.

"Let me see you." He stood, turning in circles in case he'd missed her. He ignored the dizziness that nearly knocked him from his feet.

"No." Was that a sob in her voice?

"Rachel. I'm sorry." And he was. For hurting her. For her death. For not being able to love only her.

Love only her? The words echoed in his mind and the realization stunned him. He was falling in love with Clarissa.

The air whooshed out of him, and before he could pull in another breath, a hot wind ripped through the house.

He sped for the open front door, only to have it slam shut. He tried to pull it open, but it was locked and the knob wouldn't turn. He rattled the door hard but it still didn't budge.

"Let me out, Rachel," he demanded, though he had no idea how he could force her to do so.

Silence was the only thing that met his ears. For several long minutes the pressure grew until he felt sure his eardrums would burst.

Then wicked laughter erupted. It grew until it filled every corner of the room and wrapped itself around his senses. It tore at his ears, rubbed hot against his skin, and left a bitter taste in his mouth. Bright, blinding lights flashed inside his head, pulsing to the cadence of the laugh. He couldn't escape and fully expected to feel himself explode any second.

As quickly as it began, the laughter stopped, taking the warmth with it. The air in the foyer grew ice cold. *"Tell her good-bye."* Rachel's eerie voice came from far off, followed by sobs. Why was she crying?

He'd been foolish to come here. To hell with the music box. He had to find Clarissa.

He fumbled with the door, which suddenly opened, and he rushed out into the welcome afternoon sunlight. He breathed, longing to fill his lungs with the sweet summer air and cleanse away the evil he was sure he'd inhaled. Even as his senses warmed, he felt the cold settle around his heart. He felt as if he'd lost something, and knew he'd never get it back again.

Rachel was gone—for now. And while he'd discovered his love for Clarissa, would he ever be allowed to love her? Would he ever be able to tell her his feelings?

The pain tore through him, and for the first time, he didn't fight the change. He needed to escape from himself, from this man tormented by a past he couldn't change, by the hurt he'd caused others, and away from the hurt they'd caused.

Fifteen

Clarissa stumbled up the stairs with loud urgent footsteps. At the top, she shoved at the door. It didn't budge. She turned and rattled the handle. No success.

She slammed her fist against the wood, knowing and not caring that her hand would be bruised and sore later.

"Please," she cried. "Someone help me!"

She turned, looking back down at the shadowed basement. Could she get out the window? It was small and high above her head, but surely there was a way.

She banged on the door one last time, hoping but not expecting any response. David wasn't here. Would he even hear her when he came back? Would he come back? What if something had happened to him?

Her stomach knotted. She refused to let her fears win. She'd taken two steps down when suddenly the door burst open. David stood on the threshold, his shoulders nearly brushing the doorframe as he gulped in air.

"Clarissa." His voice sounded breathless, as if he'd been running.

She ran up the steps. He grabbed her, pulling her into his arms and away from the stairs. She vaguely heard the door slam shut behind her as she stepped into the kitchen.

His grip tightened, and she buried her face against his chest. The thundering of his heart matched her own.

"Oh, God," she whispered, slipping her arms around him, clinging to him. "It's you. It's you." She couldn't stop the litany. Her fingers curled in the fabric of his shirt. His arms tightened even more, and he buried his face in her hair, breathing deeply.

"I can't..." she said, her words muffled by his chest.

"You're okay," he whispered. He smoothed his hands up and down her back, and she realized they trembled.

"Where were you?" Her voice sounded faint and pleading.

He didn't answer her. Instead, he pulled away slightly and before she could ask where he'd been, his lips were on hers. Urgent and demanding, he molded his body to hers. Filling all the empty spaces with heat.

She leaned into him. He felt so good. So alive. So real. She knew her emotions were out of control. The panic and fear fed the adrenaline that raced through her veins. She didn't care why she felt this way. All she knew was it was right and wonderful and safe to be in his arms again.

The urgency of his touch told her something had happened to him while he was gone. She promised herself she'd question him later, but then all rational thought fled as he slid his hands up her sides and under her loose sweater.

His callused fingers trailed over her ribs and encountered the edge of her bra. He didn't hesitate to reach behind her and twist the clasp free.

Anxious to be free of her clothing, to have no barriers between them, she leaned back to give him easier access and inadvertently pushed her hips against his.

He groaned, the sound coming from deep in his throat. He swept the sweater and bra over her head and filled his hands with her.

His mouth brushed hers as he cupped her breasts. "I want to live inside you," he whispered before he kissed her. His tongue swept inside, tasting and teasing until she moaned in answering pleasure.

Jumbled thoughts ran through her. All she was able to focus on was the heat of his lips, the insistence of his hands as they roamed over her, and the joy that exploded within her.

Momentary doubts tugged at her, but they were banished as his fingers played over her body. She could only breathe and enjoy. There was no more thinking.

The room warmed. David's head dipped and the damp heat of his tongue slipped across her skin.

"You're okay," he repeated.

Clarissa buried her fingers in the hair that hung low on his neck. The thick, silky strands teased her and she never wanted to let go. She urged him closer.

Suddenly, David lifted his head and slipped his arms beneath her knees. He scooped her up and walked to the living room and the wide, brass bed. As he gently laid her across the rumpled covers, the springs groaned softly.

She reclined against the pillows, enjoying the wanton feel of the air on her bare skin and the heat that flared in his eyes. Gently, hesitantly, David caressed her. He still wore his clothes, but as he knelt on the bed beside her, she reached up to unbutton his shirt.

As the fabric fell open, it shadowed his chest. She wanted to see him, all of him, and shoved his shirt off his shoulders. It whispered down on top of the covers.

His fingertips skittered across her bare skin. From her collar bone, down over the enticing slope of her breast, across the sensitive skin of her abdomen. When he reached the clasp of her jeans, he slipped his fingers underneath the band. He teased the tender skin below her navel until she longed to rip the rest of her own clothes off.

He unsnapped her jeans and slid the zipper down slowly. When her panties whispered past his hands, he stopped as if surprised.

Slowly, teasingly, he rubbed the soft silk, sending shivers throughout her entire body. When he gently cupped her, laying the heated palm of his hand against her, she moaned aloud. This kind of pleasure was more than anyone deserved, more than she dared to take. She wanted more.

A dull ache settled in the pit of her stomach and radiated outward. She wanted him there, to ease the ache.

He moved away for an instant, just long enough and far enough that she could slide his pants down over his hips and legs.

The soft swish of his jeans as they landed on the floor sent the ache within her into high gear. She wasn't sure how much longer she could bear this exquisite torture.

Bare skin to heated skin, David moved against her. The hair of his chest and legs rubbed against her, setting her aflame. She gripped his hips and guided him to where the ache was most intense.

"Now, David. Please. Now."

Without further invitation, David thrust into her, filling her and nearly sending her over the edge with that single act. For several long seconds, he lay still, letting her grow still.

"I want this to last," he whispered, his lips traveling gently, pressing against the heated skin of her brow. Oh so slowly, his lips moved over her eyes, down across her cheekbones until his tongue traced a tantalizing path over her lips. He traced a path down where he tasted the pulse that beat at the base of her throat.

Slowly, he moved within her. The heat and size of him astounded her and she responded by lifting closer, but she couldn't get close enough.

Her arms slid up around the tight muscles of his back, and she traced the taut ridges. She wanted to possess him—with her mouth, with her hands, inside herself.

He tasted of heat and sweet damp. As she kissed his face, her hands roamed his shoulders, back and thighs. She urged him on, and he responded with a ferocity she hadn't expected but which sent her spiraling toward oblivion.

"David!" she cried, her voice echoing around them, wrapping them in a cloud of passion that cushioned them as they fell over the edge and tumbled into sweet ecstasy. When the heat faded, they clung together, the harmony of their breathing soothing and reassuring.

David rose up on his elbows and gazed down at her. She wondered what he was thinking. There was pain behind the passion in his eyes. What was he worried about? Before she could ask, his lips came down on hers, nearly carrying them away again.

She felt his response and was just as surprised at her own. When he ended the kiss and shifted to hold her in his arms, she accepted her disappointment.

The night slipped in around them, and Clarissa found her eyelids growing heavy. Dim lights scattered over them, and she turned her head to gaze at his silhouette.

"Are you going to tell me where you were?" she whispered drowsily.

"Shh, later." He pulled her tighter. "Get some rest."

"I love you," she whispered and snuggled up against him. The words felt so right. Her eyes drifted closed, and she let sleep claim her. She released the smile that had been born in her heart so that it could settle onto her lips and proclaim itself to the world.

* * * *

David slept for awhile, but even his dreams couldn't compete with the turmoil in his mind. Clarissa still slept and he slipped out of bed careful not to wake her. He quickly pulled on his jeans and padded to the door. He needed air.

Quietly, he stepped out onto the veranda. He breathed deeply of the cool mountain air and stared out at the view of the city lights.

Night surrounded him, cool and crisp. Inside, Clarissa slumbered between the warm covers. He closed his eyes and envisioned her as he'd left her, the golden tangle of her hair covering the pillow, the quilts pulled up to cover the beauty beneath. He smiled as his body warmed with the memories.

She'd taught him to feel again, and he'd let himself fall into the trap so easily. Here in the abandoned town he was safe from the curse.

But he'd also been protecting himself. In the dim moonlight, he stared down at his hands. His narrow fingers looked so normal, but he knew that could so easily change. This afternoon he'd nearly lost control of everything.

The curse was growing stronger or he was weakening. Neither option sat well with him.

What had Rachel meant when she'd told him to tell Clarissa good-bye? At first he'd panicked and rushed here to make sure she was safe. In his relief at finding her, he'd wanted nothing more than to hold her, reassure himself through the only sense he knew to be reliable—touch—that she was alive and well.

She had been safe from the visions. She was safe as long as she stayed here.

But how long could they stay in this house? Life went on around them. He was sure she needed to work on her business. He had money but wasn't so independently rich he could afford not to work.

He wanted to work. He wanted a life where he gave something to the world, where he went home each night to a family. To home.

He wanted "Leave it to Beaver" and he was living in the Osborns' guesthouse.

A sixth sense told him someone was behind him, and he turned to find Clarissa standing in the doorway. The moonlight caressed her, her hair sparkled and the bare skin of her legs below his T-shirt seemed pale.

"Come back to bed, David. It's too cold to be out there worrying."

"Your psychic powers telling you that? I thought the dreams weren't reaching you here." One of the blessings of being here was the peace of mind she'd also found.

"I don't need dreams to see the tension in you. What are you worried about?"

She might not be using her psychic dreams, but she was too close to the mark for his comfort.

"My mind's too full to sleep," he admitted.

She didn't say anything for a long time. He heard her take a few steps and saw her stop at the table. "I've been avoiding this."

She sat an old book on the tabletop. He hadn't forgotten it. He'd merely put it out of his mind. Afraid there would be no answer. Afraid to get his hopes up. Afraid to learn his true fate.

The thick cover was old and worn. In the moonlight he couldn't tell its color. Not black, but some shade of gray.

He watched her slim, graceful fingers open the book. She unconsciously caressed the edges, and he recalled how she'd told him of the hours she'd spent with it as a child.

He'd like to see a picture of her from those days.

"It's here in the back." Her words broke into his thoughts, and he realized she was talking about the book. "I remember reading it a long time ago." The ragged pages crinkled as she turned them. "Here." She stopped and pointed at what looked like a handwritten page.

The contrast of the thick black ink on the white page was enough to see in the moonlight. "It's in a section labeled progressive spells. 'The cycle of life rules both man and beast. Separating the two is no simple feat. Combining them is our goal this day. As these items we join forever to stay.'"

She had read with no inflection in her voice, as if she were in grade school reading class.

"Why did you read it like that?" he asked.

"Like what?"

"So monotone."

"I don't want the universe to think I'm casting it."

"Oh." He paused and slowly reached out and touched the page that seemed to have sealed his fate. "Forever to stay?"

"That's the intent. But look." She flipped several pages then turned back a couple more. "Here. Undoing a progressive spell can be done. Set a circle. Then undo the action of the joining as the lines are repeated whole but in reverse."

"What the hell does that mean?"

Clarissa smiled at him. "We have to find that music box. Some things of yours are in it. Within in a light circle we separate them and then recite this backwards."

"Sounds too simple."

"It is simple—*if* we find the music box. Impossible if we don't." The night suddenly seemed incredibly quiet. She stepped closer and laid her cool palm against his cheek. "We'll find it. We have to."

He closed his eyes for an instant, needing to savor her touch, to believe her words. Then he stepped back and reality returned.

"I went to the mansion today." His voice was even and nearly as flat as hers had been moments before.

"You what?" Her surprise echoed in the night. "Are you crazy?" She moved closer to him. "That's too dangerous. What made you do that?"

He moved away from her distracting touch. "I can't stay here forever. I went to look for the music box. We have to find a way to either escape this curse or..."

"Or what? Let it consume you?"

He didn't respond.

"No," she said. "I won't let that happen. There has to be someone—"

"No!" He stepped closer to her. "I won't put anyone else at risk because of me." Anger flared between them. "It's bad enough I got you involved."

Her silence surprised him and stretched out painfully over the night. He looked at her more closely. She twisted her fingers together. "Clarissa?" he prompted.

She looked up then and he saw the sheen of damp in her eyes. "I've always been involved." She stepped away, turning to look at the night.

His gut tightened, and he knew he wasn't going to like the rest of what she had to say. "What do you mean, you've always been involved?"

She couldn't answer him right away. She thought back over the pictures, the dank smell and the door that slammed shut. "I was in the basement today for a reason." She shivered and rubbed her hands up and down her arms.

The night grew heavy again as David stepped closer to the spell book and stared down at it. Clarissa followed him, not letting him put too much space between them.

"The music box isn't down there." She'd looked down there on a hunch. "But there is an old box of pictures."

"Pictures? Of what?"

She hesitated, unsure, then realized it wouldn't do them any good if they weren't honest at this stage. "Your parents. You." Her voice shook, which surprised her.

She couldn't look at him. The memories were too strong, too painful. She picked up the familiar book, slowly closing it and hugging it to her chest. It's familiar weight was comforting. She stepped out to the rail and watched the city lights he'd been so intent on before.

"When Faith was here, we talked about the little boys. Remember?"

"Yeah." She heard the frown of confusion in his voice. "What about them?"

"I had a vision about a dark haired little boy, oh about five years ago. He was trapped in a dark place." She paused and fought the shiver the vision always gave her.

"I tried to find him. I had to save him. Then a couple weeks after I contacted the authorities, they found two boys. Their bodies were in an old basement. Someone had locked them in."

"Good God." His revulsion wasn't new to her.

"As I told you, I was arrested, but they couldn't prove I had anything to do with it because I didn't. They tried. Even got to a trial. Luckily, I had a good attorney and a fairly smart jury."

She sighed, her hand caressing the warm, solid book in her arms as if it offered the comfort of Granny's hug.

"What does this have to do with me?"

With us? She almost heard him think that thought.

"Those pictures. I saw one of you," she said. "My vision wasn't of two boys, or either of those boys. It was of you."

She turned and faced him. His frown had deepened. "I saw you inside that music box in the living room. That was the dark space." She closed her eyes, forcing her mind to face what she'd fought so hard for years to erase. "You were sitting with your knees up and your arms hugging them, weren't you?" She didn't wait for his answer but continued before she lost her nerve. "Tears slid down your face." And at the time of the vision, down hers. "You listened to your parents argue."

She opened her eyes. He didn't have to answer her. The shock on his face was enough.

"You kept whispering, 'Don't fight. Please, don't fight.'"

David abruptly sat down on the metal deck chair. It clattered from the impact of his weight and the force. He buried his face in his hands as he took a deep breath.

She hastily set the book down and knelt before him. Gently, she touched his arm. What was he thinking? What was going on in his mind? She tried to prepare herself for his anger or hatred, but she wasn't ready for that now—she never would be.

Swiftly, his arms engulfed her, knocking her breath away. He pulled her tight and she buried her face against his chest.

"It feels as if..." He breathed in deep. "As if I wasn't alone." Relief and an emotion she couldn't identify—gratitude maybe—thickened his voice.

She had no answer for him. It had to have been years after the actual events. He really had been alone then. She didn't know why she'd had a vision of the past, but right now she didn't care. Her eyes burned, and she let the tears fall and soak into the soft curls on his chest.

She clung to him, wrapping her arms around him, her fingers curling into the skin of his shoulders. He shook as he drew in uneven breaths. She felt his cheek against her neck.

They stayed that way for a long time. She'd have stayed forever.

David moved first.

His profile was all she could make out as clouds slipped over the moon's bright face.

"Come to bed," she whispered and rose. He took her outstretched hand and pulled her close.

His lips found hers, their coolness quickly warming.

They were halfway to the bedroom when she remembered the spell book. She pushed him to the bed, kissing him playfully and admonished, "Hold that thought."

She stepped back outside, surprised when an icy wind threw her hair across her face. She shoved the curls away just as she reached the table.

The book lay open. She thought she'd closed it. The ancient pages ruffled in the breeze. The wind stopped abruptly, and the pages settled back into place.

The clouds that had crept in shifted from the moon's face, illuminating the pages.

Handwriting she recognized as her grandmother's glared up at her. She'd seen and heard the words before, but now they seemed to scream themselves inside her head.

Trust your instincts.

Sixteen

The door opened slowly. Too slowly. David looked up. Clarissa entered the room, the spell book clasped tightly in her arms. He'd thought the moonlight had washed her skin pale, but inside the house, the pallor seemed more pronounced.

His stomach sank. "What happened?"

"Nothing...happened...exactly."

She looked into his eyes, her gaze pleading with him for something he couldn't define. He stepped toward her and then halted just inches away. "Tell me." David reached out, pushing a stray lock of hair behind her ear.

"There's a reason I found those pictures. We need to check them out."

He forced a smile to his lips. "Not having second thoughts about us?"

She tried to smile. "No," she reassured him. "I want to be with you. I do, but I'm afraid if we don't figure all this out, we'll never really be together."

She looked away from him, and he tried to read her but couldn't. This was as close as they'd come to talking about something lasting between them.

When several minutes passed, and she still didn't look at him, he slipped one finger beneath her chin until their gazes met.

He leaned closer, her lips soft and sweet against his. She pressed against him, returning his kiss with an urgency that bothered him.

After a long, silent moment, she stepped away. "The book was open on the table to a page my grandmother wrote."

"What did it say?"

"To trust my instincts."

"And what do those instincts say to do?"

"Find that music box. Maybe there's a clue in that box of pictures downstairs.

"Maybe." He stared into her face, looking for any inkling of what she felt, of what she was thinking. All he saw was a sadness he hated.

For a minute he considered telling her more about his visit to the mansion and Rachel. He just as quickly discarded the idea. If what he suspected had to be done—him returning to the mansion—he wasn't going to tell her the risks. And she sure as hell wasn't going with him. Rachel's warning had been clear.

"Let's go." He smiled, but it was more a reassurance than any true emotion.

At the door in the kitchen he stopped. "You stay up here. We can't both get locked down there if the door closes."

She resisted his command, but after a minute gave in. His argument made sense. Who knew what he would face down there? He wasn't afraid of the usual monsters in a scary basement. He was more afraid of the monsters lurking in his own memories.

Slowly, one step at a time, David descended into the shadowed, musty basement. The flashlight beam cut a swath through the dark to cast its golden puddle across the pile of photographs. He knew those photos, but he wasn't sure how they'd gotten to this house. Rachel must have brought them here.

The sound of his footsteps seemed loud and fateful as he continued down. Finally he reached the bottom. With his toe, he shoved a pile of pictures aside, seeing more images of his past. Memories captured inside neat little white-bordered pieces of paper.

The edges of many of the photos were curled and yellowed with time. A layer of fine gray dust scattered over the faces that stared up at him.

He looked down at them. His mother's face. His father's grin.

The first stab of pain surprised him as he saw an image of himself at age five. He bent and picked it up. He knew how old he was because that's when his parents had died. And that picture had been taken only a short time before.

The mental images came back to tear at his heart, and he dropped the photo. It fluttered back to the pile, leaving a trail of dust motes to dance in the flashlight beam. Then another picture caught his attention. He hunkered down and hesitantly reached out and pulled it from the pile.

The glossy finish winked in the light. He tilted it, staring for a long time at the pretty face he'd once loved.

Rachel. How long ago that seemed. Another lifetime.

He closed his eyes and fought the bitterness that threatened his clear thinking. Angry with her and himself, he pitched the photo back into the pile.

The other pictures he knew were there flashed through his mind. His parents. The house. Their trips. Germany. Paris.

His mother had written a line from one of her favorite poems on one of them. "I will die in Paris on a rainy day." She'd been fanciful and thinking of a day far away.

But die she had, though not in Paris. The rain had poured out of the sky as the bullets poured from his father's gun. Anger and disgust tore through him. Emotional pain ripped through his body, nearly doubling him over. The anguish he'd fought for so long was too strong.

Emotions threatened to engulf him, but he fought them, knowing that here he was safe from the effects of the curse.

This time he couldn't escape into another being. No angry lions. No freedom seeking stallions. No curious cats.

Just him. A man who had avoided his own torment for far too long.

His heart pounded. Sweat drenched his body. Relishing the coolness of the dirt floor beneath his bare feet, he swung the beam around the barren room. Clarissa had been right. The music box wasn't down here.

"David?"

He turned to look up the stairs. The kitchen light outlined Clarissa's form through the thin material of his T-shirt. He stood and climbed the stairs.

"There's nothing there. Just the photos." And old pain.

"I'd hoped..."

"No. Nothing." He guided her out of the doorway and closed the door. He hoped he never saw those pictures again. "Let's get some sleep."

She didn't move, just stood there staring up at him. "Are you sure? I can't believe I found them for nothing."

"I'm positive there are no clues there." He clenched his teeth to keep from losing his temper.

"Are you okay?" she whispered.

What could he tell her? "I don't know. I'm too tired to think." And he was. His eyelids were heavy and he wanted to sleep for about a week.

She fit so easily in his arms. He pulled her into them and leaned back against the closed door. Burying his face in her hair, he let himself breathe and savor her presence.

His sorrow faded in her passion. The night soon disappeared as they moved to the brass bed and forgot where they were and why they were here.

* * * *

Sated and near exhaustion, David cradled her in his arms. Clarissa's heart pounded gently against her ribs, and David felt the beat of it through his own skin. Earlier she'd spoken of love. Tilting his head to see her better, he realized she was sound asleep. Did she even remember saying the words?

At the thought, his heart soared into the heavens and hung

there for a long moment before crashing back to earth. The blazing trail it left seared through to his soul.

She couldn't love him. He wouldn't allow it. She wasn't safe.

As if disturbed by his thoughts, Clarissa grimaced in her sleep and shifted position. Carefully, so as not to wake her, David settled her against the pillows and moved away. Her hand slid across the sheets as if seeking him, and then stopped when she slipped deeper into sleep.

She looked so beautiful lying there. The dawn crept into the room and fell across the bed. Its faint light caressed her every curve. His eyes were drawn to where the shadow fell between her breasts. The sheet slipped down, bunching just below her waist, just high enough to tease him with a glimpse of darkness at the juncture of her thighs.

His body responded and he'd have woke her again except his heart threw out a warning. Fear.

Memories of the pictures returned to haunt him. His love wasn't a gift he could safely give her. He'd given it to his parents. He'd given it to Rachel. They'd been violently ripped from his life. He couldn't bear the thought of it happening with Clarissa. He knew the two of them might never survive the reality.

He picked up his clothes and pulled them on. In the dim light he fumbled around to find his shoes and belt. Then, fully dressed, he stood beside the bed where she lay so beautifully and peacefully and paused.

"I do want you," he spoke to the room and himself, half hoping that somehow it reached her subconscious. "But I can't risk you. Forgive me."

Turning on his heel, he grabbed his jacket and opened the front door. He'd left her sleeping before, but this would be the last time.

* * * *

Sunlight woke Clarissa. She relished its warmth and snuggled into the pillows, pulling the sheet up over her shoulders and thoroughly enjoying that time just before she fully awoke.

David's scent clung to the pillows and her body reacted to it. She wanted him again, now, and she reached out to tell him so. All she found was an empty pillow and sun-warmed sheets.

Her eyes flew open in panic, and she gazed about the room. From the brightness of the sunlight she realized it must be late morning. "David?" There was no answer.

Pulling the sheet off the bed, she wrapped it around her. Carefully, so she didn't trip on the long fabric, she walked to the window, hoping to find him on the veranda. There was no sign of him.

He wasn't on the front porch, but her car sat at the curb. When had that gotten here—and how? A stray ray of sunlight caught her eye, and on the nightstand she saw her keys. The light reflected off the familiar good luck charm attached to the ring.

Fear tore through her, and she hastily grabbed her clothes. Where was her cell phone? She fumbled in her purse until she found it. The battery was dead. "Damn."

She'd just finished combing her hair when a knock at the door startled her. Who could that be? David wouldn't knock. Still, anticipation made her heart skip.

She hurried to the front room, smoothing her shirt just before she pulled the door open. It took her a second to register that it wasn't David standing on the porch but an old woman.

Clarissa stared at her, somewhat surprised by her old-fashioned appearance. Her shoulders were bent, and as a result, she was nearly half a foot shorter than Clarissa. A gray hat perched atop her white hair, and a black egret feather wafted in the faint breeze she made as she walked. She wore a wool coat despite the day's warmth, and black lace-up shoes with block heels.

Clarissa cleared her throat. "Hello." She couldn't see the woman's eyes beyond the wide hat, but the deep lines in her face told of much time gone by. Her thin, pale lips pursed in a straight line that clearly found Clarissa lacking.

"Good morning, dear." The woman stepped closer, bringing the damp scent of roses with her. "I've brought the things Mr. Lorde asked for."

"David? What things?" Relieved that he was probably fine took the edge off her mood. He'd taken time to order these.

"You'll see." The old woman stepped over the threshold, a basket dangling from her arm and a secretive smile on her lips.

"Please, come in," Clarissa mumbled after closing the door.

"I won't be long. Just a moment." The woman turned back to face Clarissa. She reached into the basket and pulled out a cellophane-wrapped bundle of bright red blooms. "Here, dear."

Reaching out, Clarissa stroked the soft delicate petals that called to mind the sweet, gentle memories of the night she'd spent with him. Her heart swelled, and she pulled out a single rose to hold closer and smell its sweetness.

That's when she noticed that they weren't store-bought roses. The stems weren't thick and thornless. They were thin narrow stems, like those grown in a garden.

The tiny prick of a thorn on her finger made her gasp and then laugh at herself for being so careless. She sucked her sore finger, and the tiny wound immediately stopped bleeding.

Suddenly everything changed. The bright sunshine no longer shone in the windows. Looking outside, she noticed dark gray clouds scudding across the sky. Something felt wrong—very wrong. She turned to look for the old woman, who seemed very far away.

The rose fell from her hand, and Clarissa knew that somehow by touching the rose, she'd brought the curse here. This house that had been a haven for him. The place that had been their refuge in the war of the minds was now tainted. She was no longer safe from the illusion and dreams.

And just to prove it, her mind filled with images of David. Of the sweet love they'd shared, and of his angrily storming out of the house. Her heart ached with the pain on his face. Why had he been so angry?

You said you loved him. The voice echoed in her head and Clarissa cringed. Hadn't he wanted love? Hadn't he wanted *her* love? It hurt to see the truth as he roared away from the sidewalk, a cloud of dust rising up from the bumper of the black sports car.

When her vision cleared, Clarissa sank to her knees beside the bed. Tears flowed across her cheeks. Her heart broke and she had no idea how she was going to fix it. Maybe there was no way to fix it.

The old woman moved, as if in slow motion. Clarissa watched her build a fire in the fireplace, but couldn't move or speak to stop her. The heat and the strong floral scents seemed to swirl around her. The woman seemed oblivious to it as she stood staring, unspeaking and smiling at her.

The darkness stole up on her, then hit with a vengeance. The room vanished and Clarissa found herself standing in a dark cavern.

The walls threw off cold, and a musty-damp smell crept over her, choking her. Tears burned her eyes from all the overwhelming scents and the painful realization that she and David were no longer safe here.

The visions were all too real and terrifying.

* * * *

"Where is she?" Rachel's voice screamed in David's head though he couldn't see her.

"Who?" He had no intention of telling Rachel where Clarissa was. If she couldn't figure it out, that was her problem.

He continued his search. The large chest his mother had used to store scarves and gloves was empty. He pulled pictures off the wall, looking behind them for any hiding places.

"The old woman."

That stopped him. "Who?" Now he was totally confused. "I don't know any old woman." Except the one who had gone through the bank, taking money out of Rachel's account. He stopped his search. Something wasn't right here.

"You're lying," she whined.

"I am not lying. I don't know what you're talking about. Besides, why do you care? You've ruined my life. Wasn't that your goal?" David paced the black and white tiled foyer, fighting his frustration. He knew that if he shifted here in the mansion, he'd be lost.

He had to find the music box first. He forced himself to walk into the living room. He hated this room, and it took most of his concentration to control the pending shift.

"I've always cared," she whined as her voice followed him.

Not believing her, he stopped searching and looked for her. Was that odd-shaped shadow her? As he watched, the vision he'd seen before grew in clarity.

Had he actually once loved her? He couldn't remember how that had felt. He couldn't even remember what she'd been like when she was alive.

"That's why I want you with me forever." She seemed to move closer. *"I made sure of it."*

"Sure of what?" He stepped toward the apparition and was surprised when she moved back. She was a ghost. He couldn't hurt her—could he? He took another step, and she drifted out the door and into the foyer.

He followed. "Tell me what you did, Rachel."

She shook her head and moved up the stairs. *"I didn't do anything."*

He took another step. "You did, too. I know. I want the music box. Now." He saw fire blaze in her eyes and nearly turned away. But he had nothing left to lose anymore.

"No. It's mine. You're mine." Defiance filled her words. She drifted up the curved staircase.

He threw up his hands, wanting to reach out and grab her and what? Shake her into telling him what she'd done? Shake what? She was a damned ghost. He dragged his fingers through his hair in frustration and followed her. "You're hiding it. I need to know where it is."

"You do know her. The old woman told you, didn't

she?" Rachel drifted higher. He continued to trail her. They were nearly to the top of the stairs where Clarissa had fainted only a few nights before. It seemed like ages ago.

What had she said about a woman pushing her?

"Tell me what you did and why you need some old woman." His voice thundered, and he actually saw her eyes widen in surprise.

He took another step. She rushed toward him. There wasn't an impact, but the startling cold of her "form" rushing through him caused him to stumble. He caught himself on the rail. He'd nearly regained his balance when his fingers slipped off the polished banister.

He fell. The edge of each step tore into his ribs, his hip, the bones of his spine and finally the back of his head where it made a sickening crack.

The room spun and darkness caught him in its cold, lonely grip.

* * * *

Clarissa awoke to the sound of pounding. Belatedly, she realized it was her heartbeat in her ears.

She sat up and looked around. The small living room came slowly into focus. Quickly, too quickly for her aching head, she turned to search for the old woman.

She was nowhere in sight. Had she even been real? Had the roses? She looked down at her finger. The thorn had been real, as the tiny hole in her skin still stung.

The vision had taken her to a cavern, but she didn't know of any around here. She noticed the roses then, on the table, dead and wilted...and the spell book was gone.

Unfortunately, she couldn't remember if it had been here when she'd first woken this morning.

Had David or the woman taken it?

The woman had no reason to take it, did she? David did. She'd shown him the spell. He didn't need her anymore.

Except he did. He just didn't know it.

Her overwhelmed and sluggish mind filled with images and thoughts of the last few days, trying to piece all the odd parts of this broken puzzle together. She rubbed her eyes. She couldn't think straight.

Had she been drugged? Was this even real? She groaned. She had to believe it was, as all her other visions had become violent quickly.

David was gone. That knowledge settled in the pit of her stomach. What had he said last night? No one was going to get hurt because of him. He was trying to protect her. She admired the sentiment but knew it was foolish.

Still, her thoughts returned to the pictures in the basement. She couldn't believe she'd found them for no reason. She slowly stood. Wobbling. *What was on those roses?* She headed to the kitchen door, dreading the steps in her present condition. Her wooziness made them treacherous; still she knew she had to find what David couldn't.

Why did people have a basement if all they were going to do with it was store old memories and junk in it? Then a thought occurred to her.

Did the mansion have a basement? She stopped. She didn't need to look here.

This was the wrong basement.

Seventeen

The road to the mansion seemed miles longer than it had when she and David had driven it only nights before. Had it really only been a few days? It felt like years.

Finally, the wrought iron gates, silhouetted against the afternoon shaded mountains, came into view. Clouds shrouded the farthest peaks and a roll of thunder broke the quiet. She braked to a stop.

David's Mercedes sat in front of the house.

She climbed out of her car, staring up at the gates, asking for some divine guidance. Lord only knew she needed it—desperately at this point.

She walked the last few yards toward the foreboding house.

It looked no different, except for the eerie afternoon shadows that crept into crevices and leapt out again, and the odd dazzle of the late afternoon dew. If her heart hadn't been pounding so loud in her ears and the adrenaline galloping like racehorses through her blood, she would have marveled at the beauty. As it was, she felt time running past her.

She hurried up the front steps, anxious to get inside. Out here she felt so vulnerable. The front door was unlocked, and only after she'd pushed it open did she worry about how easy it was to enter. Would it be as easy to leave again?

The afternoon shadows barely touched the interior of the house. Bright remnants of light glowed in the chandelier and prismed about the room in fascinating procession.

"David?" she called, hoping he'd hear her and step out from a doorway, laughing at the concern on her face. When only silence met her ears, she was disappointed but not surprised.

If she found him, what form would he be in? She prepared herself for anything, then tried to ignore the animals her overactive imagination conjured up.

The living room looked just as they had left it the other night. Proceeding on, she found the library. It looked as if it hadn't been touched in years, which it probably hadn't.

She checked the nursery upstairs, and then she turned back down the hall and walked down a corridor they hadn't visited before. When she opened the door to a bedroom, memories rushed out to greet her—memories that were nothing more than the wispy fabric of the passionate dream they'd shared. An ache grew low in her chest and encompassed her heart until it nearly shattered in two. Would she ever know what was real and what was fantasy?

"Oh, David, where are you?" she said on a sigh. She felt like sinking to her knees and giving in to tears, but she didn't. She returned back downstairs and went to the kitchen.

The basement door was most likely back here. She found a door, but it was the back door. It stood ajar. She peeked out and saw what had once been a beautiful garden. The rose bushes seemed to have been recently trimmed...

She quickly stepped back inside, closing the door. A cool draft reached out to her, and she fought the urge to turn and run. She knew this was the way. This was where David would be.

A panel door sat in the back wall. Gingerly, she stepped toward it and turned the handle. It opened easily and she peered inside.

The same cool damp she remembered in the small house greeted her. Somehow, she expected to find much more than pictures and old boxes this time.

Flickers of light came from below. She hesitated. "David?" Was he down there? What was he doing? She stepped over the threshold and made her way down the timeworn stone steps.

The faint light somewhere at the bottom provided enough illumination for her to see the steps and make out the rough gouges made in the earth during the creation of the passage.

Around and around, down deep into the earth she went. The temperature dropped and she shivered, hugging the rough walls. Then it grew warmer than would be normal for an underground room.

Finally, she reached the dirt floor at the bottom. Several old bare bulb lights lined the walls. Row after row of wooden racks held wine bottles covered in dust. She pulled a bottle from its holder and rubbed the dust off the label. She might not know wine, but she knew this one looked expensive. She put it back gingerly.

Dry, dank air filled her lungs and she coughed to expel the awful taste. Adrenaline rushed through her. She leaned back against the wall for a moment, forcing her mind and body to slow down so she could gather her thoughts.

"David, are you here?" She listened and thought she heard distant voices. At first she couldn't tell if they were coming from upstairs or from deeper into the wine cellar.

She moved farther down the main aisle. The voices grew in intensity. She wondered if they were arguing and headed toward them. The claustrophobia that had been initiated in the elevator vision threatened to choke her. But she forced herself to ignore her fears and kept her feet moving.

The wine cellar had obviously been here for years, nearly eternity it seemed, from the layer of dust and cobwebs that covered everything. She heard distant thunder from the outdoors. The lights flickered and the room fell dark. Panic rose in her throat.

She yelped and stumbled. The wine rack behind her rattled with an eerie clinking as she bumped into it. Not a ray of light penetrated the thick musty air. Where was the door? Calming herself, she reached out, stepping slowly across the uneven floor until her hand touched the rough, cold rock wall.

Go right? Go left? She didn't know. One way was escape—the other she had no way of knowing where it went. She took a few steps and realized she was going downhill. As a child she'd believed she could dig all the way to China. Now she wondered if she'd end up in hell instead.

A slight breeze passed her cheek from the left and tangled her hair across her eyes. She turned toward it. The breeze faded but she knew she'd felt it on her face.

Slowly, carefully, she followed the wall with her hands. Her fingertips soon burned from rubbing against the rough stone, and she slowed, having a more difficult time feeling her way.

She moved her feet slowly, afraid of stepping on or into something unknown. As it was, bits of sand and rock slipped between her toes and the leather bottoms of her sandals.

The temperature dropped. She heard the distant drip-drip of water and found her next footfall squishy. A trickle of cold slipped beneath her fingers. This was the wrong way.

The icy water dampened a portion of her skirt. Unbalanced, the fabric swung and snapped against her bare legs in a reminder of the unseen that lay everywhere.

"Stop!" a voice echoed around her and Clarissa faltered.

"Who's there?" she whispered. No one answered her. Then she realized the mumble of voices was a distance away.

She moved a few inches then stopped again, unsure. Should

she go on? Should she stop? Was it David or someone else?

She inched along the walls. The voices rose and fell, but she couldn't make out their words with the echo in the basement. The high pitch suggested it was a woman. She waited for a deeper, masculine response, and when none came, she knew David wasn't there. Disappointed it wasn't him, and afraid of who it might be, she took a few steps back the way she thought she'd come. She needed to find the stairs. Surely if she kept going along the wall, she'd find them.

"Make it work," a woman said into the quiet and Clarissa halted.

"I...I can't," another woman said. "I...I don't know w...what you want."

Where were the voices coming from? Clarissa tried to turn toward them, but they seemed to reverberate everywhere. Her ears slowly adjusted to the odd echoing sounds, and she listened carefully.

She inched forward and scraped her knuckles on something metal. Feeling around, she realized it was the hinge to a large wooden door. She ran her fingers along the rough wood. Where did it lead?

She fumbled around until she found the handle. The metal was cool and firm against her palm. She pulled hard, nearly stumbling backward when the door opened easily.

The light on the other side of the door was blinding and Clarissa raised her hand to shade her eyes. It took several minutes for her eyes to adjust, and even then she squinted.

Candles blazed everywhere. It must have taken hours to light all of them. She looked around in amazement. The rock walls of the room were smooth and the roof blackened from soot. The room wasn't filled with smoke and she wondered how it escaped. It was as if the earth absorbed it.

An old woman stood hunched over something behind the tiers—the woman who had delivered the roses. Hastily, Clarissa backed up behind the doorframe.

"I'm not a witch," the woman said to herself.

"Yes, you are." The voice seemed to come out of the walls.

Clarissa looked around but couldn't see anyone else.

"I saw you go into the deposit boxes to get the book."

"This old book?" The woman lifted the grimoire—Granny's grimoire. So the woman had taken it, not David. "I...I went to the bank to get my mother's silver for m...my g...granddaughter's wedding."

"Liar," the voice boomed, and Clarissa resisted the urge to cover her ears.

She knew the woman wasn't lying.

"You put the book there. You're the old woman who tricked me."

"Tricked you?"

Clarissa watched the elderly woman. Even from the distance, she saw the fear in her eyes and the trembling of her body. The woman's eyes darted from side to side as if searching for the person who was speaking.

Clarissa knew she wasn't going to find the speaker.

"Don't play innocent with me."

Clarissa watched as the wisps of smoke gathered together and formed a shape. It was the woman who had pushed her down the stairs. It had to be Rachel.

The gray-haired woman screeched and backed away from the spirit until she nearly stepped into the candles. "I'm telling you the truth." Color faded from her aged face. "I don't know anything."

"You lied before when you cast the spell. You said David would always be mine."

Puzzle pieces started to fall together in Clarissa's mind. Recent events made a strange sort of sense.

"Rachel?" Clarissa spoke, stepping out from her hiding place.

The old woman spun around and the book thumped to the dirt floor. "What are you doing here? The roses should have—"

Clarissa watched the confusion cross her face. She remembered pulling only one rose from the bundle. What had been on those roses? Poison?

"Damn you!" The voice vibrated around them.

The old woman's eyes grew wide, and she trembled. "I'm going crazy, aren't I?" Her voice was soft and pathetic.

"No, you're not. You're fine," Clarissa soothed. She felt sympathy for this woman who was trapped in this mess. Now she understood David's need to protect her and others. "It's okay." Clarissa took a few steps forward. "She can't help you, Rachel. That book is mine."

"No. It belongs to that treacherous crone."

Clarissa swallowed hard. Granny had never been treacherous, but she had done some meddling with magic in her day. Had Rachel been one of her meddlings? Dread swamped her.

It was the only explanation.

"My grandmother left it to me when she died."

"Get out! Leave us! We have work to do."

"No, you don't." Clarissa moved closer, hoping to find a path through the maze of candles. None were wide enough for her to pass through. A single flame sputtered, its sound bringing her gaze back to the candles.

"That's why you kept going to the bank—to find her," Clarissa said softly, hoping to distract Rachel. "Those old women weren't embezzling. That was just an excuse to get them into the bank. You were possessing them, using them to see if they knew where the book was."

"You're wrong." Rachel's incorporeal form spun toward Clarissa. *"I knew where it was. I just needed to get it."*

"Why?"

"To fix the spell," Rachel roared angrily, as if speaking to an over-inquisitive child.

"He wasn't supposed to change into animals, was he?"

"Of course not!"

"What was supposed to happen?" Clarissa asked gently.

The silence was heavy and long. Clarissa edged closer to the old woman. Somehow she had to get her out of here.

She'd just made eye contact with the woman when Rachel finally said, *"I wasn't supposed to leave him behind. We were supposed to die together."*

Bits and pieces of the spell's wording returned to Clarissa's mind. What had given Rachel that idea? She remembered something about the cycle of life ruling both man and beast. "Maybe if you let me see the spell book, I can fix it."

Rachel laughed, the sound echoing in the cavern. *"I'm dead, not stupid. You want him for yourself."*

The flames blazed and Clarissa stepped back from the intense heat. Rachel knew her thoughts and emotions. Emotions she'd barely admitted to herself and remembered whispering to David last night. Had he heard? Would he ever know how she felt?

Realizing she couldn't successfully lie about her feelings for him, she lifted her chin and faced Rachel. For an instant she wished Granny was here, though she wasn't sure which she wanted most—her help or to throttle her for creating this mess.

She knew she couldn't lie about David, but she had no qualms about telling stories.

"It's *my* Grimoire now. I'm the witch attached to it. The spells won't work for anyone else." Her heart pounded. Was she convincing enough? She had no clue about real magic, and half expected some celestial retribution any second.

A sound that could almost be a sigh washed through the cavern. *"You don't want to help me. I can't be with David unless he dies—and you keep saving him."* On the last two words Rachel's voice roared and the flames flared.

Clarissa watched the spirit drift higher then settle just above their heads.

"You sent the kid to shoot him," Clarissa stated.

"And you warned him. I've had it with your meddling." A whoosh of hot air slammed into Clarissa and she stumbled backward. She bumped into the rough wall and a trickle of rocks tumbled down around her, burying her feet and filling the air with dust.

When the air cleared, Clarissa found herself staring not from outside the circle of candles but inside.

The old woman looked nearly as startled. She sat on the ground where Clarissa had fallen.

"Run!" Clarissa shouted. For a long minute the old woman sat there, unmoving. Then Clarissa's words seemed to penetrate and she struggled to her feet.

She hurried to the door and Clarissa heard the click of her heels receding into the distance.

"I don't need her. I've got you." Rachel's voice had turned to an evil whisper.

The smoky form faded, and Clarissa saw what she'd been hiding, what she hadn't seen from across the cavern.

She saw the entire altar now. In the ocean of flame the raised piece of stone created a pyre.

And there lay David.

Eighteen

"Tell him good-bye." The wicked voice echoed, and Clarissa looked around but found herself alone. The air felt different and she thought perhaps Rachel had left. But why—and was it a trick? She reined in her thoughts, not letting her fears of illusions distract her.

A loud roar broke through the air. Suddenly, dust filtered from overhead, black, sooty dust. The walls trembled. What was happening? Were they going to be buried alive? Something Rachel had said earlier came to mind. They could only be together if he died. Clarissa knew it didn't matter if she died.

She didn't have time to figure it out. She had to do something. She took a calming breath, fighting the panic that threatened to defeat her.

David's dark hair fell away from his face, pooling around his head in a bright ebony stream. His eyes were closed and his chest bare. She drew closer, realizing the floor dipped downward. A row of candles separated them. When she reached the edge of them, she found they were level with her waist and imbedded in a natural altar of stone.

"David?" she cried, her voice ricocheted off the stone walls. Her breath tilted the flames in the nearest row.

He didn't move. In the wavering light she saw bruises on his face and a trickle of dried blood at the edge of his hairline. Was he even—she swallowed—alive? Her heart pounded in her ears and she tasted her own panic.

Bending, she blew at the first row of candles. The heat reached out for her, not even fading with her breath. If nothing else, they grew stronger as they ate away at the wick and wax.

She had to put out the flames. She had to get to David. Had to see if...

She turned around looking for something, anything, to help her. No bucket of water. No fire extinguisher. Nothing. Were they even real, or a vision? She couldn't take the chance of guessing wrong.

Please, God, she prayed. Let him be alive. She couldn't see any movement of his chest. She needed to get closer.

"David," she cried, her voice bouncing off the thick stone walls. He didn't answer.

Kneeling, she struggled to pull a tall taper from its base.

Sweat made her hands slick against the wax. Finally it gave. She swept it in an arc through the other candles, sending them tumbling to the stone floor. Flames fed off each other, devouring the candles. Finding no other fuel, the flames soon wilted and vanished.

Expecting Rachel to stop her, Clarissa hurried to David. She leaned close. Reaching out, she touched his face and was shocked to find it ice cold.

He couldn't be dead. He could *not* leave her when she'd just found him.

A drop fell onto his shoulder, and she realized it was a tear. Her tear. She swiped at the offending dampness. Damn it, she wasn't going to fall apart now. She reached out to him again, this time placing her hand over his heart.

A single slow beat startled her. And then it was gone. *No!*

She leaned closer, placing her ear where her hand had been. His heart thumped slowly. Very slowly.

Near death, but not quite there yet.

"David," she whispered, moving up to where she could speak in his ear. "It's me."

Still no answer, but his heart thumped twice again beneath her palm. "Wake up, David," she whispered. His heartbeat quickened, and she fought the smile that threatened. It was too early to hope, even though the color seeped back into his face.

"Clarissa." He gasped, his breath loud and painful, like a man long deprived of air. His eyelids fluttered open.

Thank God, she thought and leaned closer, her smile real this time.

He licked his dry lips and tried to speak again. "Get out," were the words he finally said.

"No. Not without you."

"Get out," he repeated. This time she ignored him. She had to rouse him completely, to get him moving. She was sure Rachel wasn't far away. She had left them here for a reason, and though David was barely alive, he *was* alive.

Anger lifted its ugly head and Clarissa let it add strength to her already exhausted limbs and lagging spirit.

She'd find a way out of here—with David—or die trying. She shivered at the macabre thought.

"Sit up," she instructed him gently. He didn't move. "David?" she said more loudly, her voice echoing off the solid walls. A trickle of rocks behind her startled her, reminding her they weren't necessarily so strong.

She leaned back on her heels. Damn Rachel. Frustrated, she shook him, but he still didn't respond. Even his anger at her following him was preferable to this—except if he were angry he'd have changed into something else by now.

Her mind stopped. What if—no. It wasn't possible.

But why not?

She rose up on her knees, staring down into David's handsome face. The one she had visions of years ago. Only he'd been a child and she hadn't recognized him. A child so filled with fear. The one she'd first seen in a vision—one where he died. A man so filled with pain.

She refused to let him die. She would force him into action, and in the process, they would beat Rachel.

Clarissa smiled, knowing her own smile was as wicked as Rachel's had ever been. She leaned over David.

His lips were still cool, but they had warmed as his heart returned to its normal beat. She kissed him. Giving him all the emotion and longing and desire she'd denied for days.

And all of her love.

He turned his head away from her kiss, from her touch, from the inevitable.

"Save us, David," she whispered, knowing—hoping—the change was close. Would it be the same as before? She prayed so.

He cried out. His head fell back, and a grimace of pain distorted his face.

She moved back a step, amazed at the process she'd never really seen. Her heart tore as she shared his pain. And then, it was quickly over.

The bright candlelight washed over him.

A white stallion, as strong and beautiful as any beast she'd ever seen, stood before her.

"No!" Rachel cried out, her voice everywhere around them, shaking the walls. Another loud roar pounded against their ears as dirt fell all around them.

He threw back his head and a loud, screaming whinny echoed in the cavern. His eyes were clear. His muscles rippled, and he pawed the ground as if anxious to run free.

Clarissa climbed up onto the altar and stood waiting. He looked over his shoulder and nodded, the long mane rippling with his movement.

She climbed onto his back. "Save us," she repeated.

The horse's powerful legs shoved off the stone, sailing

them over the sea of candles to land with a resounding thud on the stone floor. The clatter of hooves bounced off the stone walls, creating a nearly deafening echo.

A chill breeze extinguished some of the candles in their wake. Clarissa turned, seeing the encroaching blackness as if it were reaching out for them.

"Wait." She leaned low against the animal's neck and spoke into his ear.

He stopped, shaking his head from side to side and pawing the ground with his right front hoof.

"The spell book. Where's the book?" She climbed down and ran through the cleared path. The book lay open between two large pillar candles. There was no sign of the music box. Was that where Rachel was? Protecting it, hiding it somewhere? She didn't look at what page the book was on, just grabbed it and ran back to him.

Ahead, the tunnel branched in two directions. Which one had she come through? She'd lost track. She remained silent, waiting as patiently as she could for David to decide which way to go. He lifted his head and sniffed the air. With a whinny, he decided. She again climbed onto his back.

Before she could say anything more, he turned to the right.

"Are you sure?" she called, listening to her voice vanish down the tunnel.

He didn't answer, and she wasn't sure she'd know if he did. Instead, he picked up his pace, and she dug her fingers into his mane and her knees into his sides. She struggled to hold on to him and the book as they raced along the rough terrain.

A loud roar came from the walls around them and the stone trembled. The faint light that followed them flickered wildly.

"Go!" she screamed on the tail of the roar, and he broke into a full-out gallop.

Dirt fell down around them and muted the light with rising clouds of dust. She held on even tighter, and he carried her through the labyrinth of tunnels, toward what she hoped was safety. He slowed only when her grip loosened or he stumbled.

The fresh scent of afternoon came toward them in a rush of coolness, and they fought for each gulp of air. They were headed in the right direction.

When they finally reached the doorway to the wine cellar, he stopped. With a shake of his head he indicated the door. He couldn't open it.

She climbed down and pulled against the heavy wood. The hinges groaned as loudly as before. She felt a shove from behind as he nudged her. "Come on." She waved for him to follow. He didn't move.

"Are you okay?" She looked into his eyes. They were wild and filled with an emotion she could only identify as fear. He raised his head, sniffing the air.

"David?" She smelled it, too. Smoke. "Hurry, we're too close to give up now."

Traversing the stairs was slow, but finally they were up them. As they reached the top, a roar came from the other side of the door, in the kitchen. The force of it slammed the door open, sending wood and broken glass with it.

They both stumbled, but David's bulk stopped them from falling back down the stairs. Heat billowed toward them.

"Let's go," she yelled as he nudged her ahead of him. She felt the heat and smelled the smoke ahead. Behind them dust billowed up in a choking cloying cloud. She went a few steps before realizing he wasn't behind her.

"David!" Panic clung to her voice. The white stallion burst through the opening. She'd give him hell later for scaring her. He stopped and she climbed on.

They'd be out of here in an instant.

The clatter of his hooves rang out. Clarissa clung to his broad back, leaning low over his neck. His mane flew in the breeze and she shoved the hair out of her face.

Breeze? What breeze? She looked up. A roar announced the fire that erupted from the back wall. The back door she'd looked out earlier was now a wall of flame. The only other doorway, the one leading to the foyer was still open but flames leapt up from the floor.

Was this real? A dream? A vision? She had no way of knowing.

"Go for it," she told him. "We have nothing to lose."

The horse leapt over the flames, landing with a crashing thud in the center of the foyer.

Heat surrounded them, flames ringing the once beautiful room.

"Stop!" she screamed. He did, pawing the ground and shaking his head, fighting his instinct to run as she dismounted.

She moved around the room, coughing as the smoke filtered into her lungs. Still she kept searching.

The music box had to be near. "It's here." The trail of flames circled the room, then led up the curved staircase.

At the top of the stairs, inside the wisps of smoke, Rachel's ghostly image stood. A smile of evil satisfaction lit her face. A crimson tear slid down her cheek. Then another fell. Each drop lit a small flame at her feet as it hit the floor.

"No! Stop!" Angry, Clarissa hurried up the stairs. Could the music box be hidden here someplace?

The walls of the house shook, and Clarissa felt as if the entire world was falling in around them. She saw the horse kneel. His eyes were filled with pain and anguish. In an instant David returned to his natural form.

"We have to get out of here," David cried, running after her to grab her hand and pull her back down the stairs. Tugging Clarissa with him, he headed for the front door.

"The music box," Clarissa shouted. "We have to get it."

"What?"

"It has to be here." She jerked free from his grasp and yelled over the flames. "We have to break the spell."

He stared at her in confusion and dread. "How do you know it's here?"

"She's here." She pointed to the wisps of smoke. Rachel was gone, but Clarissa knew she wasn't far. "Where is it?" she yelled.

"I don't know," David answered.

Clarissa hurried up the stairs, searching for any memory that would be a clue. Then a single stair creaked. The same stair she'd stepped on that first visit here. She remembered being surprised by it.

That's it. She knelt down, setting the spell book on the floor beside her. "Help me."

David ran up the few steps between them. They pulled on the stair top, hoping it would give. It didn't.

"Are you sure it's here?" he asked.

"No. But where else could it be?"

David stood, looking around, dreading the deadly firetrap that lurked so close. Smoke billowed around them and he coughed. This was ridiculous. He wouldn't risk her life to save his. He wanted to grab her and throw her over his shoulder and take her to safety. He also knew that wouldn't work.

Then he saw something that shocked him. Rachel was down in the foyer, not on the stairs as Clarissa had seen her.

He knew it was a trap. Rachel was trying to keep them

here until they couldn't escape. Until they died from the flames.

He grabbed Clarissa and did exactly as he wanted. The caveman carry was incredibly satisfying, though he'd probably pay for it later.

"The book," she screamed. He reached around and snagged it.

As he set her on her feet and prepared for her outrage, flames broke through the very spot where they'd been standing. Instead of berating him, she yanked the book out of his hands.

"Rachel?" he called, hoping for what? That she'd tell him where the music box was? That wasn't going to happen. But if she was protecting it...did that mean she was near it? It was as good a guess as anything they'd come up with so far. Then he saw a wisp again. In front of the doors to his father's study. He dragged Clarissa to the doors and turned the handle. Locked. Clarissa shoved unsuccessfully against it.

"Let me." David stepped back. Then with a run and a leap, he kicked his foot against the door. It slammed open and he dashed into the room, looking frantically for the wisp of smoke.

"Over here." Clarissa ran directly to his father's gun case. "She knew you'd never go near this," Clarissa explained. The door was locked, but the front was glass and David didn't hesitate to slam a paperweight through it. The action released long-held emotions. How could he not relish smashing the cabinet that had held the tools of his parents' destruction?

Once the latch opened, the small drawers underneath were operable. Inside the second drawer was the golden music box David remembered his father giving it to his mother. He cringed at the memories it brought back, and all too suddenly he was transported back to that day.

Mine.

"No," Clarissa screamed and grabbed the music box. She closed her hand around his arm, tugging him out of the room, back to the foyer. "Close the door," she yelled over the fire's roar.

With the door closed, he realized they were trapped. She grabbed a bouquet of artificial flowers from the table and dipped the petals in the flame. When she trailed it in front of the library doors, he grabbed her wrist, but it was too late. They were completely surrounded.

"What are you doing?" he asked as she pulled away to kneel in the center of the room.

"Kneel here." She pointed to the spot in front of her. "Now," she yelled as he hesitated. "We don't have time."

He did as she commanded. They were trapped anyway.

"Here." She pulled open the music box. Inside was a small plastic bag. She opened the bag and poured several things into her hand. She offered her hand for him to see. A lock of his hair. A piece of fabric that looked vaguely familiar—his baby blanket. One of his toy soldiers.

She struggled to flip the pages of the book.

"What are you doing?"

"It's a circle of light." She indicated the flames all around them. "Take these."

She put the items in his palm and held her hand against his. The words were familiar, if out of order. "*As these items we join forever to stay. Combining them is our goal today. Separating the two is no simple feat. The cycle of life rules both man and beast.*"

As she finished speaking, flames shot up from the floor, stealing the music box and melting it. She'd moved back quickly, but it wasn't fast enough. She cried out when the heat licked the back of her hand.

David shoved the items she'd given him into his pocket. A loud wail rose into the air. Horrendous screeching assaulted their ears and grated painfully across every nerve and emotion.

David felt something slam into him, and he nearly stumbled under its impact. He looked up. One arm of the massive chandelier had melted and fallen to the floor. Breaking the circle of flames. Before the opening closed again, he used every drop of his remaining energy and pulled Clarissa to her feet. They ran. They had to get out now. He dragged her toward the door and this time there was nothing she could do to stop him.

The rest of the chandelier crashed to the floor only inches behind them.

He'd get her out of here, and he was *never* coming back. With a shove, he sent Clarissa out the front door ahead of him and into the cool night.

Nineteen

As David and Clarissa stumbled out the front doors of the house, sirens wailed in the distance. Falling to the grass, Clarissa felt herself hit the damp ground and pull David down with her.

A large red pumper truck came through the wrought iron gates of the drive. Several smaller vehicles followed, each wailing their own answering cry.

Firefighters clad in protective gear climbed from the truck, and Clarissa stared in fascination as they fought the flames that shot high into the night sky. All around them the heavens were blanketed in smoke that reflected the dancing light of the flames.

Clarissa lay on her back on the grass, panting hard. She doubted she'd ever get enough of the cool night air into her lungs.

"You okay?" David's voice was raspy from the smoke he'd inhaled in their flight from the house.

"Yeah. I think so."

"Hey, you two." Paramedics knelt beside them, and Clarissa didn't resist the oxygen mask they slapped across her face. She'd never thought of tasting air before, but she did now, and she savored its sweetness.

She looked around and found the old woman sitting on the step of the fire truck. A blanket was wrapped around her and she smiled at them through the strobing lights and din.

Clarissa glanced over at David and saw the pain in his eyes as the flames devoured the building. She saw the loss grow in his eyes and her heart ached for him.

* * * *

The days grew into weeks, the weeks became a month. David returned to work at the bank. Clarissa spent her time here at the coffee shop, but she cut back her hours and gave them to Linda who proved to be her best employee yet. Even Faith admitted she made a better triple mocha, something she only said once at the risk of losing her "friend of Clarissa" discount.

She didn't have prophetic dreams anymore, and she hadn't had a full impact vision since that last one where she'd seen David at the mansion before the fire. It seemed like years instead of only a few short weeks had passed. She'd probably never forget the events of that night.

And if David had his way, it would be erased. He refused to discuss it. Even though he assured her that part of his life was over, she knew it still nagged at him, still filled his thoughts. Still stood between them.

She'd walked into the living room last night after he'd come to dinner to find him staring into the fireplace flames as if not really seeing them. The mansion now sat silent and empty, the kitchen, the den and the foyer nothing more than burned out ruins. The rest of the house was intact, though water and smoke damaged. He hadn't even wanted to return to remove the pictures, knickknacks and other belongings that were his. It was as if he wanted no part of that past.

Clarissa couldn't let go nearly as easily. She'd sensed the bond between David and his home. He needed to mend the pain of the past if he was ever going to face the future.

He'd sold the Dove's Hollow house. It was the beginning of a renewal project he had encouraged the bank to become involved in. Already, several low-income families worked together to build a neighborhood in the boarded-up old homes.

Clarissa hoped that someday when she returned to Dove's Hollow she'd feel spirits and happiness instead of the dreadful emptiness she'd found there. Even the diner was prospering with the new activity, and they'd replaced the broken neon sign.

Clarissa closed her eyes, realizing she was tired. She hadn't slept much lately. The delicious things David did to her until the wee hours of the morning sent charging hormones through her bloodstream. Even though she was alone in her office now, she blushed. Opening her eyes, she snapped the ledger shut and stood. It was time to go home. The paperwork could wait.

She'd learned so much in the past few weeks, not the least of which was the priority paperwork should take in her life. She hadn't taken a piece of it home since the fire.

Well, she had once, but it had languished in her briefcase from neglect. She didn't even bother after that.

As she reached for her jacket on the back of the door, a blast of cold air slid over her. She shivered and glanced at the air conditioner. It was silent.

It had been so long since she'd had a vision that she didn't expect it. She didn't even know how to react. Her barriers were down, and the vision took over her mind too clearly and powerfully.

The mansion sat in the field, empty and lonely in the late afternoon sun. *Come home,* a voice whispered through the trees, almost as if carried on the breeze.

Clarissa saw herself driving up the winding road to the house and pulling to a halt before the charred double doors. David stood in the open doorway, his arms outstretched, welcoming her into the haven of his home and heart.

"What are you doing here?" she asked him. He just smiled and beckoned for her to follow him. She did, and just as she stepped through the doors into the dimly lit foyer, the vision vanished.

"Trust your instincts," a voice whispered around her.

Her office came back into view and she shivered. Was it a trick? Or was it an answer to the upheaval they'd been experiencing lately? She didn't know what to think, but she did know one thing.

She had to go to the mansion.

Leaving Linda in charge of the shop, she raced to her car. Driving through the city, she headed toward the house. Even from the bottom of the hill, she saw the dark façade high upon it.

She continued to hear the words echo in her mind, and she knew this was the right thing to do. When she reached the ornamental gates, she had to get out of her car to push them open. The "For Sale" sign had been wired to hold them shut. She twisted two wires loose and pushed. The hinges squealed in protest.

She climbed back into the car, and once on the other side of the gates, Clarissa braked. She stepped out of the car and gasped at the sight before her.

The mansion sat nestled among the charred trees. A few brave wild flowers were trying to peek out of the ashes and the lawn was an odd mixture of black and new green.

It was oddly beautiful.

Even the wild animals, butterflies and birds were filling what seemed to be a new meadow. For several long minutes Clarissa stared sadly at the tranquil scene.

Such a waste. Such a lovely waste. David's father had built this house to be enjoyed and to be filled with a family. As she walked along the winding road toward the house, her heart lifted. She'd been called here for a reason today and something told her it would be good.

The front door stood open in a frame that no longer had any walls around it. Soot and dust covered the once polished tile and tiny animal footprints tracked across the grimy surface.

There was a silence here, but it was a peaceful silence, nothing like the tomblike quiet that had once held the house in its grip. Slowly, carefully, she walked through the rooms. She didn't sense anything other than the peace and quiet all around her.

The living room door was also open and she remembered when David had given her the first tour. She'd seen such happy visions, and now she felt compelled to go inside.

Soot had settled on the white carpet and furniture, but their beauty and elegance still remained. She ran a hand over the back of the sofa and dark dust motes rose into the air. They were suspended on the air for an instant and then settled gently back down.

Suddenly, the air grew cold and the dust settled as if plastered to the fabric. Clarissa felt her heart shake. No, she *couldn't* have been fooled. Fear gnawed at her heart and she turned to run.

But she wasn't quick enough to escape the vision that insinuated itself into her mind. The room all around her wavered and returned to its earlier splendor. She gasped. It was even more beautiful than she remembered, and then she realized why.

It was decorated for Christmas. In the corner beside the fireplace, next to the painting of David's parents, now repaired and cleaned, sat an elegant glistening Christmas tree.

The lights winked in a choreographed rhythm, and the angel perched on top sat in regal splendor. Under the boughs were dozens of gaily-wrapped presents with ribbons that reflected the myriad of lights from the tree and around the room.

Spinning slowly, Clarissa took in all the splendor. The doors into the main dining room stood open and a golden candelabrum sat in the center of the table, its flickering light glistening off the gold-edged china and flatware.

Distant giggles from children's voices echoed through the room and Clarissa returned her gaze to the fireplace. Four bright red stockings hung from the mantle, and just below the center two sat a beautiful doll with golden hair and a bright red bicycle. Its chrome shimmered with the lights.

She could even smell the scent of cinnamon and holly berries.

"Mama! Mama!" two childish voices chimed. Clarissa turned, but not in time to see who the voices belonged to. Suddenly the vision faded. The grief at the loss of the happiness and beauty gouged through her.

"No, come back." She wanted the vision to return. Melancholy filled her heart.

Slowly, she walked around the soot-covered room. She knew she couldn't let David sell this place. It meant too much to him. And yet...he'd never come here. He'd never live here again, not on his own and without a lot of prodding.

She pulled her cell phone from her purse. She was surprised when he answered instead of his secretary.

"Hello, darling." She couldn't keep the excitement out of her voice. "You'll never guess where I am."

"You're right." He sounded tired but happy to hear her voice. "I hope you're at home, waiting for me." His voice lowered suggestively. "I've been thinking about you all day."

Clarissa laughed softly, feeling the heat of his desire as it slid over her every nerve. "I've been thinking about you, too."

"Good thoughts, I hope."

"Mmm, could be. David?"

"Yes?"

"What are you going to do if the mansion doesn't sell?"

His end of the line went deadly silent. She knew she'd done as much damage with that statement as an argument would have.

"I don't think now is the time to discuss this."

"There never is a better time." She turned and gazed out over the room, reliving the vision she'd just experienced. "I had a vision today," she whispered.

"What?" His fear pulsed through the phone. Clarissa wanted to ease his fears, but she knew that was impossible. There was no turning back now.

"I had a vision. It called me here. I'm at the mansion." Silence again met her ears. "Come to the house. There's something I want to show you." He didn't answer. "David?" He still didn't answer.

"Clarissa?" A familiar woman's voice came on the line and she realized David's secretary had picked it up.

"Yes?"

"What did you say? He just ran out of here like the world was coming to an end. Are you all right?"

"Oh, yes." Clarissa smiled. "I'm fine. Would you do me a favor and let everyone know David won't be in to work tomorrow?"

Melinda's familiar chuckle came through the line. Clarissa could hear the romantic wheels spinning in the woman's head. "Bye, Melanie. We'll be in touch."

Clarissa put her phone back in her purse. It wasn't very long before she heard the squeal of David's car outside as he slammed on the brakes.

"Clarissa?" His voice was filled with worry and fear as it echoed around the clearing.

Clarissa hugged herself, joy filling her. She knew what she was about to do was so right. So very right.

"In here," she called.

He came through the doors of the living room before she'd even finished the short sentence. He stalked toward her. "What the hell do you think you're doing?"

"Dreaming."

"Dreaming?" He looked at her as if she'd lost her mind. "About what?"

"Us. The future. This house."

"Well, two out of three ain't bad, as the saying goes. This house has nothing to do with either of the other two."

"Oh, yes, it does. Yes, it does."

While she'd waited for David, she'd begun to plan. She'd mentally put the house back together and had even planned to redecorate the nursery to the grandeur it must have held when he was a baby.

"Come on, we're getting out of here. I don't ever want you to come back here."

"Don't give me orders, David." Clarissa stood her ground. "I didn't come here on a whim. I was called here."

"We escaped once. I'm not going through that again."

She watched as he looked down at his hands. There hadn't been any more shifts since they'd destroyed the music box. She knew he wouldn't shift, but did he truly believe it?

"Let's go." His anger was tinged with fear and her heart hurt for him, but she wasn't going to give in. That vision she'd just seen had been too real, too wonderful, and she wanted it. She knew it was meant to be.

"Please, David. Stay." The words were in Clarissa's mind, but from his reaction, she knew he had heard them too. He spun around.

There on the threshold of the room was a wispy white form. At first indistinct, it sharpened into two.

Clarissa gasped. David stood silent, staring, his skin pale. The image was iridescent, and a smile pulled on Clarissa's lips as she recognized them.

"Listen to her. She's offering you the life you deserve." The man's voice filled the air.

"M...Mom? Dad?" David paused, then slowly walked toward the images.

"Yes, it's us. We're nearly free."

"Nearly free?" David's voice was barely a whisper.

"The price has been paid. It's time for us to move on, but you have to let us go."

"Let you go? I don't understand."

"The music box was evil, son," the man explained. *"I brought it home and it destroyed everything."* Was that an ethereal sob?

"You didn't know, dear." His mother soothed her husband.

Then she told David, *"You broke the spell when you destroyed the music box. Now it's your pain and regrets binding us here."*

David stood staring. Clarissa watched his throat move as he swallowed. "I'm sorry. I don't understand."

His mother's spirit moved away from her husband. She hovered near David, and the pain on her face was that of a mother unable to touch her child. Unable to offer him the comfort she knew he wanted and needed.

"Don't be sorry. The evil is what killed us. Not each other."

"But I saw—" He pointed at his father. "I heard the arguments."

"It happened." The man's form moved forward, and he whispered, *"Forgive me. Forgive us all."*

"You have so much love to give. Take what she has to offer." The woman moved closer, something suspiciously like tears glistening in her eyes.

David's hand moved through his hair, leaving a trail in the dark tresses. Clarissa longed to smooth away the sign of his distress, but she knew this was between David and his parents.

There was no future until the past was dealt with.

"We love you, son. But it's time you let us go." The man moved closer as well.

"And Rachel?" The name was torn from David, as if he feared she'd join them with the mention of her name.

"She made her own choices. Not choices of love, but of possession."

"She's gone," the woman whispered. *"Forever."*

David lifted his arm, as if trying to touch them, and then let it fall helplessly to his side.

"Don't regret, David. Don't be afraid to love. Clarissa loves you. And you love her." There was a silent pause, as his mother seemed to weigh her next words. *"Give her the part of your heart you couldn't give Rachel."*

David's head snapped up and he looked at the woman's image in surprise. "How did you know?"

She reached out, but then she let her hand drop, as if once again realizing she couldn't touch him. *"I can read your heart. I always could. I never really left you. Now go on with your life. Clarissa's waiting. They're waiting."*

David stared at the images until they faded completely away. He stood for a very long time, silent and still.

Clarissa, who had been attuned to his emotions for so long, felt as if she knew him better than she knew herself. The war was just ending between his guilt and his heart.

His gaze met hers and the pained love she saw there took her breath away. His heart beat within the depths of his eyes, reflecting his love.

"She's gone. They're gone." Speaking the words helped make it real for him.

"Yes."

"And you're still here." He indicated the room and the rest of the house with a slight incline of his head.

"I'll always be here. I'll be wherever you are." She opened her arms, knowing he needed to know she was there and wanted him. David pulled her into his arms.

"You want to live here, don't you?"

Clarissa nodded, the vision of earlier appeared tantalizingly clear in her memory.

"Who was she talking about when she said 'they're waiting?'"

Clarissa's heart did a little flip, and she suddenly knew the life she'd suspected might be there was indeed real. "I think she meant our family."

"Family?" David leaned back to stare into her eyes. The answering joy in her gaze gave him the answer. "A baby?"

Clarissa nodded, tears of realization clogging her throat and filling her eyes. Suddenly the room behind David shimmered and swam, and Clarissa blinked to clear her eyes. She realized it wasn't tears but a vision forming in the room before her.

"Mama!" a golden-haired girl about seven years old cried at the top of her lungs. Clarissa saw herself rushing into the room.

"What is all the hollering about?"

"Mama, Davey is going to be bad tomorrow. It's really going to be bad. Maybe you'd better punish him now and he won't do it."

"I am not. Mama, will you tell her to stop using that magic she does to get me in trouble? It's not fair!"

Clarissa watched the little boy, who looked like an exact duplicate of the little girl, as he stuck his tongue out at her.

The vision faded and Clarissa laughed. Yes, they would be so happy here.

"What's so funny?" David gazed down at her with love shining in his eyes.

"Oh, nothing, just a passing thought." She leaned close to David and reveled in the feel of his lips as they met hers. She didn't tell him about the last vision. She knew it would be difficult enough for him to live with her psychic powers. She didn't think he was ready for the news that they were having twins, much less the fact that his daughter would have her mother's powers.

David lifted his head, staring down at her. "I love you," he whispered. "Always. Anywhere."

The pain was finally gone from his eyes.

Don't Miss

Memory Whispers

by Angel Smits

ISBN: 0-9759653-6

Recurring, sensual dreams haunt Faith McCoy. The daughter of a minister, she's uncomfortable with the sexy images. While on a trip to the colorful gambling town of Cripple Creek, Colorado, she is shocked and frightened to find not only the room in her dreams, but the man whose touch haunts and excites her. She might consider a modern-day relationship if it weren't for the fact that the room—and her dream—are set in a former brothel.

Casino owner, Cord Burke has his own dreams of the beautiful woman who seduces him. He never expected her to be real, but when he meets Faith, he's drawn to her and the past that seems to threaten her. He refuses, however, to be drawn to the forevers and promises she represents. He's been burned too many times in life to consider settling down.

Suspecting that they may have lived and loved in a prior life, Faith and Cord face the ghost of an old enemy. But how can they beat a ghost who has no fear—not even of death . . .

Available from ImaJinn Books

http://www.imajinnbooks.com

Tired of mundane romance?

Dare to ImaJinn!

Acclaimed stories of
vampires, ghosts,
shapeshifters, sorcerers,
time travelers, aliens,
and urban fantasy.

Sometimes scary.
Always sexy!

Visit our web site for
a complete listing of
our books, or call
or write us
for a free catalog.

Printed in the United Kingdom
by Lightning Source UK Ltd.
113168UKS00001B/188

9 781933 417042